The Quixotes

Novels by R. C. Hutchinson

Thou Hast a Devil
The Answering Glory
The Unforgotten Prisoner
One Light Burning
Shining Scabbard
Testament
The Fire and the Wood
Interim
Elephant and Castle
Recollection of a Journey
The Stepmother
March the Ninth
Image of My Father
A Child Possessed
Johanna at Daybreak
Origins of Cathleen
Rising

First published in Great Britain in 1984
by the Carcanet Press
208 Corn Exchange, Manchester M4 3BQ

The publisher acknowledges financial assistance
from the Arts Council of Great Britain

Hutchinson, R.C.
    The Quixotes.
    I. Title   II. Green, Robert, 1940–
823'.912[F]   PR6015.U76

ISBN 0-85635-515-1

Typesetting by Paragon Photoset, Aylesbury
Printed in Great Britain by Short Run Press, Exeter

R. C. HUTCHINSON

The Quixotes
COLLECTED STORIES

Edited by ROBERT GREEN
Professor of English
University of Swaziland

CARCANET PRESS · MANCHESTER

Contents

Every Twenty Years

On 25 January 1926, at 5.10 pm, Ralph Saronby, General Manager of the Westways Hardware Company, took his seat in a smoking coach at Charing Cross Underground station — as he had done for as many years back as he bothered to think about. From the right-hand pocket of his expensive overcoat he drew an expensive pipe, and from the left-hand pocket he took an expensive pouch. The journey as far as Leicester Square was occupied in filling the pipe with expensive tobacco, and having placed it between his costly teeth, he lit it before reaching Tottenham Court Road. From there onwards he became absorbed in his paper, which had only cost a penny. All these things had Saronby done, with unfailing regularity, since what seemed to him time immemorial.

Ralph Saronby liked and admired consistency.

'I am not a narrow man, nor an excessively conservative man,' he told his sister on those rare occasions when breakfast was just five minutes late. 'I altogether approve of change in the proper place; but I have my own ideas on some things, and I prefer to stick to them. To be a productive factor in this world one must work in a regular and orderly fashion.' He did. He was intolerably orderly. In a moment of bitterness his sister had once said to him, 'I believe no form of existence would suit you better than one in which you simply ate and slept — at regular hours.'

'I can think of other forms of existence a good deal less pleasant,' said Ralph amiably.

But on the aforesaid 25th January, which, it may be mentioned, was a Monday (of all exasperating days), Saronby's calm and well-regulated career was destined to suffer a rude shock. Somewhere in the neighbourhood of Camden Town his pipe went out. He continued to draw at it in short, quick breaths for a few seconds, scarcely believing that such a thing could have happened. It had never occurred before. The manager of an excellent tobacco firm personally blended Saronby's pet mixture, and sold it to him in neatly packed and entirely air-proof half-pound tins; nor could it have become damp in Saronby's faultless pouch. Clearly some very unusual mistake had been made by somebody, for the pipe was undoubtedly out. Saronby growled into his paper and felt for his matches. He opened the box and discovered that his last match had gone.

'The blows of misfortune never fall singly,' he murmured, trying to recall some apt epigram which would sum up his feelings. It was unusual for the General Manager of the Westways Hardware Company to borrow matches from fellow passengers who might be in any walk of life, but it was quite impossible to travel between Camden Town and Hampstead with an unlit pipe. He looked round cautiously to find a suitable person with whom to transact this delicate business.

It was then that he realized that the coach was empty.

Saronby started. He was almost certain that he remembered noticing a shabbily dressed woman who had entered at Goodge Street and sat down close to him; he had not seen her go out. Besides, at that time of day, and on this section of the line, trains were invariably full and generally overcrowded. This was to Saronby the cause of some irritation. In fact, he only travelled by 'Tube' in preference to his private car to avoid the risk of being held up at crossings, and he was constantly grumbling that the trains were too full. He maintained that big men with suit-cases and women with babies should only be allowed to travel in non-rush hours. But a completely empty coach was another matter. It was carrying things too far. It was unusual and to be deprecated as such. In this case, however, what annoyed him most was not the lack of passengers, but the lack of matches.

He was still fuming when the train came to a station and drew up. The automatic doors opened and a voice from the far end said 'All change here'. Saronby directed a withering glance upon the portrait of a smiling gentleman with a 'Bolivia' cigar, and stalked out on to the platform.

The doors closed immediately behind him, and with the customary rumble the train drew swiftly away. Saronby noticed that the other coaches as they passed him were also empty. Struck by what seemed a very elaborate coincidence, he turned to see the name of the station. Chalk Farm, probably, he thought. The red discs were there as usual, situated at intervals along the whole length of the station; but there was no name on any. Further, there seemed to be no advertisements anywhere. Evidently the station was under repair. He walked up and down, looking for some official to whom he might address his inquiries. No officials either.

Saronby swore under his breath and walked through to the other platform; seeing no one, he sat down on one of the station seats and prepared to wait. At that moment every light in the station went out.

Sitting alone in the darkness Saronby shivered. He was not accustomed to the sensation of fear, and would have ridiculed the idea of a return to the childish horror of night. Nevertheless, there was something peculiarly disconcerting in this total oblivion and total separation from any mortal being. But chiefly, he was angry. He felt that he, the General Manager of Westways Hardware Company, deserved better treatment. It was monstrous that a man of importance in the City should be lured into a temporarily disused station and left sitting there in utter blackness; it was a grossly unconventional situation. Mentally he prepared a letter to *The Times* on the subject. 'As one who has patronized London's Underground Railways ever since their opening, I feel that I have the right —' No, better still — 'It is high time that some form of protest came from the general public against the scandalous mismanagement of London's Underground Railways. Only yesterday —'

The distant roar of an approaching train cut short his meditations. He heaved a sigh of relief. The noise grew louder and a train entered the station at full speed; the coaches were fully lighted but empty. Without slackening its pace it passed through the station and was gone. Hardly had the noise subsided when the sound of another train from the opposite direction became audible. Saronby groped his way through to the opposite platform in time to see it shoot through the station. It was empty like the last, and he noticed that neither driver nor conductors seemed to be visible. He waited, and at short intervals more trains passed through, all empty, none stopping. At several he shouted, but it was useless; no one could have heard him against the din, and he could see no one in any of them to hear him. Ralph Saronby, who had lived fifty-two years and spent forty of those bullying everyone within reach, was beginning to be frightened.

'I say,' he shouted. Then louder, 'I say'. He listened. At first tense silence, then a sound of rustling and scratching, coming first from one direction, then from another. The sound, whatever it was, was not produced by human agency, and Saronby did not care to listen to it. He felt for his matches, and remembered that he had none. So he whistled to keep his feelings under control, and felt his way towards the exit staircase he had noticed while the lights were still on. On reaching the top he stepped into a passage that proved to extend in both directions. Keeping one hand on the wall, which was so damp as almost to be trickling with water, he felt his way along to the right and came at last to where the passage seemed to turn. He proceeded cautiously, since a few paces further on he advanced one foot and found no floor. He realized that he stood at the edge of a lift-shaft, and though the gates were open the lift was not there.

The escape he had had from falling added to Saronby's terror. He began quickly to retrace his steps towards the stairs, but, arriving there, he felt he could not venture down to the platform again. The sight of the trains passing through empty and heedless would make him desperate. At any rate, he must first try to find some other way of escape. To this end he started along the passage in the opposite direction, still moving with the same cautious footsteps. He thought he felt some kind of creature running between his legs, and he whistled louder; but his whistling echoed horribly down the long subway. Another ten yards, and his heart leapt as he saw, some-where in the darkness ahead, a faint yellow glow. Light at last. It was what he longed for most. Moving rather more quickly, he came to a place where the passage turned, and then he saw that the light shone dimly across it from an opening on the left. Forgetting all caution, he almost ran towards the open door.

The room he entered seemed to have been designed as some sort of station-master's office. It was only dimly lighted by a wretched yellow electric bulb in the ceiling; and a desk, some chairs, and a few oddments of furniture could be seen only faintly. But what Saronby noticed, and noticed with satisfaction, was that on the desk stood a telephone. Now a telephone was to Saronby what a rifle is to a soldier; he stepped forward and placed his hand lovingly on the instrument. When he put the receiver to his ear he felt more like Ralph Saronby, Esq., The Poplars, Hampstead, and 403–407, Barter Street. He waited anxiously, however, for it seemed almost too much to hope that the telephone would be working in this chaotic station.

'Number, please!' said a voice at the other end.

Saronby always cursed telephonists, and complained about them weekly; but he could have kissed one of them for the mere fact of her possessing a human voice. He gave the number of his home address, and waited while the customary buzzing and tapping proceeded.

Then he heard: 'Two pennies, please!'

Saronby swore again; he had not realized that the telephone was a public one. He felt in his pocket and took out a handful of half-crowns. He had no other coins. His breast pocket contained paper to the amount of twenty pounds; but not a single penny.

'I find I have no coppers,' he shouted into the mouthpiece. 'Will half-crowns do?'

'Two pennies, please!' repeated the voice without emotion.

'Exchange,' called Saronby in desperation, 'will you tell me the address of the call-office I am speaking from?'

The only answer was a long, hollow laugh, which might have been a man's or a woman's. Saronby rang again. He could get no further reply.

He sat down on a chair, mute, perspiring, listening to the scratching and shuffling. He could no longer doubt what these noises were, for, as he sat there, a large rat ran quickly across the room, dimly perceptible in the yellow glow. As he listened he heard a new noise mingled with the rustling in the walls, a regular, drawn-out, whining sound, almost like a snore. It came from the opposite corner of the room, and, peering into the shadow, Saronby saw the outlines of a couch, with a heap of something upon it. He walked towards it, and as he did so, the object moved. Bending close, he saw the outline of a human face — whether of a man or woman he could not tell. The age, too, was doubtful, for the eyes were closed and the skin so pallid that, but for the heavy wrinkles and broken lips, it might have been the face of a dead child. Yet it was partly hidden by a mass of long white hair. So distraught was Saronby that he could almost have sworn that he had seen these emaciated features before — just a shadow of a face that had been familiar at some period long past. A former typist, perhaps! Saronby had employed hundreds in his time.

He examined the rest of the body more closely. It was draped in the remains of a heavy cloak, rotted and moth-eaten beyond all recognition. Certain details made Saronby feel that he would willingly have gone without human companionship in his prison rather than endure the society of this being, whatever it was. For it was alive; of that he could not doubt, although the body stank strangely of death, the nostrils were dilating incessantly, giving vent to the whining snore which had first attracted his attention. He drew away, overcome by the nauseous odour, and preferring to look on from a distance. As he watched, the eyes opened and blinked; the eyes, as far as he could see them, were moist and feeble; but they were not the eyes of age.

Suddenly they fell upon him, and immediately the figure sat upright, uttering a long, hoarse peal of laughter. The peal subsided and was followed by another, and another, till Saronby thought it would never end. He stood there, silent, wondering what he could do to calm the frightened creature.

'Pardon me, Madam,' he said at last — for he now saw that it was a woman, 'can you tell me at all where I am?'

She broke off in the middle of her hysterics and looked fixedly at him, her whole wasted body quivering. 'Hell,' she cried shrilly. 'You're in hell, hotter than fire, the place of the damned!'

'To be rather less metaphorical,' said Saronby gently, 'I take it that I am somewhere in the proximity of Chalk Farm?'

The woman did not answer. Instead, she took something from the couch where she had been lying and began to gnaw it savagely. Saronby shuddered when he noticed that it was the body of a rat. He tried again.

'You must excuse my bothering you with questions,' he said, feeling strangely at a loss to manage so unusual a conversation, 'but can you by any chance tell me when the next train leaves this station?'

'Trains,' she murmured, this time in a lower tone, 'always trains, night and day, train after train, always going through the station. But they never stop, always empty, never stop.'

Saronby coughed. 'This is very irritating,' he said. 'I have an engagement this evening, and my sister who keeps house for me will be anxious.'

His companion continued to stare at him vaguely; into those filmy eyes came the shadow of a thought — a wild, passionate struggle to recall the past. Suddenly she stepped forward and seized him by the arm.

'Listen,' she said hoarsely, grasping him with her long fingers, 'who are you?'

'My card,' said Saronby, extracting one from a waistcoat pocket with his free hand.

'Card,' muttered the woman, her eyes vague again, 'card? — oh yes! Gentlemen, ladies, name on card!'

'Exactly,' said Saronby, 'my card. And may I ask your name?'

'My name? I have forgotten,' was the hesitating reply. 'No, I remember, it was Erse — Erse — Erse something.'

'Ursula?' Saronby suggested.

'Yes, Ursula Lockhart.'

'Ursula Lockhart!' Saronby knew the name, or thought he did. He shook himself, fearing that some madness was coming upon him, to make names and places seem familiar which he could not place accurately in his mind.

'How did you get here?' demanded the woman suddenly.

'I came by train,' replied Saronby, 'and was foolish enough to be led into getting out at the wrong station.'

'Twenty years ago I got out at this station. I have been here, alone, ever since.'

'Indeed,' said Saronby. 'Then, presumably, I am right in thinking that you occupy an official position in this very uncomfortable establishment?' She shook her head. 'At any rate, having been here for twenty years, you are no doubt acquainted with the place pretty thoroughly; I shall be much obliged if you will show me the way out, since no trains appear to stop.'

'There is no way out,' she said.

'My very good woman,' exploded Saronby. 'This is London, not Mexico. There is always some way of getting from one place to another in London.'

She shook her head again. Saronby clicked his tongue. The presence of a gabbling lunatic did not enhance the situation.

'How do you get your food?' he questioned, struck suddenly with a way of approaching the matter methodically.

'I eat only these creatures,' the woman replied simply. 'I have forgotten their name. There are many which have died here.'

'Rats!' said Saronby, horrified, 'you eat nothing but rats?'

'That is the name — rats!' she echoed.

'But you must drink something?'

'There is water running in the — the passage out there; it is not good water, but you can drink it. I have drunk it for twenty years. Soon I shall die. I think I am thirty-seven.'

'How do you know that?' demanded Saronby abruptly. 'You don't seem to have a calendar here; do they deliver newspapers?'

She pointed to a clock hanging on the wall.

'That thing,' she said, 'it always goes. And the light always burns. I have marked on this table the days and the years. I was seventeen, when —' She broke off into a fit of hysterical weeping, her body shaking with sobs.

Saronby felt an emotion which he had not been conscious of for years. Moved by a sudden impulse he stepped forward, took the quivering creature in his arms, and carried her back to the couch. Sitting there, he held her close to him, while her sobs grew fainter. A strange feeling passed over him. His loathing for this dreadful wreck of humanity, withered and actually preyed on by creeping insects, had given place to pity — more than that, to some strong feeling of tenderness which he thought had died out of his life. Dimly he remembered a time when to love and to protect were his strongest desires, great and beautiful. He had thought since then that they were the whims of a boy. Now he realized that as a boy his perspective had been clearer and truer than his vision of life as a man.

'Is it true?' he whispered to her. 'Are we to stay here, alone together, for ever?'

'For ever,' she said, choking. 'They never stop; always empty, always passing. They never stop.'

He sat still, grasping slowly the full meaning of the truth. The darkness, the rats, the noisome odours, the trains which passed ceaselessly, but never stopped. His brain worked feverishly, trying to devise a means of escape. He pictured his companion, a young and beautiful girl, groping her way round and round the long dark passages — in vain. He saw her living there throughout the long years, alone, rapidly becoming an old woman. He put his burden down on the couch and began to pace up and down the room, stopping occasionally to listen to the monotonous ticking of the clock. The white-haired woman watched him in silence. Wearying of his pacing, he went to the far side of the room and sat down upon a wooden box.

The woman started. 'Do not sit there,' she said.

'Sit here, why not?' he asked vaguely, feeling that he was losing all command of his reason.

'My baby — I buried him in that box,' she replied.

Saronby turned abruptly. This was more than he could stand.

'You swear that what you say is true, every word of it?' he demanded. She nodded. 'Then,' he added, pronouncing each syllable slowly and with emphasis, 'if the trains will not stop for me, they can at least kill me.'

She gazed at him piteously.

'You will not leave me now?' she implored. 'I have waited here, alone, twenty years. And now you have come. You cannot leave me now.'

Saronby reflected. He tried to recall his normal way of facing any situation that arose in his business life. Then he made a decision.

'You must kill yourself, too,' he said quietly.

She did not reply, but sat there, cowering.

'We must both die,' he said again.

'You cannot die,' she replied. 'I have tried. You cannot die here.'

At that moment Saronby became aware that the light in the room had brightened. Then he ran into the subway. It was fully lighted.

'The lights!' he gasped. 'They have come on again — it may mean that a train will stop.'

He ran back into the room and found the woman groping her way towards the door.

'Come!' he cried. 'Come quickly.'

'I cannot see,' she faltered. 'The lights have blinded me.'

Ralph Saronby remembered that he had always prided himself on being a man of action. He seized the woman by the hand, he almost dragged her down the passage. As they came to the top of the stairs he heard the rumble of a train entering the station. Unmistakably it was slowing down. He heard the whistle of the suction brakes as it came to a standstill.

'It has stopped!' he shouted. 'Mind — steps — buck up!' And he ran down, pulling her with him, half stumbling, half falling.

The automatic doors of the train were open.

'Quick!' he cried, dragging her towards the nearest. She hung back, pulling her weight against him.

'No!' she shrieked, 'I cannot; it is too much. I cannot face the world again.'

'Fool,' he panted, 'you must — we must both be saved out of this hell.'

'I can't!' she cried. 'Leave me here. I would rather stop here.'

Saronby did not stop for argument. He picked her up bodily and ran for the doors, which began to slide as he approached them. He thrust her between them, but before he could follow they had closed with a snap.

Immediately the train slid forward. He tried to push back the doors, but his strength was not enough. Wildly he looked for something to seize hold of as the train gathered speed, and then realized that he was left. He ran after it shrieking, and hurled himself against the windows of the last coach, only to be thrown back, stunned, upon the platform, as it disappeared from view.

He stumbled to his feet, looking dazedly around him. Then, high up on the tiled wall, he saw a notice, neatly printed in very small letters:

FROM THIS STATION.
ONE TRAIN, EACH WAY,
EVERY TWENTY YEARS.

Then the lights went out. Saronby gave a groan.

The General Manager of the Westways Hardware Company felt a touch on his arm, and a woman's voice said:

'It's all right, sir, only something gone wrong with the electric; they'll come on again presently.'

Light again, all in a flash, and the roar of a train, and the feel of motion. The coach was full, and Saronby, blinking, saw the woman who had woken him gazing fixedly into his eyes.

'Ralph!' she said suddenly.

Looking back at her, he remembered.

'Ursula,' he whispered; 'it is a long time since we last met. How long?'

'Twenty years,' she said.

The Wall not made with Hands

Hamilton Priest leaves the club every night at half past ten — usually not one minute later. That is the only reason why his friends refrain from calling him the complete and perfect bachelor.

I have at one time and another asked most of them if they knew the reason for this peculiarity in his behaviour, but none ever enlightened me. Other members of the club — and by 'members' I mean those who were elected within the same decade as myself, not the youngsters who have paid an entrance fee and drop in for a drink — leave at eleven or thereabouts; they live in distant suburbs, and their movements are governed by the London transport companies. But bachelor-members who, like Priest, are owners of luxurious cars with well-paid drivers, do not, as a rule, leave before twelve; particularly if, like Priest, they live no further from civilization than the W2 area.

Let it not be thought that I have ever considered this eccentricity a vicious trait in Priest's character. A bachelor must be allowed at least one eccentricity, and no one could say that my friend is not loyal to the club. He is among us from dinner-time onward each night, he gives us freely of his good humour and his superb wit, the air of the observant traveller which he carries with him. He notices our absence when we are ill, and sends inquiries. Having no sons of his own to get into debt or develop a *penchant* for literature, he interests himself in ours. His name is on every subscription list, not at the top, blatantly, but hidden far down among those of junior members, and usually with the word 'envelope' against it in the amounts column. Five times out of ten his hints about the National prove correct, though he is not to be trusted so implicitly with regard to Newmarket. He dresses well, he makes more money by his handling of a leather concern than he does from his investments. He is shrewd, well-preserved both physically and mentally, and possesses himself so completely that he does not mind being possessed by us.

Priest has given me more good dinners than I care to remember. It is perhaps one of his most charming qualities, and very typical of the man, that he understands how to do this so often — not only for me, but for others also — without ever giving us an excuse to realize that the reason why he pays the bill is that he is much richer than we. He succeeds, time after time, in making me feel that I do him a favour in dining at his expense. ('Hullo, this is a bit of luck! I've pulled off a double, and I was just desperate for someone to join me in celebrating.') But when, a fortnight ago, he entertained me at his own house, it was for the first time.

I was alone in the Justices' Room, sitting with my feet on the fender and turning over the pages of *Punch*. I had seen all the drawings, and read A. P. Herbert's article, and was wondering whether there were any good shows I had not seen. Priest, coming in suddenly, evidently detected my boredom, and said impulsively,

'You look as if you're rather fed up. Would you like to come round to my place?' '

When I assented, I thought I saw on his face an expression to indicate that he regretted his impulse. But it was gone in a moment, and I believed then that I had merely imagined it.

I had often wondered, vaguely, what Priest's 'place' would be like. It was known to me only as a number in a square I had never happened to visit. My picture of it was of a small service flat, arranged to serve every requirement of a man who had only his own comforts to consider, and could afford to consider them thoroughly. It would, I had imagined, be well filled with rarities of some sort, pictures or antiques, since bachelors collect such things, and this was the only reason I could think of for his not living at the club.

'We don't have many visitors,' he said, as we drove along Piccadilly.

We! So Priest kept with another fellow!

'I don't know what you'll think of the house,' he went on, 'it's an odd place.'

It was quite plain now that he wished he had never invited me. His manner, I thought, was peculiar. Some essential part of the personality I knew at the club had departed. I felt awkward, and wondered for a moment whether to suggest an alternative programme in the shape of a theatre. I could not, however, think of any polite way of phrasing the suggestion.

'It's very good of you to cheer me up like this,' I said, 'but I hope I'm not inconveniencing you in any way. My own establishment's wrapped in an inferno of spring-cleaning at present, and yours may be the same.'

He took no advantage of the loophole I had offered him.

'Inconvenience? Of course not! My wife will be delighted to see you.'

'I beg your pardon! I mean — you're married? I didn't know.'

It seemed ridiculous to say such a thing to a man I had known for twenty years.

'Of course,' he replied easily. 'One does marry, you know.'

Certainly one married. I had myself twice suffered the process. But Priest! Well, it was hard enough to imagine Priest doing many other things that he must certainly have done. No doubt he had lain in a perambulator and howled, been christened, studied Latin in a dingy form-room, and fallen off horses. By a severe mental effort I could visualize such things as these. But Priest married! Even when the first shock was over and I had started to think about the news steadily, I found difficulty in making myself believe it. I could not see Priest embracing any woman — let alone a wife. I could not hear him complaining about the food in the soft tactful way which husbands know is the only one that works. Least of all could I picture him declaring to a woman his willingness to hand over the vital part of his being to her guardianship. Each new condition which the term 'husband' connotes seemed less in keeping with the individuality of Hamilton Priest.

He was talking about the traffic problem now, and I punctuated his theories with remarks which conveyed my agreement. But I was still ruminating on my strange discovery. Theories were forming themselves rapidly. He had married beneath him, and his wife preferred to remain in tactful isolation. But that was impossible for anyone married to Priest. Granted that he should have married at all, he might well have chosen a wife of lower rank, but he would never have allowed himself to see that she was not his social equal. She might be an invalid. That was not unlikely. Priest, if he had met a woman who was blind, deaf, and dumb, would have done anything possible to help, and failing any other means would have married her. Perhaps it was a very old lady. There were many cases of romantic chivalry, of the kind which men thought funny and women called disgusting. A lonely old person was just the kind that —

'Here we are!' said Priest.

It was a very narrow-fronted house, with the three steps and tall portico which one associates with five-figure incomes. When I went inside I was surprised to see how far back it extended. There was a long hall, and a door at the end. Half way along this hall he turned to the left and led me up a short flight of stairs, then right, and up a long flight.

'Two front entrances to this house,' said Priest, as though answering a question. 'Come along!'

He crossed the small landing, and opened a door which faced the stairs.

I believe that many people would think for quite a long time before realizing what is peculiar about the room we then entered, though its oddness would strike anyone but the desperately unobservant at first glance. To me — perhaps it was a relic of my training in the furniture business — the thing which made it curious was apparent at once. It was actually not one room but two. True, a single carpet ran the whole length of it, and the wallpaper was the same all round. Moreover, the furniture, made in a connoisseur's wood that is sometimes mistaken by the uninitiated for mahogany, was in the same style throughout. It was his furniture, nevertheless, which gave the clue. The part in which we stood was a man's room; heavy, comfortable furniture, a wide roll-top desk, cartoons on the wall; the other end, with its small chairs, its little table covered with silver, its watercolour landscapes, had been arranged by a woman. In the centre a round, squat table (of the kind known commercially as 'smoker's utility'), standing next to an ivory statuette in the earlier manner of Semovini, indicated that the room was divided into two exactly equal parts.

Pretending to ignore the phenomenon, I turned towards the side of the room where fully two-thirds of the wall were covered by bookshelves. The habit of examining a man's books is one of which I cannot cure myself, and as Priest, I knew, did the same thing himself, I had no compunction. There were many works on architecture, novels in all languages and of all ages wildly assorted. There was a whole row of Balzac, but, oddly enough, no Lucas, no Leacock, and as far as I could see, no Dickens, though Thackeray was prominent on the easy-reach shelf.

'Execrably arranged!' was Priest's comment.

'I prefer them thus,' I answered.

At the far end of the room there was another small bookcase, which, from the distance, appeared to contain several series of the modern 'uniform' editions, small books very beautifully bound.

'What have you there?' I asked, and started to walk across.

'I say!' he said quickly, so that I stopped. 'I'd rather you didn't go over there if you don't mind. You see, it's my wife's part. You can't go, as a matter of fact, because there's a piece of glass which divides the room into two.'

I stared. There was no sign whatever of glass.

'It must be very fine glass,' I said, 'I can hardly believe it's there.'

'It's cleverly fitted,' said Priest. 'I don't quite know why we have it. It was put there shortly after we married.' Then, drawing my attention away, 'Look here, I don't suppose you'll believe me when I tell you that this is Rembrandt. He did nothing else like it. I copied it myself in a gallery in Antwerp which most people didn't know about.'

He was talking of the Flemish School, making me marvel as usual at his powers of memory and his knack of being interesting, when his wife came in through the door at the far end of the room.

'Talking pictures, I suppose,' she said, and the glass which separated us seemed to take nothing from the delicate inflection of her voice.

She was young in appearance, clear-skinned and with perfect teeth. Her hair was light as that of Scandinavian women, her eyes of a very light blue, and ignoring the usual canons of effective contrast which would have demanded a dark-coloured or bright-coloured dress, she was wearing a flimsy, pale-yellow thing which made her look unreal. It was the device which many shy women will adopt to make certain of securing the very small section of males who like ethereality in the fair sex. But Mrs Priest was not a shy woman. She had dignity, and the briskness of a hardened bazaar-opener. The bow she gave me was one which I recognized as having been assiduously practised for the benefit of worthier persons.

We drew our chairs together — she on her side of the glass and we on ours — and talked of finance, of aviation, of musical comedies. So interested was I by the personality of Priest's wife that I soon forgot the strangeness of our positions, and for some time did not notice that both of my hosts addressed themselves exclusively to me. As one knows that one has been aware of a clock ticking the moment after it has stopped, so the fact that they had hardly once addressed each other occurred to me first of all when the rule was broken. Priest was speaking at some length about the new Electricity Bill when his wife interrupted him.

'Oh, Hamilton, did you remember to turn off the landing light?'

'My wife is a sticker for petty economies,' said Priest with a smile. 'To tell the truth, I'm not sure if I did.'

He put his hands on the arms of his chair, preparing to rise.

'Let me go!' I said.

'No, of course not, don't bother,' Priest protested.

'I am two years your junior,' said I, arriving first at the door.

'Impudent youngster!' he said, and returned to his chair.

I went out, leaving the door slightly ajar. The landing light was still on. For some time I could not find the switch, and was almost ready to go back and ask, but I determined not to be beaten, and started to search again. I came across it at length — it was actually beneath the arm of an oak figure mounted on the top post of the balustrade. 'Old devil,' I thought, 'he's given me a lesson in the correct behaviour of a guest.' I walked back softly over the thickly-piled carpet, and stood for a moment outside the door, listening for Priest's chuckle. I heard none — evidently his merriment had exhausted itself. Pushing open the door (it swung on pre-war hinges), I re-entered the room, and then stopped.

It was a strange sight, a sight which made me stand motionless like a statue. Priest and his wife were standing at opposite ends of the boundary-line, and both were pushing frantically against the glass.

For a few moments neither was aware of my presence, and I was trying to think of some less obvious way of attracting their attention than the usual cough, when Mrs Priest first saw me. Her recovery was so quick that it almost deceived me, despite its transparent futility.

'My husband is showing me how Blackheath trounced the Harlequins,' she said. 'I am proving to him that a team of athletic girls would have trounced Blackheath.'

'You found the switch all right?' Priest asked.

'Yes. I didn't know that your house was a kind of St George's Hall.'

'One of Hamilton's ridiculous gadgets. We wondered how long you would take to find it.'

And so we started to talk again, and talked for an hour or more, they apparently delighted with my society, and I genuinely delighted with theirs. The extraordinary barrier which separated us seemed to spoil our pleasure not at all; it was, after all, invisible, and what did it matter therefore? I had concluded that it was simply an eccentricity of the Priests. Most families had their eccentricities — a habit of putting a squeaking cushion on a guest's chair, an absurd family game with cards and dice and complicated rules, a time-table of gong-soundings which has no relation to that of meals. Priest, obviously, had been nervous about how I would take the eccentricity of his household; but finding that I had, in a few seconds, become just as accustomed to it as the club was accustomed to his nightly departure at half past ten, he had immediately regained his ease. And his wife, she, with her long experience in handling situations, had been confident in her own personality availing to carry off this one. She had given her husband sufficient time to notify me of the phenomenon, and had then brightly ignored it. I gained an inkling, that evening, as to how candidates make their way into Parliament on a programme which, written down in black and white, would not deceive a fourth-form schoolboy.

At eleven o'clock I rose, for the second time, to take my leave.

'You must have some port before you go,' said Priest.

Port was, I think, the only form of refreshment I had not already been offered.

'Of course you must!' his wife agreed. Then, to her husband, 'I'm afraid you'll have to get it, dear. Bythorp has probably gone to bed.'

Priest, ignoring my protests, went downstairs.

'I wonder,' said Mrs Priest, 'if you'd care to see my books. I've got some rather nice editions.'

I was rather nonplussed.

'I should like to very much,' I replied, 'but — the glass!'

'Come along,' she said simply, and I walked over to her side of the room. 'I expect you know this edition of Barrie's plays. It's rather jolly, isn't it? I do so love Barrie.'

She stood close beside me as I opened the books one by one and admired them. Then, as I was bending to examine the printer's mark in a collector's edition of Kipling, she raised her head suddenly and whispered in my ear.

'You see, the glass isn't there at all. It's just a quaint idea of Hamilton's.'

At this moment we heard his footstep on the stairs, and putting her hand on my shoulder she gently pushed me.

'Quick!' she said, under her breath. 'Please get back to the other side.'

I returned to my chair, and as Priest came in received an understanding smile. She had got back to her own chair like lightning.

'Bythorp hadn't gone to bed,' said Priest, placing a tray with the glasses and decanters on the smoker's utility. 'He was waiting to lock up. He belongs to the old class of servant, Bythorp.'

'Did you tell him he could go?' his wife asked.

'Yes, but he didn't seem very anxious to.'

'I suppose Watson has gone?'

'I don't know. I heard voices in the kitchen.'

'Watson belongs to the new type of servant,' said Mrs Priest, with a wry smile. 'If you'll excuse me for one minute I'll just go and see.'

'My wife isn't happy about that girl,' Priest said when she had gone. 'Stays up late talking to Bythorp and scrambles the early work next morning. Nuisance!'

He was pouring out the port very slowly, looking intently at the glasses as though he feared that something would happen to the precious liquid if it were not carefully watched. He replaced the stopper in the decanter with that elaborate delay which serves to intensify the action of a screen-play. Rather ceremoniously we raised our glasses together, and then he put his down abruptly.

'There's something I ought to explain to you,' he said quietly.

He stopped, pulling in his lips, and raised his hand to his chin, placing four fingers on top and his thumb underneath. Contrary to custom, he was evidently finding difficulty in the management of his words. His mouth widened, and he began suddenly to laugh, with long silent laughter that had no mirth in it. His next words were thrown out spasmodically between his gusts of noiseless, meaningless merriment.

'The glass — you see — it's not there at all really. It's just my wife's imagination.'

He became quiet again. The wave of hysteria had passed away as quickly as it had come.

'That's the devil of it,' he said, and repeated, 'that's the devil of it.'

A Rendezvous for Mr Hopkins

He was always on deck, except when the weather was cold. The steward carried him up, and settled him on his chair — an odd, small figure, covered to the shoulders with thick scarlet blankets, white head protected by a yellow panama-hat.

He smiled at all of us, and we smiled back, and wished him 'Good morning'. But he seemed so individual, so much apart from us all, with a certain pride in his fragile loneliness, that none of us ever talked to him; at least, for a long time none of us did. We were only a few days outside Port Curtis when I ventured one day to approach him.

I offered to lend him a book — he seemed to have nothing to occupy his time on deck.

'It's very good of you,' he said in his quiet voice, 'but my eyes won't let me read nowadays.'

I asked: 'Would you like me to read to you, Mr —?'

'Mr Hopkins. Oh, thank you, thank you very much! But my mind wanders rather, I'm afraid I should be a poor listener. I should be so pleased, though, if you would sit with me for just a little while.'

I fetched another chair and put it up beside his. It was rather difficult to start a conversation, and he gave me no help.

'I suppose you're travelling for your health?' I asked at length. A weak beginning but it served.

'No,' he answered simply. 'I am travelling to Temelhurst to die.'

I suppose there is some good answer to a statement like that, but I couldn't think what it was. I smiled in a foolish way, I said:

'Oh, the trip will do you a lot of good. You won't feel like dying when you get to Temelhurst.'

He looked at me with his peculiar smile.

'It would hardly do, not to die,' he said. 'You see, I can't afford to live. I've spent all my savings on the fare, everything but a pound or two. . . . It's getting rather chilly, don't you think. I wonder if you'd mind sending for the steward to take me down?'

On the following day he beckoned to me as I passed him, and asked:

'Do you know when we're due in?'

'They say we ought to get there about Thursday midday,' I told him.

'Not before?'

His face was very anxious.

I said: 'Well, you never know your luck. Sailors are always pessimistic, just to put themselves on the safe side. Are you in a hurry?'

'Yes: I have to meet someone at Temelhurst. It's very important that I should get there quickly.'

I thought for a moment, then I said:

'Look here, if you feel up to it I'll get a car at Curtis and drive you straight through to Temelhurst. That would get you there much quicker, and it won't take me much out of my way.'

'You're very kind,' he said warmly. 'Of course I'll pay for the car myself, I can still just run to that.'

'I'd rather have you as my guest!' I said. 'When have you got to be there?'

'When? Oh, it isn't any particular date. It's just a matter of lasting out till I get there. It's going to be — rather close work.'

'Your friend couldn't meet you if you telegraphed?'

'No.'

He was silent for a time, and then he began to speak in a very methodical way, precise, restrained.

'I've had to time things very closely, it's taken me such a long time to save enough money for this voyage. Everything I saved seemed to melt away in doctors' fees. In the end I had to give up the doctors. I got much worse, but I was able to save much quicker. It's been a bit of a gamble.'

'You deserve to pull it off,' I said.

He went on: 'I suppose I oughtn't to burden you with my troubles, but it's so nice to have someone to talk to. It's like this. When people suffer as I do they often kill themselves. The pain's so great, it seems madness not to escape. Well, it would be so easy for me — suicide, I mean. I've only to stop fighting.' He laughed softly. 'It's a struggle, you know! But I must keep my appointment.'

It was not till Thursday evening that we reached Port Curtis. I arranged with the chief steward that Mr Hopkins should be taken to the Hotel Melbourne while I went in search of a car. I was lucky enough to get a good one, a powerful tourer, beautifully sprung, with oversize tyres; and I was round at the hotel with it in less than half-an-hour.

I found Mr Hopkins looking paler than he had ever been on board. But he still smiled.

'I expect you'd like to start straight away?' I said. 'I've got some food with me.'

'Oh yes,' he said, 'Yes — I don't need food, I never take anything but a little gruel. . . . But you, I expect you'd like some dinner before you start?'

I said I'd had a good meal before landing, and with the help of one of the porters I carried him to the car. We put him on the front seat, wedged him in with cushions, and covered him up with rugs. His luggage — one dilapidated suitcase — went in the back. We left Curtis by the old waggon road which goes as straight as a ruler for twenty miles or more across the Brayson flats, and in spite of the broken surface we travelled very smoothly. The cool evening air which came over the windscreen gave a little colour to Mr Hopkins' face. He sat very still, half anxious, half contented. We reached Croak's Point, and the sky had darkened, before he spoke.

'If you wouldn't mind stopping just for a moment, I'd like to show you something.'

I pulled up, and with a good deal of wriggling he got out a little note case from some inside pocket. Out of that came two pieces of faded paper. He gave me one of them and I held it under the dash-lamp.

'It's a plan of Temelhurst,' he said. 'I can't see it clearly myself, but you see the place on the edge of the town which I've marked with a blue cross?'

'Yes, I see it.'

'That's where I want to go. Do you think you can find it?'

'Oh, quite easily! The map's perfectly clear, and in any case we can always ask in the town.'

He smiled contentedly, and I drove on.

Throughout the night I do not think Mr Hopkins spoke at all. But I knew he wasn't asleep because he constantly stretched out his hand and squeezed my arm. It's a strain to drive at night on a road like that, which for mile after mile never alters and hardly turns. For thirty miles or so the bush gathers to the stature of a forest, and then at McCarthy's Crossing the trees fall away and you've nothing to see but the road's red surface and the cattle-wires eternally converging.

But I never felt like falling asleep that night. Every time those thin, cold fingers touched mine it seemed as if a current of new energy passed into me from the shrivelled creature at my side; till I felt as if the power that drove us through the darkness came not from the purring engine but from him. The car and I, we were both of us slaves to the master who sat beside me, his eyes always open, his body very still.

At half-past seven in the morning we had still fifteen miles to go. And Mr Hopkins, his smile all gone, was shaking his head.

'Fifteen miles, are you sure?' he asked faintly.

'Rather less now' I told him.

'I'm afraid — I can't quite do it.'

I put an arm round his shoulders. I said: 'You'll do it all right!'

'If I don't last,' he whispered, 'you'll take me there all the same, won't you!'

I promised that, and half an hour later, when we reached the centre of Temelhurst, he was still gripping my arm with a strength that seemed almost impossible in a man so puny. I stopped to refresh my memory from the map, and then I took the road leading eastwards out of the town. It was an easy route to follow, and in ten minutes we reached the little chapel, surrounded by a graveyard, which Mr Hopkins had marked with a blue cross. I stopped the car.

'Here we are!' I said.

His eyes were closed and he did not move. I took one of his wrinkled hands and gently rubbed it. Presently he stirred, and opened his eyes, and looked about him.

'Yes,' he said, 'this is the place. I've always pictured it like this.'

His hand crept into his pocket and he pulled out the second of his faded papers. I read on this: 'The second path on the right, then the first on the left.'

'Quickly!' he whispered, trembling with excitement. 'Take me there quickly, please!'

There was no one about to help me, but I picked him up in my arms and carried him to the path he wanted. There was a seat there, I put him down on one end of it.

'That's just right, I can see it from here!' he said. 'Thank you so very much. I should like you to leave me here. Thank you, thank you very much.'

I left him, and went into the chapel, a hideous building of yellow brick, where I knelt, feeling a peculiar happiness. I stayed for about ten minutes, and then, fearing that Mr Hopkins might not be covered warmly enough, I went out into the sunshine again.

Mr Hopkins was no longer alone. A girl in a rather old-fashioned blue dress, whom I had not noticed before, had come to sit beside him. In a brief glance I had the impression that she was English, with fair hair and very fair skin. She was pretty, I think, though her beauty was not of the noticeable kind. She sat very close to him, holding one of his hands in both of hers, her head resting against his shoulder. Neither of them saw me, and I fancied that if an army of men had tramped along the path those two would not have noticed them.

To give them a little time I went off to the car and got out a thermos flask which I'd brought from Curtis. When I got back to Mr Hopkins the girl had gone.

I went and stood beside him.

'Who was it?' I asked. 'Where has she gone?'

He didn't answer. His eyes had closed again, but again he was smiling: a smile of triumph.

He was buried next day, beneath a stone on which I could faintly decipher the words: 'Here lies Ethel, wife of Joshua Hopkins, of Enfield, England. Died at Temelhurst, March 8th, 1886, aged twenty-five years. WE SHALL MEET AGAIN.'

Mr Harptop rings the Bell

They came at intervals of a minute or two, a 12, a 5, a 7; but no 13.

Mr Harptop sat down on the steps of his club. He had never done such a thing before, but the long bout of influenza from which he had only just recovered had left him rather weak, and he had been waiting now for over ten minutes. Perhaps the 13 buses stopped running earlier than the others; but it was not midnight yet. Should he go and ask the club porter about it? Well, his position was fairly comfortable, if not altogether dignified. He would wait another five minutes, anyway.

He moved to the other end of the step and put his back against the wall, having arranged his newspaper so that his clothes should not be soiled. Ah! that was very comfortable, and, with his overcoat buttoned up over his scarf, warm as toast. Much better than waiting inside the club and probably missing it when it did come — that had happened before! He stared across the street, down a narrow gap between two buildings, trying, for amusement, to see how many of the features of the alley he could remember.

Another bus came into view, swinging round out of Marriot Street. Mr Harptop, intent on trying to think how many windows you saw at the end of the alley, did not notice it until it was less than seventy yards away, and even then he could not make out the number. His sight was not good. It came thirty yards nearer before he could see — yes, it was a 13. He stepped out into the road and held up his hand, but his signal was not noticed, and the bus passed him without slackening its pace. Gathering his strength and courage, Mr Harptop raced after it, seized the handrail, and swung himself on board.

Most irritating of them not to have stopped! The bus was empty, inside, at any rate, so there was no excuse. The conductor, apparently, was on top. Mr Harptop sat down in the corner seat next to the entrance and began to read his paper.

'Fares, please!'

Without looking up, Mr Harptop held out sixpence.

'Newstead Boundary,' he said.

His fare was taken, and a ticket placed in his hand. Anxious to know why the eighteen-year-old tennis champion had committed suicide in a churchyard, he read to the end of a paragraph before he spoke. Then —

'There seem to be fewer buses on this route than there used to be,' he remarked.

There was no reply.

He glanced up, to find that the conductor had gone. 'Must be slippy on the feet, that chap!' he thought. 'Skipped upstairs in no time.' He went on reading.

'Do you mind moving down a little?' said a voice on his left. 'I'm a wee bit squashed.'

He turned his head sharply. No one there.

'Extraordinary!' he thought. 'I could have sworn — Let me see, I only had two glasses, and they were both well diluted. Perhaps even those were unwise, after the flu. Strange, though; nothing like that has ever happened before.'

Mr Harptop began, all of a sudden, to be afraid of being alone. What if he should faint or something? Not unlikely after a severe illness. Why, in any case, was the conductor staying on top so long? He would see for himself.

Having mounted the stairs, he stood at the top for fully a minute before he could convince himself that the outside of the bus was as empty as the inside. No passengers, no conductor. But what had happened to the fellow?

It then occurred to Mr Harptop that the bus was, perhaps, being driven to the garage for the night, and that they had not meant to take any passengers. It was queer that the conductor should have taken his fare, but this seemed the only sort of explanation, and he must have jumped off subsequently.

He went downstairs again and jerked the bell viciously. It rang, loudly enough to have been heard by everyone in the houses facing the street, but the bus did not stop. On the contrary, it increased its pace. 'It's scandalous,' thought Mr Harptop, 'We must be doing over thirty-five.' He rang again. The bus went still faster. This was monstrous — the man must be drunk! He went toward the front of the bus, stumbling as he did so over what felt like a heavy boot.

'Sorry!' he said instinctively, and realized at once that the boot was his own imagination.

'All right,' said a voice.

Mr Harptop did not stop to consider this new phenomenon. He

made one leap to the front, banged on the window, and shouted, 'Stop!' Then, staring hard through the glass, he felt a cold draught over his shoulders, up the back of his neck and over his head. There was no driver.

It was at this moment that Mr Harptop lost his head. He stood, holding a strap with one hand, frantically pulling the bell with the other, and gasping, 'Stop, stop! You're going too fast, I tell you, you can't go like this, you'll kill us, stop, stop, stop!'

A chorus of voices broke out behind him.

'Oh, Billie, he's going so fast, I'm frightened!'

'It's all right, my dear!'

'One of these young drivers, I suppose!'

'Make him stop!' panted Mr Harptop.

'It's a scandal, this kind of driving!'

'Oh, Billie, if the level-crossing's closed he'll never be able to pull up.'

Mr Harptop stopped speaking. He was still articulating words, but none would come out. He was gazing through the window straight ahead at a red lamp in the middle of the road.

The level-crossing was closed.

Like a runner entering the straight, the bus again increased its speed, hurtling forward as though the red lamp was its winning-post, faster, still faster. The men's voices rose, and above them a peal of wild, idiot laughter. Then every other sound was drowned by a woman's shriek, long, piercing, devastating, turning the flesh into ice, shriller and shriller, and ever more horrible.

Mr Harptop did not hear, only felt, the crash as the gates were shattered. But he saw quite clearly and almost coolly the long engine swooping upon them. Yes, saw it, although he had only one-fifth of a second to do so. Then blackness.

'It's the 12A you want, sir,' the club porter said. 'They've changed the number. You see, people were superstitious after that accident at the level-crossing.'

James returns

1

The first knock at the door was completely drowned by the noise outside. The second, coming in a brief interval of silence, was heard but not recognized. Dr Strong had to bang once again, and with some violence, before the passage light went on, and he could see, through the frosted glass, the huge form of James Winter coming to open the door.

When the bolts had been drawn back and the latch unfastened a nervous face peeped round.

'Oh, it's you, Doctor — thank goodness! I thought it was a constable come to tell me that I had a light showing. Come in, sir, it's not safe outside.'

'I just thought I'd see how your wife was getting on,' said Strong, shutting the door behind him and taking off his overcoat. 'Better switch this light out, or it *will* be a constable next time.'

James did so. 'It's good of you to come, sir,' he said, 'but you shouldn't have troubled. It's risky being in the streets, and it isn't for ten days yet, is it?' He led the way into the kitchen, and bent down to encourage the last glowing coals of a sinking fire.

'My wife's away, and I wanted company really,' Strong replied. (He had his own reasons.) 'So this visit won't be on the bill,' he added brightly, dropping unceremoniously into the one comfortable chair which the kitchen afforded.

'Mary'll be down in a minute,' said James. 'They always must tidy up a bit, you know, no matter what's happening. I hope you'll excuse the kitchen. They say that the pipes from the boiler give you some protection. I don't know if there's anything in it, but it helps to keep Mary calm, you know. Cigarette? Or would you rather have your pipe?'

Strong preferred his pipe. 'It's bad luck on you, this,' he said, stuffing the bowl with delicate fingers, 'having your leave spoilt. It's only three weeks, isn't it?'

James struck a match, and lighted both pipes. 'Yes, three weeks; it would have been less if I hadn't had dysentery. They took pity on my cheesey face, you see.' He pulled at his pipe vigorously for a second or two to get it under way. 'Well, I wouldn't mind all this business, only —'

A tremendous report, followed by another, silenced him for a moment. When the windows had stopped rattling he continued, 'Only it gets on Mary's nerves so. And I do so want her to have no worry, just at this time. Of course we're not getting proper sleep. Three nights in succession is hardly playing the game, is it?'

He laughed, and went upstairs in search of his wife. They came down together, she in rather elaborate négligée, looking very pretty, Strong thought.

'Will you excuse me being like this?' she asked. 'I thought it wouldn't matter really, you being a doctor.' She smiled at him mischievously. 'You've done splendidly with the fire, James. Doctor, shall I make you some tea? I could boil a kettle in no time. Oh, there they go again! The noise is awful, isn't it?'

Strong watched her as she rattled on. 'It's bad,' he thought, 'she's all nerves.'

'No, I won't have tea, thanks. Yes, it's a beastly hubbub. Reminds me exactly of my little Vera playing scales.'

'Oh, it's not really so bad,' said James, in what he honestly considered a soothing manner. 'We get much worse row on the other side.'

He saw at once that his words had had the wrong effect, and changed his tactics.

'I expect they're trying for Hendon again,' he continued lightly. 'They must be rotten shots. The nearest they've got so far is Potters Bar.'

He stopped, saw that he had blundered again, and fell into confused silence.

'Talking of Vera,' said Strong, 'she seems to be having a fine time at Bath. She wrote the other day and said that if only daddy and mummy and Mrs Winter were with her she'd be in heaven. You know, she always remembers how kind you were when you were looking after her.'

(James, immediately, began to wonder why he had not thought of Bath for Mary, and whether the doctors there were frightfully expensive.)

'She's a sweet lass!' said Mary.

The guns were still rumbling, but the noise had grown less.

'They've chased them off,' said James. 'We'll get the all-clear presently.'

Strong racked his brains for conversation. He was tired. 'The fire's jolly, isn't it,' he remarked. Then, stretching out his legs and thrusting his hands deep into his jacket pockets he felt something hard. Salvation!

It was a pocket edition of *Three Men in a Boat*. Strong nearly always carried Jerome; he had read *Three Men in a Boat*, from cover to cover, some fifty times, and the *Diary of a Pilgrimage* nearly as often. One or other of these books invariably provided the slight cerebral massage necessary for his complete enjoyment of the last pipe before going to bed. He read them, too, whenever the crush in a railway carriage made a newspaper impossible. Jerome was Strong's Marcus Aurelius. He came to him for soothing and comfort when the misery of the long wards had made his heart sick. And now, once again, his Marcus Aurelius was by him in time of need.

'Would you like me to read to you?' he asked briskly. 'I expect you know this off by heart, but it's worth reading again, I always think.'

He was cut short by a terrific detonation, a noise like that of a dozen bass drums thumped in unison. It felt as if the window-panes curved inwards with the force. 'That's a bomb,' said James to himself. 'One of the blighters must have got separated. They're chasing him and he's getting his own back.'

'Yes do, Doc,' he said hastily.

Strong opened the book at random, and leapt into the middle of Uncle Podger's picture-hanging activities. The guns in the neighbourhood had started again now, at full strength. There was a series of double reports, and very soon the second explosion began to follow the first more closely. Skipping on, Strong started the Hampton Court maze episode, glancing at Mary over the corner of his spectacles.

James laughed heartily. 'That's good, Doc!' he roared, every time Strong paused. 'No one writes such good stuff nowadays. By Jove, that's funny, do go on!'

A mighty effort, this. He was watching his wife so carefully that he had not heard a word. She, in her turn, was tittering bravely, not having the faintest idea what Strong was reading.

There was silence outside for a few moments, while the doctor, reading quickly, was dealing with George's shirt. James thought that he heard a buzz overhead, and laughed still louder so that Mary should not notice it. Then the guns opened up again, and this time the second explosion came from the opposite side of the house.

Strong went on reading. 'This is a good bit, about Montmorency's performance in Oxford.' (Thank God! the noise was dwindling away, perhaps that really was the last.) He came to the end of the chapter, and hunted feverishly for another real screamer. Silence now. Surely they would hear the all-clear soon.

Then came the biggest noise of all, sudden, deafening, over-powering. It seemed to claim the whole world for itself, making silence a mere intruder.

What happened was not really much. Ten panes of glass broke simultaneously, the pieces flying inwards. The dresser fell forwards, crashing the china on to the floor. And the table, as though it had been sharply kicked from underneath, jumped six inches into the air.

James stood up, and remained motionless for about ten seconds. Then he gave one glance at his wife, lying back, white, in her chair, with the doctor bending over her; gave a little, frightened cry; and walked out of the house, into the darkened streets of Southgate, along the Epping Road, past Waltham Cross; bareheaded, no overcoat.

At seven o'clock next morning, the hour when his wife died, he was still walking, northwards.

2

'You are taking a very serious risk,' said Mrs Strong. 'After all, he's happy enough.'

'No, he's not happy enough,' her husband contradicted. 'He's cheerful, perhaps, but so are his hens. You can't allow a man to go on living with an imitation soul; and I can't bear the way he treats Joyce.'

'But he's not unkind to her.'

'Oh no, he's kind enough, but he won't realize who she is. The child can see it, and it depresses her horribly. You see, she's twelve now, and old for her age, so she understands the situation pretty well. I just can't bear to see them together.'

'I suppose you must do it, then.'

'You can trust me, my dear. I'm not an ignoramus in these cases. You must remember that I worked with Henriques for a year, and he never had a failure . . .'

3

James did not mind the east wind that had swept over Hertfordshire for three days. 'It stings you and warms you up, Mrs Strong,' he said, his face glowing with it. And certainly there was little reason to complain, while the sun shone down from a naked sky, licking away the last traces of the previous week's snow. There was that in the air which makes the world young, as it is young only in the autumn of Hertfordshire; where, beneath the falling leaves, cars are racing along the brittle roads all day long; out towards the Berkshire hills and back home before theatre-time to where the shop-windows, in November, are already being filled with the bright frilleries of Christmas.

James put down the buckets of mash he was carrying in both hands, to the loudly-expressed annoyance of his expectant hens, and turned to face the doctor.

'No!' he said for the third time. 'I don't want to go anywhere near London. I've never been there — except once when I was a boy, I believe — but it's a noisy place by all accounts. I prefer to stay here.' And picking up the buckets he set off again down the cinder-path.

'But won't you come for a drive?' Strong pleaded.

'Yes, daddy do!' his daughter chimed in.

'You mustn't call me that!' said James. 'I told you when you came before. You make me feel old.' He stopped to gaze at her with the piercing eyes which had rather frightened her at first. 'You're rather like a little girl I once knew, I can't remember where,' he murmured.

'But won't you come?' Joyce persisted, as he wandered off to the other side of the hen-run.

'Well, there's no harm in it,' he said, as though the suggestion had only just been made. Actually he had spent the whole afternoon refusing.

'That's right!' said Strong. 'Come along.'

By dint of helping and cajoling they had him in the back of the Morris-Cowley in ten minutes, sitting bolt upright like an old lady more accustomed to a Victoria, all muffled up in a heavy overcoat and woollen scarf, smiling just a little, as a child smiles who feels the excitement of a first pantomime but is too young to make head or tail of it.

'Quite comfy behind?' asked the doctor. He drove off in the direction of Hemel Hempstead, glancing every few moments in the driving mirror to see how James was taking it. James took it well. He was obviously pleased at seeing the scenery race by him, and kept filling his lungs with deep draughts of the fine air. He was silent most of the time, but he glanced continually at Joyce, and each time moved his lips as though preparing to speak. 'New experience for me, this — he's a nut at driving, Mr Strong,' was all he actually said in the first half-hour. Joyce prattled whenever she could think of something to prattle about, pointing out odd bits of scenery, talking of other motors she had ridden in. His sudden glances made her stop, but she was learning to smile under his gaze. Once she detected the glimmer of a response in his eyes, and was overjoyed. Joyce had observed the world shrewdly in the course of twelve years.

Strong carried out his plan fearlessly. At Hemel Hempstead he turned right, towards Redbourn, and a few minutes later, turning right again, joined the stream of cars flashing towards St Albans. At Barnet they stopped for tea. James was silent throughout the meal, but ate heartily and still seemed happy. Then, as darkness fell swiftly, they drove southward again, through Enfield. The doctor had his first feeling of nervousness as they came into Southgate. He could no longer see James's face, and he would have given a great deal to do so. Every moment he was expecting to hear a sudden sharp cry, and was regretting that he had brought Joyce. But the sharp cry did not come. Actually James was staring vaguely at the lamps which hurried by, thinking of nothing but a bit of wire fencing which had to be mended; and Joyce was asleep.

'We'll just pop in here and warm ourselves up,' said Strong casually, as he brought the car to a standstill in front of 14 Ashby Road.

'Well, I'm not cold, but you must be tired after all that steering, Mr Strong.'

That was all James said, as he followed the doctor into his old home. And there was the same worn carpet, the same hall seat, the same wallpaper slightly more faded, the picture of Nelson dying, and the special middle-class suburban odour.

A fire had been lit in the kitchen, and they sat round it, James pleased with its cheerful warmth, Joyce rather pale, but holding herself steadily with the conscientiousness of a child on the stage, Strong watching them both.

'Shall I read to you?' he asked, when they had sat in silence for a minute or two.

(Curious this — no response! Was it too severe on the child? A mistake to have her, perhaps, but her presence would help and she was doing awfully well. Surely James would break through presently!)

'Just as you like, Mr Strong.'

Strong took *Three Men in a Boat* from his pocket, and read through the Uncle Podger episode. James stared into the fire; he did not seem to be listening. Strong went on — the maze at Hampton Court — Montmorency at Oxford. Joyce giggled a little, and James gave her one of his quick glances. Then back went his eyes to the fire.

4

Four small boys, very reluctant to miss a firework display in Mr Laming's grounds, but buoyed up by a sense of duty fulfilled, were assembling at the scout room in Warbeck Street. Tonight, Mr Waters said, they must see if they could get the reveille perfect. They put the bugles to their lips and puffed like Scots pipers. The improvement was not noticeable; not, at least, by Mr Waters. But the noise was terrific. It burst out of the scout room and went echoing through Southgate, waking the local babies and infuriating the local listeners-in. It drifted into the kitchen at 14 Ashby Road.

'It's all over, thanks be!' said James. 'I think we'd better get to bed now, Doctor. Come along, my dear.'

5

He stayed at Southgate for two days, running errands to the shops, helping to dry up, treating Joyce very affectionately, rather perplexed by Mrs Strong's presence in the house. With great rapidity he began to lose his mystified expression, and to talk a little more, asking why there were white lines on the roads and commenting on the size of the buses. He never mentioned his hens. On the third day he disappeared.

Strong scoured the neighbourhood, and made more than one trip into Hertfordshire. He found no trace. On the second night after the disappearance an SOS message was broadcast, and an answer came through in twenty minutes. Mr Taylor, employed in one of Thomas Cook's offices, had, on the previous day, seen a gentleman answering to the description given. Yes, Winter was the name. He had behaved rather strangely; he wished to go abroad without a passport, declaring that he was travelling in the King's service. Mr Taylor had been quite unable to make anything of what Mr Winter had said, but had managed to obtain a passport for him, and had sold him a ticket for Boulogne.

They found James a fortnight later, very haggard, trudging along the road from Nieuport to Ypres, looking for his company.

At Grips with Morpheus

'I'm awfully sorry to put you fellows on to this,' Sanderson said, 'but it just can't be helped. I know you've had a stiff day, but there's no one else I can send.'

We said we understood, which we did.

'I take it you're clear as to the position?' he went on. 'It's this blue line I've drawn,' pointing to the map, 'that we want to stick tight to. Actually the Boche are some way further back, but we haven't enough men to coop them up there. The point about this line is that it's fairly easy to hold. They've had a very nasty drubbing, and I don't think they'll feel like rushing into the great open spaces. But they may try their luck at sneaking along those three roads, keeping in the ditches, with the idea of deploying when they get into the wood. See?'

We saw.

'Well, it's the centre of those three roads that I want you to look after. The observation people say that there's a house or barn of some sort standing where I've put a red cross. That ought to be quite a good spot to watch from, and it won't be difficult to find. I'll lend you my compass, which is a sound one. Now I don't want you to start a dooce of a great Armageddon without any reason. But if you see any cheery fellows sneakin' down the road, just blaze at 'em with the Lewis. We want to give them the idea that the whole place is pretty strongly fortified.'

With a few further brief words of introduction he dismissed us. He was as fagged as we were, poor devil, and his night's work wasn't over by a long way.

Ten minutes later we set out under a rather unenthusiastic moon, with maps, torches, compass, revolvers, light rations, and a Lewis. We cursed the Lewis. That part of the country was new to us both, but we had visualized the map pretty clearly, so finding the way wasn't difficult — to begin with. I can't say it was easy going, though. Thick mud all over the place, and masses of wire. Uphill, too, most of it. We just tramped on mechanically, too tired to speak except for an oath or two when one of us fell over something. Dickson seemed on the whole to mind it less than I did — he could always keep going for hours and hours on end, that chap. And he insisted on taking more than his share in carrying the Lewis, bless him!

We had gone about half a mile when the fog came. It just dropped on us suddenly, like a cloak thrown from heaven, and simply blotted out everything.

'This puts our show right out of it,' Dickson grunted. 'We can't stop them if they try to counter under this. I only hope they all fall over something and break their ruddy necks.'

I endorsed this sentiment.

'There really isn't much point in our going at all, when you come to think of it,' he added.

'There's no point at all in this rotten war, if it comes to that,' I said. 'We've got to get there, all the same.'

'If we can,' said Dickson.

And certainly it was a problem. At least, I thought at first it would be easy enough, but as we progressed — if 'progressed' is the right word — things became rapidly more involved. I was supposed to be 'navigator', and keeping my eye on map and torches I selected immediate objectives, and passed them on to Dickson. Thus —

'In about a hundred yards we will come to a brook.'

We travelled two hundred yards, and then came to what seemed to be a road of sorts. The brook didn't appear for another quarter of an hour. Dickson was too sleepy to be in his best form, but he cursed me as jauntily as he could.

'I suppose you are not holding the map upside down?' he suggested.

I retorted to the effect that all names on the map were readable, which seemed to indicate that I was holding it correctly.

'You do know how to read a compass, I suppose?' was his next comment. 'The south is indicated by the letter S, the east by E, and so forth.'

'Righto, you have a go, since you know so much about it!'

He took the map, and handed me the Lewis.

'Ah,' he said, after a minute's scrutiny. 'You've got all muddled up. We've just crossed over a sort of cart-track, haven't we? and about five minutes ago you very carelessly hurt yourself against a wall. Well, that places us exactly on the spot which, for reference purposes, I shall call Z. We now proceed in a Nor-nor-ee direction, and we shall shortly come to what used to be a railway embankment.

Bien! Continuons, messieurs!'

We covered another half-kilometre or so, a most unpleasant one, and came to a thin coppice, which Dickson and I identified on the map about four kilometres north-west of his 'position Z'. I asked him if he had ever studied map-reading scientifically, or had merely attended general lectures on the subject.

It was the same all along. The artillery had not only completely wiped out every vestige of natural features, including hills. It had created new features, using its imagination pretty freely. And when, in the treacly fog, trees looked like houses until you actually bumped into them, picking up landmarks was an exhausting business. We knew we were going in the right direction, and we knew we must eventually come on to the road we wanted. But that was all. And time and again we began to think, quite seriously, that we had gone over the beastly thing without noticing it. You can do things quite as silly as that when you are fagged out, and can't see five yards ahead of you.

It was when Dickson developed a limp, which he tried to hide, that I got wind-up. He said it was nothing — boot just a wee bit tight or something. But I could see that the poor fellow couldn't go on much longer — a tired man can't put up with pain indefinitely. I suggested that he should sit down a few moments, while I scouted ahead. But he pointed out, very sensibly, that we'd probably lose contact altogether. So we plugged on — it was agony, and five minutes later I felt and heard loose stones under my feet. For a moment I hardly dared hope that it really was the road. But a brief inspection relieved my doubts. It was an obvious main road, apparently very straight, as the French roads usually are, and moving along it eastwards we came to the house in less than half a mile.

We thought it must be the house we wanted. There were jolly few of them still standing in that part of the world, and it answered to our knowledge of its locality pretty well. It was right on the edge of the road, surrounded by the remains of a wall, and another wall led off at right angles across a meadow behind. This I found by a tour of inspection, which cost me some effort. There was not, as there should have been, a clump of trees on the other side of the road, nor any sign of the fact that they ever had been there. But the fog had played us a good many tricks, and we both suspected by that time that the maker of the map had been nothing but a practical humorist, so the absence of a few trees didn't worry us.

If there's one thing I hate more than all others, it is entering a deserted house after dark. I mean to say, it's bad enough if you know quite well that the house *is* deserted. But when it may possibly be occupied by a lot of irritable Huns, I just hate it. Stupid, perhaps, but there you are. In this case I was too weary to feel as nervy as usual; in fact, I flashed my torch about in most suicidal manner. The rooms below were empty, and the stairs intact, bar a few boards and the banisters. I crept up cautiously, making, with my mud-clogged boots, a noise like a whole regiment. I found that the upper storey had been pretty well smashed up, but one room had escaped — it had even a door. This I opened, and my torch showed three men lying in the corner. Not men, though, on closer inspection — only sacks. Yet I could have sworn that one of them had moved!

Dickson followed me up, and we planted the Lewis in the window, which fortunately looked over the road.

'We take it in turns to keep a look-out, I suppose,' said I, when we had consumed a portion of our rations.

'Righto! I'll go first — I won't be able to sleep just at present, this foot's giving me gip. It's now twenty-three thirty, just after. I'll wake you up at two.'

'All right,' I replied, settling myself with as much comfort as the bare floor afforded.

'I hope,' Dickson continued, 'that the blighters haven't got through already. According to schedule we should have been here nearly two hours ago. I should swear if they had. All our day's work undone, and those topping fellows pipped for nothing.'

'Hope not,' I murmured and went to sleep.

Dickson shook me. 'Your turn,' he said, 'Sorry old man, but I can't keep my peepers open any longer.'

'Wha' d'you mean?' I asked.

'It's two o'clock.'

'But I've only just got to sleep.'

'You've been snoring like a hippopotamus with influenza for over two hours.'

I got up — it felt like pushing a ton weight off my chest.

'Have you seen anything?' I asked.

No answer. Dickson was asleep.

I had been sweating in every limb when I got to the house, but it was cold now, fearfully cold. No glass in the window, of course. I was rather thankful at first — it helped me to keep awake, but after ten minutes I began to be afraid that I should get stiff with it. My greatcoat seemed useless against the draught. Fog still as thick as ever.

How did one keep awake? There was some business of fixing a bayonet so that it dug into your chin if your head dropped. But I was too tired and cold to fit up anything so ingenious as that. I tried all kinds of things, kicking my ankle periodically, pinching my wrists, repeatedly shaking my head. But I was getting sleepier and sleepier. The rousing effect of getting up and standing in the window was wearing off.

I pricked myself sharply with a jack-knife. I dared not go deep, in case the flow of blood should have a weakening effect. But I longed for sharp physical pain — anything would be much easier to bear than straining against this overwhelming power.

The difficulty was having to watch. If I could have paced up and down, it would have been much easier. But if I didn't keep my eyes glued on the road I might just as well not be there at all. And one couldn't even light a cigarette. My eyes seemed all out of focus. Incessant blinking made no difference — they just *wouldn't* hold that tiny patch of road that was visible through the fog. And my ears seemed to be smitten with deafness, though I turned my fingers in them every half-minute.

I glanced at my luminous watch. Only twenty minutes had gone. Dickson was sleeping very uneasily, evidently. He was murmuring the whole time; it sounded like poetry, and I thought I caught a line of Swinburne, jerked out in the rhythm of a slow train going over a badly laid track. Must be the bad foot worrying him!

The road! Good Lord! I had taken my eyes off it, and was looking straight into a patch of fog level with the window, a patch which seemed to go round and round like a whirlpool.

I fixed the road again, now with a fierce concentration. Yes, it *was* Swinburne. 'Grow straight in — The strength of — Thy spirit —' and with the cadences, some spoken and some snored, the road rose and fell, coming towards me, receding, and being lost till I recalled it by savagely rubbing my eyes.

Grow straight in — up — The strength of — down —

I did wish he would stop, or at any rate try something different. I was sick of Hertha. Should I take his boots off? He had been too sleepy to think of doing so. But that would mean losing the road for a minute. One couldn't let the Boche get through. It was just wasting good lives.

The fog grew no thinner. The road still rose and fell. It was getting the better of me, and soon I should lose it altogether. Had I better wake Dickson? No, not fair to do that. Besides, it would take a lot of doing. He was at it again. 'Grow straight in — The strength of —'

The road rose again, higher this time, right to the level of the window, and a man stepped from it on to the sill.

'What do you want?' I asked him.

'I'm Sleep,' he replied.

'Then clear out!'

'No, you can't get rid of me that way.'

'Get out!' I roared again. And seizing him bodily I threw him down on to the road. He was gone. It only needed determination, after all. The road was clearer now, steadier. I saw the fellow hiding in a patch of fog a bit to the right, but he evidently funked me.

A few minutes later, or was it an hour? the road was clearer. I held it now, quite firmly. My eyes seemed to have got into focus at last, and without any effort they kept the road in its position. The cold wasn't so bad now. I had got to the stage when it didn't matter. And everything was much more restful. I did hope no Germans would come along to spoil the peace of it all. After all, watching wasn't such a bad business. Not much to do.

The ditch on the far side went back a little, making the road wider. Someone was coming now. A car swept into view, bearing head-lamps which shone mauve, no wheels, but it glided over the rough road like a barge towed at a gentle pace by a powerful horse. And inside was Amarita; yes, I knew she would be there.

'Can you give me a lift?' I asked.

'Of course,' she answered. How clear and jolly her laugh was! 'But you can't sit with me. You'll be quite comfortable in the back, if you put your head on the side.'

Yes, it was fairly comfortable.

The road turned, and we swung into Piccadilly. I leaned forward to speak.

'You mustn't come so near,' cautioned Amarita. 'Danger!'

Well, that didn't matter. It was so very exhilarating to be anywhere near Amarita. I felt a warm, pulsating sensation right through my body. Awfully cosy.

'I only wanted to tell you,' I said. 'I'm looking out for Germans.

We mustn't let any pass, you know.'

'They won't get past here,' said Amarita, as we raced along the Thames at Burnham. 'There are heaps of policemen.'

Yes, there were, heaps of them. And one of them was Sanderson.

'You're keeping your eyes skinned, Bobby?' he asked.

'Yes sir, quite all right. Seen nothing so far.'

'Grow straight in — The strength of —'

The road darkened again (we had just been through Ealing) and I saw Sleep wink at me as he darted into the thickest part of the fog again.

I raised my head sharply — it had fallen on to the window-sill. Then I looked at my watch. Good God! It was a quarter to four, and the last time I had looked it had been just after three. Had I been sleeping? Was I awake now? Yes, wide awake now, and devilish cold and stiff.

So I had been asleep. That was one of the choicest crimes in the whole military code. To sleep on duty! What if someone had got through! Well, it was rather beastly, all that firing-party business, but it didn't take long. The trouble would be — the other side. Tommy would be awfully decent about it. He would say, 'Of course I understand, old man.' But there would be just a look in his eyes which said, 'It wasn't much good us getting plugged, since you mucked the whole show afterwards.' Horrible! but perhaps a good lie would save my skin, it would at least put off the evil day. I could say the Boche had skirted that bit of road. The war had made morality a pure farce, anyway.

I did so want to go to sleep again. It seemed a harder struggle than ever now. But that wouldn't do.

The crackle of a branch somewhere disturbed my thoughts. Was it just my imagination, or was it down the road to the right? If so, that meant the worst. Someone had got through. Should I wake Dickson?

The fog was lifting a little, at last. I peered into the waste of darkness, and thought I caught a glimmer of light, just a tiny flash, as though someone had lit a match, and quickly extinguished it. There, another!

I bent down and shook Dickson by the arm.

'I can't turn out today,' he mumbled. 'Tell Matron I've got a spot of flu.'

I shook him again, and then violently, but he only cursed me sleepily, and wouldn't wake up.

I craned my head into the darkness, and now the place seemed to be alive with noises. Nothing very definite, a little crackle, a slight hissing noise like a snore. Just my nerves possibly. But I could see things now, as the air became clearer, slight movements of dark mass. That couldn't possibly be all imagination. I reminded myself how often I had got jumpy over what had turned out to be a bush swayed by the wind, or a stray hungry dog prowling about in the deserted fields. But that wasn't any comfort.

Ugh! it was wretched, these noises. Daylight would be ever so much better, even if it revealed the whole German army, massed a hundred deep right round the house, with Hindenburg in the middle, brandishing a fiery sword. The uncanniness, the shapes without form, the noises produced by no earthly agency. That was what made me feel like a nursery kid, longing for its mother.

Still, there was really no point in waking Dickson. He deserved his sleep, poor chap!

The dawn came at last, and the remains of the fog went with the darkness. I've watched the sunrise pretty often, but I've never seen one quite like that. A dull purple glow on the horizon, changing its colour like those 'rainbow-caramels' that a child sucks, but much more quickly, becoming brighter and brighter. It threw out a long soft tongue, and licked the tips of everything. Every bush, every blade of grass, was just tipped with gold. The cold wasn't coldness any longer, but freshness. The world, waking, was just full of life, and it was nice to watch it, feeling so dead sleepy, and yet somehow in harmony. It was worth waiting for, that sunrise. And now it didn't matter so much being shot. I had tasted for a few minutes the deepest and most exhilarating wine of life. *Demain? Ça n'importe!*

No sign of animal life anywhere. A slight wind was stirring the trees, but there wasn't even a thrush or a lark to share the drama with me. So it *had* been all imagination!

When the light was full I scanned the landscape, but my scrutiny revealed nothing. Well, there had been no row, except guns in the very far distance, so they couldn't have got through, thank God! I might have saved myself a lot of wind-up if I had thought more logically before.

I was congratulating myself, and wondering whether to risk a cigarette, when I heard a noise right below me. Fool that I was! While I had been philosophically surveying the view from the window someone had come up from behind. Was it a scout or a whole blinking section?

Someone stamped up the stairs. I covered the door with my revolver, and as it opened said in my schoolboy German.

'Halt! Drop your arms!'

'All right — English!' said a Harrow-faced young captain laconically, 'and what the hell are you doing here, anyway, if I may ask?'

Sanderson apologized to us both quite effusively, when he interviewed us four hours later.

'My fault, entirely,' he said. 'I accidentally gave you old Burton's compass, which is a dud. Yes, you were about half a mile inside the line. No, they didn't try to counter —'

The Last Page

In February 1922 I was in Ypres on business. I almost laugh when I think of doing business in Ypres — Ypres, the memory of which is fixed for ever in my mind as that of ruin, uncanny desertion, and bleak discomfort, the ghost of a town that had been. But the fact remains, it was necessary for me to interview Paul Desmatres, and he, that massive emblem of cold reality, was to be found in the town which I still think of as belonging to a horrible dream.

I had booked a room in a little hotel in the market-place, from the windows of which today you can see the Menin Gate. In the tourist season I believe this place does a very thriving business in forty-franc *déjeuners* for charabanc parties, but in mid-winter it is almost empty, and you get good attention from the superfluity of servants. When I signed my name in the register I found that only four other visitors had arrived since the beginning of the month — one from Amsterdam, two from Boston, Mass. (I long to find a hotel where the name of that city does not spring at me from the register) and one from London.

The name of this last visitor, written in a very bold feminine hand, made me jump. It was 'Mrs John Colquortson'.

I suppose that if you went to Somerset House you could discover any number of Colquortsons — the fact that there is one denotes the probability of there being many others — and I imagine, further, that some ten per cent of these may bear the baptismal name of John. These considerations, however, did not strike me at that moment. I felt certain that there was only one Mrs John Colquortson in the world, and that this was she. As to the latter, I happened to be right.

I think I should have remembered John Colquortson if I had known him only for a few hours; as a matter of fact our friendship had lasted for several months. 'John Con' we always called him; the nickname, I fancy, was started by one Lieutenant Horford, who flippantly maintained that 'Con' was the correct pronunciation of Colquortson. Actually it is pronounced Coltson, I believe. I remember John Con for his unnatural cowardice and his unique heroism, but above all for his tremendous sanity.

It was this last quality which made the war so very hard for him. He always sought a reason for everything he did, and was worried when he could find none. He could never, as other men do, forget everything but the work or the passion of the moment and plunge himself into it. Plunging was, in fact, almost a logical impossibility for him. He went into each new passage in life with his eyes open, looking round cautiously, weighing things up; which is good enough tactics for a schoolmaster (John Con's job before the war) but not wholly satisfactory for an officer on active service.

He was, as anyone might expect, a violent pacifist. Over and over again he would say, 'The important question is not who started this rotten war but why we are all carrying it on. If we and the Boche and everyone else just refused to go ahead with it, why, the thing would stop. That's a truism. Well, why don't we? Why do we all do all we can to slay a lot of poor blighters when we've absolutely nothing against them except that they're under orders to slay us?'

'Well, why do you?' I asked him more than once.

His reply to this question was always very long and complicated. I can only give the gist of it.

'Pure funk,' he would say. 'I could hardly bear to have people sneering at me as a war-time conchy, and I certainly couldn't stand them sneering at my wife for being married to one. But I have a sort of moral justification; at least, sometimes I think I have, though I suppose it's casuistry. You see, I funked fighting even more than I funked not fighting. I loathe loud noises — I couldn't bear crackers when I was a kid — and until recently I used to faint right off whenever I saw a spot of blood. I can't bear discomfort, I detest filth, I abominate lice, and the thought of pain makes me sick. So you see, I had something else to get the better of besides moral scruples before I joined up. I really won the stiffer battle, if you see what I mean, so I come out with good marks for quixotry. I don't know if that's really much comfort.'

I did not wholly understand him. His mind was more subtle than mine, and it moved so rapidly that he was only able to throw out a scanty scent, difficult to follow. But from what I was able to understand I couldn't help admiring the queer chap.

I met John Con's widow at dinner. A short, rather plump little lady, about thirty-five as far as I could judge; very lively in manner, a face whose charm was partly in its slight tan and general appearance of healthiness; a smiling, whimsical mouth, which contrasted oddly with a tired look in her eyes. She was dressed, rather poorly, in grey.

We were sitting at adjacent tables, side by side, as it were, with only a yard or so between us. (We had both shifted our tables so as to be as near as possible to the fire.) She asked my help when she was in difficulties with a waiter whose quite extensive English vocabulary apparently included no words relating to eating.

'Excuse me, can you tell me what this is?' she asked, pointing to an item on the menu.

'I cannot translate it,' I replied. 'In fact, I doubt if there is any English equivalent, but it means a piece of meat of some sort stuck up on a piece of toast, covered with white sauce, and tasting exclusively of garlic.'

She thanked me, and later we fell into conversation. She asked me if I knew this part of the world well. I said that I had known it much too well when it was another world altogether, and she became rather excited over this.

'You were here during the war?' she asked.

'Yes, in 'fifteen.'

'Then I wonder if you ever came across my husband, Captain Colquortson?'

I hesitated for just an instant.

'Yes,' I said, 'I knew him quite well. I saw your name in the register,' I went on, rather confusedly, 'and I wondered if—'

'But why didn't you introduce yourself?' she demanded.

'I wasn't sure if you were the right person, and — well, I was rather shy, you know,' I explained a little lamely. Actually my reasons had been quite different. 'I will remedy the omission now; my name is Barlow.'

'Major Barlow?'

'Formerly.'

She held her lips tightly for a moment, while, as I could see, she forced back memories that were darting into her mind.

'He often spoke of you in his letters,' she said.

Later in the evening we met again in the tiny lounge, and Mrs Colquortson became confidential.

After manoeuvring the conversation with some dexterity and determination, 'I wonder if you could help me over something?' she said.

I was very ready to do all that I could. Probably, I thought, she was here to search for her husband's grave, and did not know how to begin.

'You will think,' she said, 'that I am completely insane, but I must carry this through and I can't really do it without your help. I suppose you remember roughly the positions that you and my husband were in? I mean, what lines you occupied, and so on?'

'Well, only vaguely. You see, I travelled about a good deal, and everything's completely altered.'

'Still, that's better than nothing,' she affirmed eagerly, 'if you will help me. I want to try and find something — I know it sounds hopeless, but I'm going to try.'

'May I know what it is?' I asked her.

She hesitated before she replied.

'Well, yes, of course you must,' she said slowly and with curious shyness, 'but please don't tell me I'm a fool, though of course you'll think I am. It's — it's a portion of a letter.'

To this day I cannot think how she failed to notice my start of horrified surprise.

'One of his letters,' she explained, 'the last one I received, and therefore the most precious, was incomplete. There were four foolscap-size pages, written on both sides, and at the bottom of the fourth page are the words, "There is one thing which I meant to tell you about before, but —" and there it ends. Somehow he forgot to put the last page in the envelope. Well, that's what I'm going to hunt for, whether you will help me or not.'

'Of course I will help you,' I said, 'but — certainly I would not call you a fool, I can quite understand how you feel about it — only I'm afraid, frankly, that there's not a ghost of a chance. I mean, anything solid one might find among all the litter that's still left, though that would be only a million-to-one chance. A piece of paper, on the other hand, couldn't possibly have survived, when you think of all the muck, and the clearing up that's been going on, and the weather and —'

She cut me short. 'I know it sounds absurd,' she said, 'but things just as delicate as paper have been preserved for thousands of years. It's within the range of possibility that this sheet got rammed into a tunic pocket or an ammunition pouch. There must be piles of stuff like that about still — things that were beneath the notice even of curio-hunters. And I must, must find it. I feel, somehow, that I shall.'

God is kind to widows, you know. You will admit, now, won't you, that there is a chance in ten thousand?'

'One in ten million, I'm afraid,' I said, trying, all the same, to keep the hopelessness out of my voice.

Liar that I was! I could have told her, there and then, precisely what had happened to the last page of that letter.

As I sat there, staring into the fire, my mind formed a picture of John Con's face; rather curiously, it was a clean-shaven face, though hitherto I had always thought of him as having a heavy moustache. He shaved this off a few weeks before his death, partly, he said, 'in case the trench-bugs adopt it as an attractive domicile,' and partly to make him feel a bit younger. Round that face, with its very piercing eyes and half-cynical lips, a scene gathered itself.

It was a dancing place in Paris. John Con and I had wangled a short leave there, after a long period 'up for'ard', as our sergeant (late of the merchant service) termed it, when reliefs had been scanty and nearly everyone had been put on to double shift. We had made our way thither by lorry-jumping, choosing Paris because, though you could not get away from the war anywhere, the good folk in that city did try to keep some of their proverbial gaiety going for the sake of the wounded *poilus* who were there in thousands. We stayed in bed most of the mornings, spent the afternoons in seeing so much of the serene beauty of the place as was not under sandbags, and let ourselves go properly in the evenings. We sought out revues, and roared with laughter at the senseless jokes, happy simply in knowing that within a radius of some miles no one was being murdered. To one of these revues we went three times. We joined the little bands of cosmopolitan soldiery in the *cafés* and sang foolish songs with enormous gusto, putting our own words to the tune when we could not follow the French ones. And, on our last evening we went to the hall I have already mentioned, a place glorying in the title *Grand Dance Club de Londres*.

It was a smoky, garish little hall. We dropped in there because I thought that flashy music and colours were more likely than anything else to put a little spirit into John Con, but at first it seemed quite a failure. For a long time we sat at one of the little tables, I making a meaningless remark every now and then, he gloomily silent, smoking one cigarette after another. He started speaking at last, when I asked him if he would have another cognac.

'No, thanks!' he said shortly, then, 'The trouble is that alcohol's no good to me. I loathe wet drinks of every kind, and I can't force myself to drink even enough to make me high-spirited. You see, I'm blessed with an infernally strong head. I can drink as much beer as would put most men under the table without feeling any sensation except nausea at the sheer nastiness of it. That's the whole trouble. Other fellows have got alcohol to help them, I've got nothing.'

He paused.

'I tell you,' he went on, 'I'm feeling fairly low in my ghost. I try to keep all this sort of thing to myself, but at the moment I feel I must cough it up. You know, I dam' nearly made tracks during the last chukkah. I don't know why it is, but somehow this business gets me in the small of the back. Every time a strafe starts I'm perfectly certain that my turn's come. I spend the whole time imagining what a bullet would feel like if I accepted it in the stomach; alternatively what a twisting bayonet feels like. I can hardly sleep at all when I'm in the line, and when I do I dream foully. Frankly, I don't see how I'm going to stick out the next round. It's all right for the chaps who've got no imagination.'

He would have gone on longer in this strain, but we were interrupted. A girl came and asked him to dance. She had the figure of an over-developed child, with a stage prettiness in her face; she was very scantily clad.

John Con, rather to my surprise, accepted. He obviously did not want to dance, but his politeness never failed him. I had never seen him dance before, and I was astonished that he did it so well, with real grace and all the vivacity which the camouflage gaiety of wartime Paris demanded. I saw, moreover, that he was talking quite brightly to his partner, and laughing when she corrected his clumsy, schoolboy French.

When the music stopped he took her to a far corner of the room and gave her a drink. They were together again for the next dance, after which the girl was claimed by another partner and he came back to me.

'Sorry to have left you alone,' he remarked, and I noticed that his tone was more cheerful.

'Not at all!' I answered. 'Pleasant girl?'

'Yes.'

He lit another of his cigarettes.

'She wants me to give her supper. Do you think I should?'

He put the question like a boy asking whether he should spend his savings on a new cricket bat.

'Do you want to?' I said, evading him.

'Yes, I do,' he answered emphatically. 'The point is, ought I to? You see, it's probably not only supper she's after.'

'I imagine not,' I agreed. 'Well, ethics isn't my line; I'm sorry, but I can't advise you.'

'It's the only thing which would make the next few hours go past,' he said meditatively. 'Anticipation is even worse than the thing itself, and I can't stand the idea of the darkness. If I don't go with her I shall have to sit up all night reading, and that's not good enough, really. I feel that I must have something that acts like alcohol. Oh, if only I could drink like an ordinary human being!'

I realized then, more strongly than ever before, the tragedy of a well-developed moral sense in a religious agnostic.

In the end he took the girl to supper.

He spoke very little as we travelled back next day, making the journey in one train, one Press car, and three lorries. We parted at Brigade HQ, and I did not see him again till a week later, when we happened to meet in what we called the Tic-Tac Office.

It was then he gave me a letter addressed to his wife.

'If anything should happen,' he said — and his tone was unwontedly cheerful, 'you might send that off for me. So long as you're on your present job you're not likely to get sniped. You won't lose it, will you? It's important.'

I promised that I would not, and put the letter with two or three others I had of the same nature. Since being put into a 'valuable-brain-to-be-handled-carefully' job I had become quite a pillar-box for these letters, which were always being demanded for rewriting. In that little world where we made a point of joking over everything serious, it became a byword. 'Hard up for a job? Then get your important letter from old Barlow and polish it up.'

'By the way,' John Con said. 'I've told my wife in that letter about that girl I danced with.'

That was the last time I saw him. He was killed, I heard, while reconnoitring alone on German ground, in the small hours of the morning. It was ordinary, routine reconnaissance, but knowing what I did of John Con I wondered whether anything braver had been done in the war than those little Tom Tiddler's Ground trips of his. It is worthwhile recording that Benson, one of his sergeants, told me afterwards, 'He probably wasn't careful enough. Captain Colkyston, of course, he was one of those chaps that don't know what fear is, as you might say.'

I didn't send the letter off as soon as I heard the news. I had formed, before that, a nasty picture in my mind of his wife receiving it. All next morning I felt a dread of seeing the mails orderly. At the last moment, after a conflict of thought, I steamed the letter open, glanced over it, destroyed the last sheet, and put the rest back.

It was a sunny morning when we left the hotel, Mrs Colquortson and I, to begin our search. There was never, I think, a stranger search, both of us looking for what she knew intuitively that we would find, and I knew positively that we could not.

Despite the insane futility of our mission, I somehow felt obliged to lead her as I would have done if it had not been quite so hopeless; and, starting from the village of Dorgue, we worked our way south-east towards Anjou-Carillême, which I knew would lead us right across the territory where John Con had done his last service. Having done this once, we turned round and made our way back, choosing a slightly different route. Then back again, with a short stop for a picnic lunch, and so on throughout the day.

Apart from my general idea of the locality, I was no more use as a guide than a blind man. I had served in so many different sectors, seven years makes havoc with one's memory of places, and everything seemed just as different as the 'before-and-after' figures in an advertisement. There was hardly a thing which I recognized.

My companion talked very little, but she never lost her calm cheerfulness. It was almost unbelievable, and yet I could partly understand it. For all these years her thoughts had been concentrated on the missing page of that letter. The determination to find it must have grown and grown until the thing desired had become a possibility and finally something so essential that no power could deny it. Probably, I reflected, she was badly off, and had to do work of some kind, as a governess, perhaps, to make ends meet. In that case it might have been difficult to find the money and the time for this little trip to Flanders. Having achieved so much she must have felt as though the worst obstacles were surmounted, and meeting me at the hotel had surely seemed to her to be providential. For all that, I

was amazed at her good spirits as we plodded over the heavy
ground, stopping to poke in every little pile of debris in the hope of
finding a piece of paper which only a miracle could have produced,
even had the circumstances been as she supposed.

'I'm afraid this is terribly tiring and boring for you,' she
apologized more than once.

I assured her that it was not, and tried desperately to capture
something of her happy zest; but how could I possibly appear
cheerful, miserably occupied as I was?

'I've a week to hunt in,' she told me, 'so I'm not downhearted yet.
Of course, now that you've shown me roughly where the place is I
won't have to drag you out again.'

I determined, however, that even if it drove me mad to tramp up
and down on that useless quest, I would not leave her to hunt alone.

Darkness fell suddenly, and with it a fog.

'I'm afraid this must end today's search,' I said. 'We've combed
one piece pretty well, anyway. Better luck to-morrow, I hope.'

I said the words without remorse, because my mind had become
centred on the problem of finding our way home. I had no compass,
landmarks were few, and we might easily wander in a circle, as I
knew from experience was really possible.

We kept walking in what I thought was the same direction as that
in which we had been moving when darkness came down; and we
proceeded thus for some twenty minutes, hoping to strike the little
road which leads from Dorgue to the mill a mile away. It was just
when I was beginning to grow a bit nervous that something caught
my foot and I prostrated my six feet two inches face downwards.

I lay where I fell, motionless, for perhaps four or five seconds.
Thinking it over, I can see now why I did so. I had come just such a
cropper seven years before, and, the old instinct returning, I lay still
for a moment or two for fear that a star-shell should make me an easy
jack-in-the-box target.

'Are you hurt?' my companion asked anxiously.

'Not a bit!' I said, getting up. Then I bent down to see what
tripped me.

It was the end of a shaft, sticking up through the ground, and
belonging evidently to some agricultural machine which had
become buried deep in the soil. With a sudden curiosity I struck a
match and examined it more carefully. It was ironbound, and when I

had rubbed away a little of the rust on the binding I could just read the word NOGG.

'That's queer,' I said. 'I tripped over that very shaft seven years ago.'

'Are you quite certain?' she demanded, and for the first time that day her voice had a note of nervous excitement in it.

'Quite certain,' I replied.

'Then this may help us to get our position more definite.'

I thought hard.

'I doubt it,' I said. 'I can't remember at all on what occasion I fell. I only remember walking rapidly, falling, and then looking to see what had tripped me. When I saw the name NOGG it at once made a niche in my memory; it's such an odd name. That's how I know it's the same shaft.'

'Do think again!' she implored.

I did so, for a couple of minutes, and then the incident which I remembered widened out a little; with that I caught a little of her own excitement, forgetting for the moment the futility of our chase.

'I'm not certain,' I told her, 'but I've got just an idea. Look here, will you wait here while I make a detour? I won't go out of earshot.'

She agreed. I calculated my direction, and had gone no more than sixty yards when I came upon what I sought. It was a gully, about a hundred yards in length and thirty feet in width, which had, as I had formerly surmised, been cut long ago by some industrious road-maker who found the steep rise of the muddy ground too much for his horses. It had played its little part in one of the retreats, that gully.

'This way!' I called, and she came to me at a run, stumbling and sliding most dangerously. We traversed the gully together, I feeling along the side with one hand and holding her arm with the other. It was damp going — a messy place as it had always been. I was now quite breathless with excitement. Would it be there, or had it been finally blown to atoms by one of the shells it had dodged so long, secure in its snug hiding-place? It was there. We almost walked right into it as it suddenly jumped at us out of the fog — the Tic-Tac Office.

It is a little hut built of solid stone, and it will probably stand there for another fifty years at least as it must have stood for nearly a hundred already. The roof was gone now, and the windows are no more than gaps in the wall, but when I saw it last the door was still there, and swung quite evenly on its rusty hinges. For what it originally served I can only guess.

'I don't want to make you hopeful,' I said — for some unknown reason whispering the words — 'but I believe that your husband's letter was written in that hut.'

She leant forward and gave my hand a squeeze.

'Thank you!' she said. 'I think, if you don't mind, that I'll go in alone. Will you wait for me?'

I climbed up the bank a little, found a comparatively dry spot in which to sit down, and lit my pipe. I sat there until it had gone out, thinking of John Con, wondering, strangely, whether at that moment he was thinking of me. It was not till over twenty minutes had passed that I called out, and receiving no reply, went into the hut.

I found John Con's widow lying in a dead faint on the ground.

It was chiefly through luck that I found my way back to Dorgue, more or less carrying my companion, and perhaps I was still luckier in finding a man to drive us back to Ypres in an old Citroen used for carrying milk-cans. Mrs Colquortson never spoke a word on that journey, and I did not hear her story till the following day.

I had reached the toast stage in an English breakfast when, to my astonishment, she came into the dining-room, looking none the worse for the adventures of the previous evening. She seemed, in fact, even more sprightly and cheerful than she had been on the morning before.

'I thought you would take a longer rest,' I said. 'Are we going to continue the hunt straightaway?'

'No,' she answered, smiling, 'the hunt's over.'

'You mean — you've given up?'

'No, I've found what I was looking for.'

I asked no more questions, but when she had finished her coffee and rolls she told me everything quite simply, with complete calm.

'I knew,' she said, 'before we came to the hut, that I was close to the place that I had dreamed about for all these years. I knew what I should find in that hut, and I found it.'

'You found — what?' I asked.

'I found my husband. He was sitting at a table, and though it was quite dark I could see him clearly. He was writing. I went up to him and looked over his shoulder to see what he wrote. I saw that clearly, too, but I need not have seen the first four pages, because I knew them off by heart. I knew all the time what he was going to write next.'

'And the last page?' The words came from my lips, I believe, without any volition of my own.

'Yes,' she replied simply, 'I saw the last page too.'

I looked into her eyes, and though I am a fool at reading the thoughts of women, though I could make nothing of the vision she had described, I somehow saw that she had read the last page as it had been written. I was silent for a few moments, and then, looking away from her, I spoke.

'You must realize,' I said slowly, 'that war is a greater strain on a man's nerves than anyone who has not fought can possibly realize. It is a still greater strain for a married than for a single man. You see —'

'You are not married yourself?' she interrupted.

I replied, 'No.'

'Then, just as I can't realize the nervous strain of war, you can't realize what the companionship of a man and his wife can be. You can't begin to realize how close John and I were.'

'I suppose I can't,' I answered. 'But you must remember, he had the courage to write and tell you about — about —'

'About the tonic that he had to take when his nerves were in a desperate condition! My dear Major Barlow, it does not require courage for a man to tell his wife that he has broken a piece of china.' She paused. 'That's what I mean,' she said quietly, 'when I say that you haven't any conception of the strength and depth and height of married union. And that's why I forgive you for having kept me waiting seven years for my husband's words of farewell.'

She was not scornful; her voice was truly forgiving. But if she had taken a pistol and shot me through the heart I should have been happier, that moment, as I looked out through the window towards the scaffolding poles of the new Cloth Hall.

In the Dark

The station was very badly lighted — only murky oil lamps every twenty yards or so — and when I got into the train there were no lights in any of the carriages. I had to feel my way carefully, in case someone should be there already, and it was some time before I could be quite certain that my carriage was empty. I thought that it was going to remain so, but just as a hustle and banging of doors indicated that we were about to start, the door was jerked open and another passenger climbed in.

I could see none of his features. I knew only that he was a short man, thin and wiry. A hat, rather too large for him, was pulled far down over his eyes. These were the only impressions I gained from a brief glimpse of his figure, hazily silhouetted against a misty Bovril poster, before he plunged from the twilight into the heavy darkness. It surprised me that he did not step on my feet.

The commotion died away, and nothing happened. I was not surprised, as I had travelled on this line before, and knew, as a shareholder, that the company who owned it was not one for brisk efficiency. I was impatient, however; I do not like darkness, and my Saxon suspicion of strangers was intensified by the presence of a stranger I could not see. He did not speak to me, nor I to him. I regarded his taciturnity with suspicion, and as my suspicion increased — he kept so still, that man, so stiff and tense — so I grew less anxious to talk to him. The spirits, they say, are silent until we address them. I prefer a spirit to be silent.

We waited for five minutes or ten perhaps, and then a porter peered in through the window.

'Where for, sir?' he demanded, domineering.

'Tillyharry,' I said. My fellow-passenger, properly, I thought, allowed the darkness to hide him and ignored the man.

'Change at Nether Wells,' the porter commanded, suggesting by his tone that I should have known this. He moved on to the next carriage, but I called after him.

'I say, aren't we going to have any light?'

'It'll come on in a minute,' he replied impatiently over his shoulder. At the same instant as myself, he noticed for the first time that the other carriages were duly and correctly illuminated, and this discovery so far impressed him as to make him walk back.

'Queer!' he said.

'Yes,' I agreed.

'Something must've gone wrong with the gas in this carriage.'

'It seems probable,' said I. 'If you'll open the door, please, I'll get into another one.'

'Too late now, sir,' he replied, with the satisfaction of the downtrodden creature who suddenly finds himself able to summon vast power to support him. He stood back. The train gave a jolt forward, stopped, quivering, while each coach in turn inherited the motion and butted noisily into the one in front, and then, encouraged by this impetus, snorted out of the station into the outer world; a world so dark that the platforms we had left seemed by comparison to have been brilliantly lighted.

There was no moon that night, and a mist hung over the country-side; I could barely see from the light thrown out by the other carriages when we were in a cutting and when on an embankment. The jerking motion which we had collected in our precipitate exit was stimulated by a series of badly laid points, and it was some time before the horrible jolts and clanging gave place, gradually, to the rhythmic *turradadum, turradadum*. By this time, my thoughts devoted solely to my own discomfort, I had forgotten my companion's existence. I started violently when he spoke.

'Tillyharry, did you say you were going to?'

His voice was high-pitched and quavering, rather like that of a woman from the south side of the Thames. I did not like the voice. I should have detested it, had there not been something to pity in it; as one pities a garrulous beggar, not because he is poor, but because he fails to see how ludicrous is his begging.

I said yes, Tillyharry was my destination.

'A fine town,' he remarked.

'Indeed!' I said. 'You know it?'

I had never been there myself, but Hugh Mattersol had described it to me as 'a one-horse, back-bush, hick-and-hayseed little village, every cottage in it rotten and foundering, but so much dirt that you can't see the decay.' I had not looked forward with any pleasure to my week's sojourn in Tillyharry.

'Born and bred there, lived there twenty-three years,' my companion said.

'Perhaps you can help me then,' I said quickly, for fear he should become autobiographical. 'I'm staying at the King's Arms. Is it close to the station, or shall I have to take a cab?'

'Cab? No, not unless you've got a very heavy bag. It's only forty-five paces down the High Street. When you come out of the station, turn to your right along the pavement. In about twenty yards you come to a lamp-post, and it's best to cross the road there, as there's usually a policeman on duty. A lot of traffic on that street nowadays. You'll see the High Street, straight in front of you. It's a cobbled street, a fine old street. There are tall houses on both sides, oh, three or four storeys, I should think. The King's Arms is the tallest of the lot, I fancy. It's a fine hotel, that.'

Again I recalled Mattersol. 'You might try the King's Arms, it's a dingy little pub, but there's nowhere else. Personally I'd rather find a field and pitch a tent. It would feel more civilized.'

'Yes, it's a fine hotel,' the stranger went on. 'Five steps up to it, and two doors before you're inside. A swagger place. Of course it smells of ale rather, more ale than champagne like there is in some of the London places they talk about, but they've got a proper waiter and everything. You'll like the Arms.'

'I'm glad of that,' I said, speaking as one who has told the bedtime story for the third time and devoutly hopes the child is asleep. I did not want to talk to this man. When the sun rose on the morrow, I should know all I wished to know about Tillyharry. I could then count the storeys of the houses myself, note the grandeur of the hotel, remark its proximity to the station. In the meantime I did not want to hear it described. My companion's description might be more accurate than Mattersol's — certainly Mattersol was seldom right about anything — but what did it matter? I could not get away from the idea that the man wanted to unburden himself of a tale long stored up. He had the weightiness and prolixity of a beggar. He seemed to believe that I should doubt his words if he did not make his story still more unlikely by verbose embellishments. It was unreasonable, perhaps, to think thus. No doubt the darkness and chilliness of the carriage were depressing me so much as to make me a little inhuman. The fellow had not said a great deal, so far. It was simply his tone of voice which made me suspect the bore in him, the bore who has calamities to share out with any chance acquaintance. Worse still, I could not help suspecting that he was not altogether sane. It seemed to tell me so much, that voice.

'You will see the cathedral, of course?'

I was right. It would not be checked, that voice; it would persecute until the next station brought relief, or until that dark figure, the outline of which I could only just discern against the window, began to move nearer and nearer, until I felt it leaning over me and —

'Cathedral?' I said. 'I didn't think there was a cathedral at Tillyharry.' I intended my voice to be bored only, but I knew that it sounded frightened.

'No, no! I'm wrong. It is not a cathedral, only a church. But I think of it always as a cathedral; it is so tall and majestic.'

I needed no other proof. Nothing but sheer madness would make a man talk of a country church as a cathedral. Streaks of blue light darted into the carriage, leaving it dark again. We had impudently passed through a station. I wondered when the next would come; the stations were, I supposed, about two miles apart; we were moving at, perhaps, twenty-five miles an hour, certainly not more; that would bring the next station in about five minutes; but we might not stop there.

'Yes, it is a fine church, St Mary's at Tillyharry. You go in through a wide door. It is a heavy door, covered with leather and little brass knobs, but it swings quite silently when you push it. When you are inside, you walk six paces and then you turn and look up the nave. The nave is very long and the high roof is supported on fourteen pillars, seven on each side. You feel how cool and spacious it is. It is like being in a garden, when the sun is behind the clouds, only there is incense instead of the smell of flowers, because God dresses differently when He is in His churches. You go up the nave to the transept, and then you are in a pool of sunlight which comes in through the south window. It is like the sun coming out after a shower. I always knelt there, to keep still and feel the sunshine. There are priests walking round, up and down the long aisles, and the skirts of their robes swish past you. They are wonderful, gorgeous robes. They go up into the chancel, and you turn your head after them. I have never been in the chancel, there is a rope across it when there is not a service, but I know that it is all marble; they stand there, their wings touching and their heads bent forward. Sometimes the organ is playing, and I think they nod their heads very gently to the music.'

All this he had said in the same high monotone, the tone which frightened but was beginning to fascinate me. Then his voice changed suddenly. It became more excited, more tremulous, but softer. An ecstasy of beautiful remembering seemed to take away its harshness.

'The sun moves round gradually, and the pool of light travels away. It travels up the steps and across the barrier, and shines right on God's face, as He sits there up in the chancel. And then God smiles.'

Though I could not see his face, I knew that my companion, too, was smiling.

I felt the train slowing down, and heard the hiss of the suction brakes. A jolt, and then a voice calling, 'Nether Wells' brought me back into reality. I jumped up, put on my hat, pulled my bag from under the seat, and stepped on to the platform. 'Good night!' was all I said to my companion. I wanted food, and warmth, and above all, bright, mundane light. I wanted to get away from a man who saw God in a church. At the barrier I stopped to fumble for my ticket, and as I did so heard the eerie voice again. 'I want some chocolate with nut in it. I don't think this piece has any nut.'

Impelled by curiosity I turned round. He was not an old man, after all, not more than thirty, I guessed. His face, now seen clearly under a station lamp, was thin and bearded. His moustache looked as if it had been allowed to grow long to hide an ugly twist in the lips, a twist that might be caused by a physical defect or by long suffering only. He spoke to me again.

'Yes, I was born like this,' he said, and smiled bravely. He must somehow have sensed my fixed and curious gaze, for he could not have seen it through those white, unlighted eyes.

'I do hope you will like Tillyharry,' he added.

Last Voyage

From Monday to Friday I live in a queer club which is hidden behind the tall business houses in Victoria Street. From Friday night to Monday morning I am at Staunchstones. I have what I call my third home, which I occupy in the time elapsing between these two periods. It is called, crudely, the five-fifteen.

When I pass through the booking-hall every Friday at five o'clock I turn to the left and walk precisely forty yards, which brings me to a spot where there is a tobacco stall on my left and a door with the figure 'one' on my right. The latter (my grandfather the brewer having died recently) I enter, and, removing the hat which my friend Bob keeps for this special purpose, I take the corner seat next the corridor. There I stay, reading my paper until William tells me, just past Feversham Magnum, that my dinner is ready.

On the Friday before last William spilt my soup — not, fortunately, on my trousers — and after wondering for a moment whether there was some convention about throwing spilt soup over the left shoulder I began to reflect that William must be getting on in life. For fifteen years William had never spilt anything. He may, of course, have upset porridge on the breakfast passengers, he may even have poured gravy on those who dined on Wednesday; but, so far from spilling soup on my table, he had never, to the best of my knowledge, upset anything on a Friday evening over either the just or unjust.

I said, while the cloth was changed, 'The track's getting very bad, William. Not as smooth as it was when we first knew it.'

'I am very, very sorry, sir!' was his only reply.

His manner, I thought, had more than the conventional restraint, but this was not enough to prepare me for the shock to follow.

A few minutes later, when he was pouring out my wine, William bent down a little lower than the task required and whispered in my ear, 'I shan't be serving you again, sir!'

'William!' I said sharply, 'why not?'

'My time's up,' was his reply.

For some moments I found it hard to believe his words. It seemed perfectly absurd that William should cease to be in my service when I had given him no notice. It dawned on me gradually that William was rather old — ten years older than myself, perhaps. I had known him first as a rather handsome man, spruce and sun-tinged enough to remind me that he was an ex-mess sergeant. The steady change of his hair from black to grey and then to a complete white had almost escaped my observation. It had never occurred to me that a man who could still hold the vegetable dish so steadily as we lurched drunkenly over the points at Mayorshott was subject to the same decaying influence as the rest of mortals.

'How old are you?' I asked.

'Sixty-five, sir,' — and he hurried off to get a roll for a pink-cheeked subaltern at the opposite table.

When I had finished my coffee I stayed — contrary to my custom — to finish my cigar where I sat. It was a bad business, this, I reflected. The long chain of pleasures which came on Friday evening to reward me for my week's work — the swift rush into Northacres tunnel, the glimpse of Muscaugh Castle, often in the sunset, — and the final drive up the cedar grove of Staunchstones — none of these things would ever be quite the same without William's voice murmuring 'Sole or plaice, sir?' If a change had been made on the menu, and William had offered me cod-or-whale, even if the five-fifteen had stopped at Mashford, these irregularities would have seemed trivial by the side of the one which faced me now.

I called William to my side and begged him to take the vacant seat opposite me, but this he would not do. ('Oh, no, sir! It would be a bad example for the young fellows, thanking you very much, sir.') He consented, nevertheless, to stand by me and talk while he pretended to polish an ash-tray.

'Well, William,' I said, 'I hope you'll enjoy as long and happy a retirement as you deserve.'

'Thank you. I hope so, sir.'

He gazed over my head at the Teerwell, which was leaning against the embankment, coyly receding, diving underneath us, and reappearing to catch on its surface a fresh hue which the sunset had prepared for it.

'It won't be quite the same without the five-fifteen, sir,' he said. 'I shall always look out of the window at half-past eight and expect to see the first lights of Haiseton. I shall be putting my right leg back a bit then, ready for where the Foote line comes in, and I'll be saying "Black or white, sir?" No, sir, it won't be the same.'

I tried to comfort him by talking of the gardening he might be able to do, and not having to get up early. He agreed that it might be nice for a change, but he was still remorseful. The light was almost gone now, and as the air coming in at the window became sharper, as the sparks from the engine began to be visible, I, feeling and hearing the solemn power which impelled us forward, sympathized deeply with William.

'It's the — it's its being the down journey gets it crooked,' he said.

I failed to understand. 'Why that?' I asked him.

'You see, Jane died two years ago come next month,' he began to explain.

'Jane?'

'My wife, sir.'

So William had been married!

'We used to live in London, you see, and so it was the up journeys I always liked. That was going home, you see, sir. I always hoped that my last journey would be on the up train. But I'm living in the North with my daughter now, so this is the last journey. You see how it is, sir?' — and suddenly encaging his voice again he added, 'You'll be wanting your bill, sir?'

Mechanically — for it needed no mental effort — he scrawled the incomprehensible ciphers on his pad and handed me the carbon sheet. I gave him a five-pound note, and (my grandfather having brewed very good beer) went back to my carriage without waiting for change. I wished I had not done this, as it made things so much harder when William came along to my carriage to say goodbye.

At ten minutes to eleven, with the certainty which it shares with the chimes of big Ben, the train began to slow up. I took down my bag from the rack, placed the novel I had been reading inside, and put on my overcoat. This I was buttoning when a sudden fearsome jerk threw me into the arms of a passenger sitting opposite, knocking my head against the wall of the carriage with a force sufficient to produce a bruise which I feel still.

When I had recovered myself I walked, rather dazedly, into the corridor, which was full of men talking excitedly. Everyone was asking questions, receiving no reply, making conjectures. In the next carriage a woman who had fainted was lying, white-faced, on the seat.

It was some minutes before we learnt, from the guard, what had happened. Some mistake on the part of a pointsman had put a couple of trucks, which were being shunted, on to the main line. Our driver had barely pulled up in time. Some people farther up the train had been badly shaken.

'No one seriously hurt?' I asked.

'I'm afraid so. A man was flung against a door and killed.'

'A passenger?'

'No, a waiter.'

With Bob's help I found William's daughter, and with her willing consent I arranged that he should be buried by the side of his wife at Stoke Newington. Thither his body was taken — on the up train.

The Quixotes

The news came through slowly, as news does come from a back street in a small Ontario town. From a briefly-worded post card Armitage Cegraine learnt that he had been three weeks a grandfather. It was a month later that he heard of the girl's death — Dorothy, was that her name? — though the second event had taken place only a few days after the first. Three more weeks passed by before he heard that she had taken her child with her, away from the world which she had found so bitter.

The two successive shocks had moved him, coming as they did like a challenge to his faith in a certain order of things. Cegraine's moral beliefs had been founded on a mixture of Kantian severity and Leibnitzian fatalism. He had maintained that there was a certain path of duty, which, if followed unswervingly, led to a result which was good, whatever it seemed. A streak of scepticism told him now, whispered, as it were, into his unwilling ear, that things were not thus ordered. In the course of his life several men had told Cegraine that he might be wrong. He had never before admitted it to himself.

He was returning from his bank when the last blow fell. He had pulled out a bundle of cheques from the back of his passbook, and examined them eagerly to see if a particular one was there. The first doubts of conscience had made him write this cheque; it had not been cashed. With a smile so grim that it might almost have been a frown he returned the cheques to their pocket, leant back into the deep cushions of the car, and opened an evening newspaper. In a column headed 'Items from Overseas' a name caught his eye. It took a few seconds to refold the paper so that this column could be brought under the roof-light. Then a paragraph in very small print told him that a young man named Charles Mason, believed to have lately immigrated, had hired a dinghy on the shore of James Bay, leaving a small deposit with the owner; and that the dinghy had been towed in, empty, a few hours later.

When Cegraine reached home he found a letter bearing the postmark of Toronto and his sister's handwriting. He did not open it at once. It was his custom to leave letters till after tea, and on this occasion he was not anxious for his sister's lengthy outpourings.

Several times, however, when he stopped eating to pour out another cup, something made him stretch out his hand towards the envelope and turn it over, as if in doing this he could fathom something of its contents without feeling the brunt of it.

Habit and will-power prevailed. The tea things had been cleared away, and Cegraine had carefully filled and lit his pipe before he opened the letter with his penknife and spread out the five thin, closely-written sheets.

Judith Cegraine, four years older than her brother, might have been his twin. They were remarkably alike in appearance, and though her mind was more subtle and penetrating than his, they thought in the same tempo, carefully, without haste, only wrongly when their premises were wrong. They had lived together for most of their lives. They had no conscious affection for one another, but they moved in harmony, having been joined together not by a priest, but by an act of nature. Judith Cegraine was the only woman who had ever argued with her brother; he had let her do so because he hardly realized that she was a woman. He thought of her almost as of a part of himself. When he read her letters he felt no more emotion than when reading a newspaper. If what Judith wrote agreed with his own ideas it was natural; if it did not, then some illogical twist which she had in common with the rest of the skirted sex had misled Judith.

The first page of the letter he was reading now, holding it in one hand and stretching the other towards the fire, contained only an account of a trip to Winnipeg. 'Winnipeg is a pleasant place, I think you would be interested in the planning and architecture. Very different from towns on the Eastern side of the Atlantic.' (Strange, how Judith always noticed that in France the people spoke French!) Halfway down the second page she began to mention his son, and she did so as he himself would have done — three months before; as if she were writing of events in an outside world.

'I never saw Bill at all, he was very elusive, but he wrote two or three times. He signed himself "Charles Mason", he stuck to that name, I don't quite know why. He told me he had had a cheque from you, I wonder what made you send it? but he destroyed it apparently, he had a terrible pride. . . . Under-nourishment, apparently. Neither of them would admit they were badly off, in fact, no one knew until the flat was examined after Bill had gone. The ghastly thing, to me, is that Bill was offered quite a decent job two days after he had lost them. If the letter which told him about it hadn't gone astray in the post he might have borrowed money on the strength of it . . . he admitted that he hadn't eaten anything himself for three days before Dorothy went.'

'So that,' thought Cegraine, 'is the result of my system of duty.'

It was — though he had not realized it at the time — Bill's quietness and steadiness which had made him feel so right. In the last, cold interview he had felt like a teacher reasoning with a wayward disciple. 'I'm sorry our views disagree, father. I'm afraid we must leave it at that.'

In the practical issue he, Cegraine, had been proved right; ironically, it was because his predictions had been so right that he was now being forced to own himself in the wrong. 'You believe that you can, as you express it, "get away with it". My only course is to let you try.' Bill had tried and failed. His failure had simply served to show all the world that by every reasonable canon of ethics his father had been wrong.

All the world? No! That, fortunately, could be prevented. The finest thing Bill had done was to change his name. Of course, people were inquisitive; there were scandalmongers and blackmailers and busybodies; but, thank God, Canada was still a long way off.

Cegraine turned over the pages of the letter, glancing through them rapidly to see if there were anything else of importance. The last part was something of a shock. Judith had always been out-spoken. On some occasions she had lapsed into a moral tone. But here she was speaking to him as one who claims the right of admonition. Was something wrong with the girl? She seemed to be taking some standpoint different from his own, whither she should only have ventured after deliberate debate with himself. 'You know, I have never agreed with you about Bill . . .' Well, no, she had not. She had said so plainly; they had labelled the matter 'point of disagreement' and locked it away in the 'arguments settled' drawer. But this — 'The cheque, of course, came too late. It arrived when hard circumstances had made him dogged. You know — Shakes-peare or someone — "you can't beat a man when he's tired". The trouble with you, brother A, is that you're too lazy to put yourself in anyone else's position. I think I told you that before. You've never experienced WANT. You've always had everything you desired and you will go to the grave satisfied and ignorant. You don't mind my being blunt, do you, dear? Something's rather got out the tiger in me, maybe the heat. Ninety-five in the shade here at present. I don't mind so much about Bill, because there was something clean and fine about his departure. But the girl and her kid. I don't like to think about my niece being starved to death . . .'

Cegraine was not given to melodramatic actions, but he tore the letter into four pieces, threw them into the fire, and sat holding the sides of his chair, his lips together, eyes lighted. Had the letter come from anyone else the matter would have ended with its destruction. The whole college of Bishops would not have made any impression by preaching at Armitage Cegraine. But Judith, in her odd, unfeminine way, had sometimes been right. More than once, when he had beaten her soundly in an argument, he had gone to bed realizing that she was right. Judith — here was the trouble — having once been more right than he might be more right again.

Plain nonsense, of course. It was Bill's fault for having destroyed that cheque. Bill's ridiculous quixotism — it was the quixotes who were at the bottom of half the trouble in this world. But wasn't he a quixote, in his own way? 'Disregard your own feelings. Obey the dictates of duty.' That was a fine motto, his motto, fine and Spartan and impracticable; the very badge of quixotism. Damn it, was there any sense in things at all? Could you ever get away from the cross-currents of emotionalism?

A clock struck the half, the three-quarters, and the hour, while Cegraine sat thinking. In his methodical way he grappled with the question of want. It was true, he had never experienced want. He ought to experience it. But how? How could he make himself uncomfortable? He could give away one of his cars and not be seriously troubled by the loss. Supposing that he were to impoverish himself entirely? It could be done. He was not as rich as he had been, now that increased cost of living and an iniquitous super-tax were making inroads on his fortune. He could build a hospital for ten thousand, endow it with another ten, no, twenty, say. That would leave precious little. There was Judith to be thought of, but she must swallow her own prescription. The question was, would another hospital —?

A maid brought him a card on a brass salver. 'Mr Ernest Pittway' — no address.

'Who is this gentleman?' he asked curtly.

'I don't know, sir. He didn't state his business, only asked if he could see you.'

Cegraine pondered, twiddling the card between his fingers.

'Mm! Better bring him up.'

The young man who entered the room a few moments later was tall, dark haired, neat in dress. He stood a little awkwardly just inside the door, holding his hat in both hands. He was curiously like Bill.

'Your name,' said Cegraine, 'is — I think — Mr Pittway. May I ask what you want?'

The young man had prepared his formula.

'I have come, sir, to offer you the sincere condolences of the editor of the *Sunday Gazette* on your tragic loss.'

'I have never heard of the *Sunday Gazette*. I don't know the editor of that periodical, and if I did I should not want his condolences.'

Cegraine delivered the speech like three rounds of rifle fire, took up a book, and started reading. To all appearances he had, in three seconds, forgotten the young man's existence. The young man, however, remained where he was. His profession had so hardened him to rudeness that he scarcely noticed it. Cegraine gave him two minutes' grace, then glanced up.

'Well, sir, what are you waiting for?'

'I thought perhaps that you might care to give me some details of the accident.'

'Why on earth should I?'

'Well, perhaps from courtesy, sir, or —'

'Courtesy!'

'Or perhaps to avoid wrong stories getting about. You see the public believes what it reads in the *Sunday Gazette*, and if other papers float the idea that there was something fishy about —'

Again Cegraine cut him short.

'If newspapers start false rumours I shall not require the aid of the *Sunday Shriek*, or whatever your rag is. There are well-defined methods of legal procedure in cases of libel. Look here, let me make this quite plain, so that you can repeat what I say to your editor. I've had a good deal of experience of this infernal publicity, and I do not intend to let it get me in its claws. I'm sorry to inform you that you belong to a despicable trade. You are one of a brand of men whose business it is to rout out all the unpleasantness you can find, and to publish it abroad; where you can't find unpleasantness you suggest it. You're the scavengers of the earth, you collect dirt, you make dirt, and you retail it to a dirty-minded section of the public. Well, that's all I have to say.'

The reporter looked at him as a pupil sitting at the feet of a philosopher.

'I will not admit, sir,' he said with every appearance of humility, 'that my profession is as you describe it. But even if it were, I would ask you to admit that someone must do the world's dirty work.'

'Must do it? Nonsense!'

'May I just ask you, sir, if you have read *Mrs Warren's Profession*?'

'Yes, I have read it, and I do not want that humbug Shaw quoted at me.'

Ernest Pittway knew that he was beaten. No good arguing with this fellow — stubborn as they made 'em — much better get back to the town and pray for a street accident! He moved towards the door.

'I'm sorry, sir, that our views disagree,' he said. 'I'm afraid we must leave it at that.'

The book which Cegraine had pretended to read was still lying on his knees. With a sharp movement he pushed it on the floor.

'Just one minute!' he called.

The reporter, about to close the door behind him, came back.

'How much do you earn?' Cegraine asked abruptly.

'It usually works out about two pounds a week, sir; occasionally a bit more.'

'How do you mean, occasionally?'

'Well, every now and then I get a bit of what's called a "scoop", you know.'

'I see. You intended this to be a scoop?'

'Not a scoop, exactly, but I won't deny that anything you told me would have ranked as first-class matter. You see, the public is interested in distinguished men.'

'I know that!' Cegraine remarked bitterly.

He paused, staring at the disconcerted reporter as if at a wide landscape. Then, again jerking out the question, he asked, 'Are you married?'

'Yes, sir.'

'How long?'

'Three months.'

'You said you got two pounds a week?'

'About that, sir.'

'Do you write shorthand?'

'Of course — I mean, yes.'

'Well, take this down!'

Cegraine leaned back in his chair, stretched out his legs, and closed his eyes. He began to dictate, smoothly, never pausing for a word, never using the wrong one, as one who is used to dictating.

'The most ironical thing in life is that each generation copies the mistakes of its predecessor with the greatest fidelity. Since the days of Moses — and probably earlier — men have conceived systems of morality which they believed to be flawless. Every one of those ethical systems has failed. I, eagerly seizing the undying torch of folly, devised a system which I thought was perfect and beyond all question. I have failed, like the rest . . .'

Pittway, as Cegraine's deep voice rolled on through sentence after sentence, took down the words automatically, wondering almost, if he were dreaming. Of course, elderly men developed odd notions and were liable to lapses of reason; but how could this man, who had seemed so sane and cynical, fall suddenly into sheer madness — the madness of a man who tears off his clothes and flings them to a passing beggar? Well, that wasn't his affair. Here were riches being poured out to him, and he could only gather them in without stopping to think if they were a madman's gift. For six, seven, eight minutes his pencil leapt and cantered over the pages of his notebook.

'. . . and thus the death of my son, the death of his wife, and the death of my grandchild, are as much to be laid to my account as if I had murdered them with my own hands. The law, indeed, cannot punish me; but if God punishes the terrible arrogance and folly of a man, then surely I shall be punished, and so surely shall I not dare to cry for mercy.'

The long, steady flow of sentences finished suddenly, and there was silence for half a minute.

'Shall I read it through to you, sir?' asked Pittway nervously.

'No, don't bother.' Cegraine had resumed his briskness. 'Tell your editor to publish it in full under my name. How much will he pay for it?'

'I don't quite know. He will probably ask you for a price.'

'What's a story like that usually worth?'

'Well, as it's exclusive, I should think you might ask for five hundred.'

'Very well, we'll have a thousand. What is worth five hundred is worth a thousand in business. That's a good principle for you to remember. Being an artist, and not in the workhouse, like most artists, I understand all about business.'

'I understand, sir. I'll put your proposition up to the editor —'

'Tell him,' said Cegraine, 'that he's to give you a thousand or send me back the copy. He's to give the cash to you, see? I'll write that down and sign it.'

'Then shall I send you a cheque, sir?'

'Cheque? No, a thousand pounds doesn't mean anything to me.'

'But — it's awfully good of you, sir, I can't begin to thank you, but —'

'No need to. I don't mind having wasted ten minutes.'

'But it wouldn't be the money that would count, really, sir. It's the kudos I'll get. If you land a thing like this they put you on to bigger stuff, you see, sir, and —'

'I must say goodbye, I'm afraid,' said Cegraine. 'I've got some letters to write.'

When the young man had gone he sat still in his chair, staring in front of him, motionless. An hour later the maid who came to tell him that dinner was served found him in the same posture, and he dismissed her absently. He was feeling exultant. He had done his penance, and though a faint vision of a dying girl would haunt him for many months he had done something to efface the horror of it. He had paid the full price of his wrongdoing, sacrificed the thing he valued more than anything in the world.

He had, moreover, given Judith some subject for meditation. This pleased Armitage Cegraine.

At this moment Ernest Pittway, who had walked four miles through a biting wind to save a taxi fare, was warming his hands by the fire in the station waiting-room. The fire blazed for a few seconds more brightly than is usual with the fires in waiting-rooms; for Pittway had thrown in six sheets torn from his notebook.

Slaves of Women

From the porch of Knight's Hall hung a lamp, quaintly fashioned, which looked as if it were lighted with oil but which was actually lighted by a small electric bulb. Beneath this lamp stood a car of the type known to those who know about cars as a sportsman's coupé.

Into the sportsman's coupé Morton put first a suitcase, then a tennis-racket, then a trouser-press, then a sponge-bag, and then the top half of a pair of pyjamas. From this succession of events it may be judged by those who have keen detective powers that Andrew Blair, the owner of the car, had packed his belongings very quickly indeed and wished to leave Knight's Hall in a hurry. This was so.

Andrew Blair, having rewarded Morton in a manner altogether out of proportion to her small services stabbed his foot sharply against the self-starter, engaged a gear noisily, and precipitated his car down the drive so rapidly that Morton's ecstatic acknow-ledgment was anwered only by a wink from the tail-lamp. The only thought in Andrew's mind was to shake the dust of Knight's Hall from off his tyres before the church clock had struck the hour of eleven.

This he succeeded in doing, but when once the massive pillars which marked the boundary between private property and public roadway had been passed he began to consider the possibility of returning with equal haste to the house he had just left. He thought better of this, however. If Denise had said with proper severity that she had not a heart to bestow upon such a man as Andrew Blair he would certainly have returned. Indeed, it is doubtful if he would have left Knight's Hall at all, at any rate without packing both parts of his pyjamas in the correct fashion. No, Denise had simply said, very gently, 'You see, I've never thought of you in that way at all, Andrew.' That, and the sympathetic smile which Denise had smiled, seemed to Andrew quite final. Each time his foot strayed towards the brake he heard the words again, and quickly returned it to the accelerator.

These were a very bad few minutes for Andrew. Until now, from the time that the blow had fallen, he had been well occupied. Rather dazed, and conscious only of the general idea that he could not possibly meet Denise at breakfast — it never occurred to him that Denise herself would avoid this awkwardness by means of the usual headache — he had roamed round and round his bedroom seizing his possessions one by one and flinging them into a suitcase. Then there had been the business of sorting things out, finding his keys, and writing a note to his hostess with a fountain pen which alternately ran dry and released pools of ink on to the dressing-table. Cursing a fountain pen is good for the soul of a sad man. But now, he had time to think.

Everything which his headlamps lit up led his thoughts along unpleasant paths. He had driven Denise along this road only three nights before, on the way home from a ball. And every cross-roads, every inn, every curious formation of trees, brought to his mind some remark of hers, her soft laugh, or the presence of her close beside him. Now, Denise was dead — worse than dead, in that she would come along this road again sitting by someone else. Driving here without Denise was ghastly. A world without Denise was more bitter than death.

If only he could get away from the memory of her! He would never come into this county again, that was certain. It would probably be best to leave the country altogether. But would that be enough? His thoughts would fly to her every time he heard one of the sugary dance-tunes which the perverse Americans had so remorselessly spread over every quarter of the earth. Other women, by their very inferiority, would make him picture Denise. He would dream of her night after night, always waking to find her gone from him and to endure the agony over again.

Collecting himself for a moment Andrew switched on the dash-lamp to glance at his clock. Twenty to twelve, and only at Beesmere! He must have been dawdling. There was another fifteen miles to cover before he got to Southorn, where, with luck, he would get decent accommodation for the night at the Bull. It would be a wearisome fifteen miles. Knowing that he would get no sleep at the end of the journey he was none the less faintly conscious of being very tired.

Well, the road was better for the last bit; and he was getting near Maseley Common, with its straight, ten-furlong stretch. That would be rather refreshing. He would let her out there, and try to drown his feelings with the furious rush of cold air. With a piece of real luck a lorry might butt out across the road suddenly from the Warmouth turning. Deliberate action, of course, was sheer cowardice. But if gentle fortune did the whole thing for one — well, that would be pretty decent.

Round the bend came the sportsman's coupé, and there, straight ahead, the headlamps showed nearly half a mile of road, gloriously smooth, straight as the back of a colonel. Andrew knew that there was more to come — he could quite safely gather speed all the way to the farthest point he saw now, and further. He pressed his toe down firmly as far as it would go, and the note of the engine became higher and higher. The needle was creeping round steadily when, two hundred yards ahead, a dark object appeared in the centre of the road, arms outstretched like those of a scarecrow. Andrew hooted. The figure did not move. Andrew put on his brakes.

The man standing in the road saw that the car was slowing down, but did not trust to its stopping. He held his position until it had come within a few feet of him, then: 'What in blazes do you want?' Andrew shouted.

'A lift,' was the reply, 'and judging by the way you were coming half a mile back,' the speaker added, 'it will be in blazes.'

'Get in!' said Andrew curtly. He was furious at having his run stopped, and the last thing he wanted was company.

The stranger took his seat in the car.

'Sorry to have made you stop,' he remarked easily, 'but my car has been stolen, and I dislike walking. I left it by the roadside for half a minute, and two fellows calmly pinched it — practically under my nose. I have a gadget fitted for cutting off petrol every few miles. Not knowing where the release switch is they won't get very far, but it's tiresome.'

He lit a cigarette. Andrew, driving on, glanced at him sideways. A curious devil! Probably a ruffian — the story about a stolen car sounded a bit hackneyed — but in the circumstances it didn't much matter. A sharp blow on the napper at that moment would be precisely what the physician had prescribed.

'My name is Blair,' he said. 'May I ask yours?' Not that he cared two straws, but the chappie seemed intrinsically civil, and one had to say something.

'Loughton,' his companion replied. 'My name is Loughton. Since my godfathers and godmothers were lacking in the barest rudiments of aesthetic culture it is Archibald Loughton. And since my late parent put up the boodle for an elderly alderman to stand as conservative candidate in the borough of Weesedale, it is Sir Archibald Loughton.'

Loughton! Andrew had heard the name at Knight's Hall. He seemed to remember connecting it with wealth, but any other detail had escaped his memory entirely.

'By nature I am somewhat hard and unsympathetic,' Sir Archibald continued comfortably, 'and thus I am inclined to look upon your present unfortunate situation with the detached melancholy of the gods looking down upon mortals, rather than with genuine pity. Life, as Horace Walpole said — but you've probably heard that remark quoted before!'

'Misfortune?' said Andrew, rather puzzled.

'I don't mean misfortune in having me as your companion,' Sir Archibald explained hastily. 'Admittedly it is annoying to have to apply one's brakes on a good stretch of road, but as I am the best conversationalist to be found in any club in London you are quite amply rewarded.'

'Then what precisely do you mean?' Andrew demanded. His irritation was returning. Without introspection, he felt vaguely that he was being rudely pushed into a role different from the one he was scheduled to play at this moment. It was painful, yes, to dwell on the scene of an hour or two before, but he felt somehow that it was his duty to do so. He had worked himself into a mood for recalling every feature of the incident over and over again, and he had the feeling that a few more hours' real bitterness of spirit would make matters easier. And now a loquacious bore, who had something confoundedly interesting about him, was drawing him into a rough-and-tumble of silly back-chat.

'I assume,' said Sir Archibald, 'that Miss Denise Marshall has just turned you down.'

'What the devil do you know about that?' Andrew gasped.

'My dear young friend,' was the suave reply, 'you must surely realize that it's impossible to go down this road any night when there's anything of a moon without meeting half-a-dozen young men who've been turned down by Denise Marshall . . . all right, don't stop, I'm quite comfortable. In a sparsely populated part of the country like this everyone knows all about the affairs of their neighbours for miles around, so, of course, I got to know that Blair the rugger Blue was staying at Knight's Hall. In fact, the moment I saw my car and its unauthorized occupants disappearing, I said to myself, "Well, there's a good moon; young Blair will be coming along presently." When you appeared, driving as though the devil was after you, and acceded to my request for a lift in a very sullen fashion, I just boarded you as one would board the local bus.'

'You form conclusions very rapidly,' said Andrew coldly. He was conscious of a reflex action trying to promote laughter, but, dash it all, one didn't laugh within a couple of hours of having one's heart broken.

'I don't claim to be a Sherlock Holmes,' Sir Archibald said, 'but when I find an empty sardine-tin at the foot of the Victoria Monument I don't trot in to Buckingham Palace and ask a sentry if the King has dropped anything.'

'Well then,' said Andrew, with the air of a greengrocer coming down three farthings, 'your wild assumption proves to be correct. If I steer into a stone wall in a minute or two, as I half contemplate doing, you will realize that there are times when flippancy is superfluous . . .'

Strictly speaking, dignity demanded complete silence for the rest of the journey. There was no need to ask the passenger where he wished to alight — the passenger would certainly not fail to pull the bell-cord when he wanted to. After a short distance, however, it proved necessary to reopen conversation. A red light showed that the road was blocked, and Andrew, forced to take the by-pass, came shortly to a fork which left him undecided.

'I've lost my bearings,' he said briefly.

'Left!' said Sir Archibald, and a little later, 'Left again!'

They were now on what Andrew classified as a fifth-class road, and he began presently to doubt his guide's knowledge.

'Are you sure you know the way?' he asked.

'I should do,' the other replied, as the road passed between two pillars of brick and became a private drive, 'since I've lived here all my life.'

The next moment they were in front of a tall house, built, in accordance with Bacon's remarks, without any regard to beauty or to the economy of labour, but for the solid comfort of such as were able to keep an extensive domestic staff.

'I've no objection to driving the village bus to your door,' said Andrew, 'but you might have said something about it beforehand.'

'That would have spoilt the pleasure of surprise,' said Sir Archibald. 'Life is nothing without dramatic dénouements. Come along in. Bush will look after your car. Bush!'

'Sir!'

A man appeared in the patch of light which fell through the front door.

'The Daimler has been pinched. It will probably be at Frontworth police-station now. Collect it in the morning, will you? In the meantime take this gentleman's machine and give it a feed of oats, please. Come along!'

He strode into the house.

'It's very good of you, sir, but I think I'd better not stop,' said Andrew, hurrying after him like a railway coach which has just been slipped.

'Of course you must stop. It's past midnight, and there's not a decent pub within miles. This house has ten visitors' bedrooms, all empty. Take off your coat. Hang up your hat. Come in and get out of the moon. Want a wash? No? Come in here, then.'

He led the way to a room which should have been the drawing-room — thirty couples could have danced there comfortably — but was furnished as the smoking-room of a club is furnished, with the addition of those personal touches — charcoal caricatures, an oar, several guns — which are not within the scope of an ordinary club secretary's imagination. Andrew found himself in a chair, long in the seat, around which the arms and back were ranged as the hills are set about Jerusalem.

'Sherry will meet the occasion, I think,' said Sir Archibald, and rang. 'Sherry please, Murison, and you might put another log on this fire. Mr Blair will sleep in the Dean's room.'

Andrew had hitherto been acquainted with two sorts of sherry, good sherry and bad sherry. He had regarded it, at its best, as distinctly inferior to port, and at its worst hopelessly inferior to ginger beer. He now tasted sherry for the first time. Raising the glass to his lips he stopped, not by way of imitating the connoisseur as is the manner of schoolboys, but because something bade him step slowly and cautiously across the threshold into the sanctuary beyond. Feeling the gentle, caressing fluid on his tongue he stopped again, and held it there, unwilling to let it pass down his throat. He took another sip. It proved more mysterious and sensuous than the last. He was in no mood for enjoying things, he told himself, but still, there was no argument for denying the flesh because the spirit within was broken. Thoughtfully, he drank again.

Andrew was tired. Sitting upright and holding the steering-wheel rigidly, as one whose thoughts are sternly occupied, he had become stiff in the limbs; it was pleasant now to lean back in the armchair and stretch his legs in front of the fire, to close the eyes which had become watery with following the bright headlamps. Already the sherry had begun to stir up a warmth in his body, and the inward glow, against all logic and against all dignity, was forcing a feeling of contentment.

'Like that stuff?' Sir Archibald asked.

'The best I've ever had.'

'That,' said his host, 'is another glimpse of the obvious. The man who created that wine was cleverer than Plato, and did more towards the advancement of civilization. Have another glass. You can drink as much as you like of this, because it devotes all its attention to the brain, and does not romp in the stomach as lesser wines do.'

'Thank you,' said Andrew.

He drank more quickly this time, finished the glass, and pushed his body back farther into the infinite recesses of the chair. Looking at his companion through half-closed eyes, he decided that the man was a good sort. Conceited, perhaps, but sound. By lowering his lashes a little further he made everything in the room recede into the far distance. The face of Sir Archibald became distorted, like the reflection in a silver dish-cover. The blazing fire was unreal, and like a very splendid sunset. He opened his eyes, slowly, and everything assumed its normal shape again. It was rather pleasant, pushing everything away and pulling it to you again like this. Gradually there came over Andrew a sensation of power. The words of Henley's 'Invicta', which he had always thought pure tripe, came into his head, and he was conscious of a feeling that he had written them himself. He wanted, at this moment, to slay a dragon, to make a speech in Parliament, and to rescue a large number of female persons from burning buildings. He knew that if he could run in the Marathon now he would come into the stadium fully half an hour before any other competitor. It was nice, however, to sit quietly in this extraordinarily comfortable chair.

'More sherry?' asked his host. 'No? Well, I will now preach you a sermon.'

'Fire away!' said Andrew.

'I will first ask you to survey your surroundings,' said Sir Archibald. 'They will serve as my text. Here you have every comfort that man can devise, and they give me no trouble whatever. The servants do everything necessary in this house. I do not have to give them orders, or pay them, or dismiss them. My butler does all that for me; consequently I can devote myself to the things which interest me. Now, I am not really a rich man. I am simply a man who knows how to get the fullest possible enjoyment out of a moderately decent income. I am, in fact, a bachelor. I am my own master. If I want to travel, I do so. When I return I find things as I left them, everything prepared for my comfort. The whole point is this. I spend my money on myself, instead of diffusing it over a family.'

'I see,' said Andrew. It was not very interesting or particularly uplifting, all this, but the fellow had a decent enough voice, and like an expensive gramophone he was not really disturbing. 'The moral of your sermon doesn't seem a very high one, though,' he added by way of stimulating the conversation.

'No doubt you are one of these young men who regard Mill as out of date,' said Sir Archibald with some severity. 'Well, he may be, but his conclusions seem to me to have been extremely practical ones. You may split hairs till you're past the resources of an oculist, but the fact remains that to increase the sum of the world's happiness is a very worthy object. I do so by increasing my own. Supposing I married and had a family. I should not be able to keep so good a cellar, or to travel so frequently, or to buy rare editions. My wife would not be able to have anything approaching the luxuries which a woman naturally — and I suppose rightly — demands from her husband. My children — there would probably be eight of them — would probably get scrappy educations just good enough to render them fitted for the most dismal professions, such as business or the stage. None of us would be really happy. Now I *am* happy. Personally I can see no flaw in my simple ethics.'

'Except this —' Andrew put in. (He did not feel in the mood for heavy reasoning, but the old thinking-box seemed to be ticking over quite nicely.) 'You're talking of happiness as if it was static. It's not, it's dynamic. You've got to be doing something all the time to get happiness. You've got to keep moving. That's why you play apparently ridiculous games like rugger. You go through something damned unpleasant for the sake of the satisfied feeling you get afterwards.'

'I see,' said Sir Archibald. 'You recommend action as a recipe for happiness. Your suggestion is, I take it, that I should marry a wife, produce children, and enter into the same humdrum rut that nearly all the rest of my sex enter. That I should take up some steady, safe job, to make sure of leaving enough money to provide for my family if I happen absentmindedly to cross the Etoile without a policeman to look after me; that I should, in fact, work in an office from nine to six for fifty weeks in the year, spend Saturday afternoons playing golf, and Sunday afternoons pushing a pram. You call that action. I call it death.'

'Well, bringing up a family is a fine work, after all,' Andrew protested. The remark was, he felt, sententious and a little foolish.

'Fine work? Well, yes, I suppose that, regarded from a certain angle, it is. It's self-denial, and self-denial is always something to admire. But it's been done too often — everyone does it. When you marry you just fall into a routine that's been working since creation. You obey the scheme of things without question and without any exercise of free will. *Mater Natura* wants existence to go on. She's prepared an elaborate trap — moonlight and soft curves — which does the business perfectly. It's so old that you'd think anyone could spot it. But men keep on falling into the trap every day and will do so until the end of time. Upon my soul, it's cleverly thought out — I could hardly have invented anything so simple and satisfactory myself.'

He paused to punch another cigar and light it with the precision of a craftsman engaged in a piece of delicate work.

'The whole trouble is that in creating a family you are making a wild speculation. You *may*, of course, produce a genius. In opposition to the eugenists I believe that rather fatuous people *should* be engaged in this task, in the hope of creating something more worthy than themselves, on the off chance of bringing it off — just as the pedantic Dean of Lichfield brought off Addison. But if you feel that you've got any sort of Divine spark in yourself, why waste it in the routine of reproduction? Of course Chatham begat William Pitt and Dumas *Père* begat Dumas *fils*, but throughout history you find remarkably few cases of one great man producing another.'

'But supposing that one doesn't feel any Divine spark —'

'A fellow of your stamp and education must. At least, you're pretty gutless if, at your age, you don't feel that you've got it in you to do something fairly big.' (Andrew, as it happened, was suffering from a violent attack of that feeling at this very moment.) 'It's up to you to try, anyway. If when you're thirty-five you haven't done anything and don't feel likely to, then by all means marry some sensible girl and pray for a brilliant son. In the meantime, the finest pictures of the world have not yet been painted; the finest poems haven't been written. No one has yet made a motor-boat do a hundred and fifty miles an hour. No one's made a tyre that can't be punctured. Everything in the world wants doing, but as all the best youngsters have so little self-restraint that they can't struggle undefeated through the sex age, it just doesn't get done. Have some more sherry?'

'He's got it all wrong,' Andrew thought. But somehow he could not put his finger directly on the fallacy. He thought that if, at this moment, someone had asked him to solve the most complicated of all mathematical equations he would have done so without faltering. He felt brilliant, inspired. But the particular part of his brain detailed to frustrate the sophistries of Sir Archibald Loughton was not functioning as it should.

It hardly mattered, anyway. The facts of his case were clear. There was only one thing in the world that he wanted and that was Denise. But Denise had gone from him. She had been suddenly removed as a limb is amputated, and that part of his life was over. Women no longer meant anything. The old fascination — soft laughter, daintiness, the aroma of perfume and prettiness was nothing more than a body under post-mortem examination. One had to look for something else to fill the gap. Perhaps, after all, there was something in what this garrulous old bachelor said.

Sir Archibald, having once again poked the fire with demoniac vigour, sat down again.

'I have a brother,' he said slowly, 'who is an even more remarkable person than I am. He is at present in Pirazi, on the West Coast of Africa. Some twelve hundred miles from him there is a district between two rivers which covers about four hundred square miles and is inhabited by several thousand people who would all be as rich as I am if they knew that their territory is just soaked with oil. But they don't know. All they know is that when a man dies they must burn about twelve women alive in order that he shall be well provided with dancing partners when he arrives at the local Valhalla.

Between my brother and this country there is a marshy waste so poisonous that few Europeans are so foolish as ever to cross it. Now he proposes to build a railway-line between there and Pirazi. If he succeeds, which is unlikely, he will introduce all the more pernicious features of our civilization into a hitherto unexploited territory. But with the greedy oil hunters there will come doctors and policemen. Once the policemen are there, there will be no more widow-burning except *sub rosa*. So on the whole I think it's worth his trying. Do you?'

'It is, of course.'

'Of course! Well, that's encouraging. If *you* go out there you will probably be more a nuisance than a help, but I'll pay your fare if you feel like it.'

Andrew sat upright.

'You mean that —?'

'Well, let's talk it over. Help yourself to another cigar.'

The barking of many dogs woke Andrew shortly after six o'clock. Emerging abruptly from a dream in which he had been back at school, he was first relieved, then puzzled, then enlightened, and with the realization of where he was his thoughts went back to the previous evening, arriving precipitously at the blackest point. He sat up in bed, the effort helping to thrust back the cloud of gloom.

He was wide awake, and his head clear, as though he had walked in hilly country all the previous day and gone to bed at nine. The window was open, and a breeze caught his face. That was good.

Lying back again, he closed his eyes. Denise, probably, was still asleep, curled up as he had seen her once when he had crept along the balcony at dawn, feeling hardly a gentleman but something of a poet. He forced the picture into the remotest corner of his brain, replacing it with a scene which he had conjured up the previous night. Himself being wheeled in a chair from a long white house with a veranda, beneath a blazing sun. A long straight line with a ribbon across it. An engine hurtling along and breaking the ribbon. A tall, grave man in a sun-helmet congratulating him. A telegram from Windsor —

But in the meantime, effort, effort, *effort*. He kicked off the sheets, found his way to the bathroom, and stood beneath the shower for half a minute . . . Quite a decent feeling, although he had always despised the clean-and-manly-life fans. Twenty minutes later he was out of doors, breathing the cold air with relish. Now, for the first time since that agonizing moment of the night before, he felt completely himself again, calm, sane, able to review his position intelligently.

It *had* been a knock-out. It had left him shattered, deprived him suddenly of the whole sense of existence. But here was a new world, a world where the keenness of the wind was pleasant to the senses. It was not such a fresh world, of course. The cream had been skimmed off, leaving a pallid, bluish liquid beneath. But his feeling of youthfulness had been changed, strengthened by a sense of maturity. It was not an intolerable world. Perhaps there was something after all in that stupid speech of an exiled king they had made him learn at his prep. school. Shakespeare was an allegorical blighter. He had a habit of pulling one's leg.

'Good morning!' said a voice behind him.

'Good morning, sir. When can I start?'

They had reached the marmalade stage when the telephone bell in the hall rang querulously.

'Damn the thing!' said Sir Archibald. 'Why do people ring up at this unholy hour?'

'Someone wishes to speak to Mr Blair,' said the butler.

'Me?'

Andrew, wondering, followed him into the hall and took up the receiver.

'Blair speaking.'

'I say, Andrew —'

'Denise!'

'Yes, it's me.'

'How did you know I was here?'

'Someone rang us up early this morning. I say, Andrew, I want to talk to you. I've been awake all night — it's been rotten. Could you —?'

'All right, I'm coming!' said Andrew.

He returned quickly to the dining-room.

'I say, it's awfully rude of me, but I must — can I get my car?'

'You'll find it by the steps,' said Sir Archibald. 'All right, no need to apologize — liberty hall, you know!'

He put the remains of a piece of toast in his mouth, wiped his lips carefully, and went to the window.

'Just one thing,' he called out. 'Beware of ever falling into the slavery of women. They drag you down, they stifle you, they murder all ambition. However, I suppose it's no good my philosophizing.'

It was not, for Andrew was already halfway down the drive, almost hidden in the blue haze of his exhaust.

Sir Archibald rang the bell.

'Did Bush get the Daimler all right?' he asked the butler.

'Yes, sir. The thieves abandoned it about a mile from Frontworth. It was undamaged, and they don't seem to have taken anything of value.'

'Good! Tell Bush to be at the station a few minutes before twelve. Your mistress and Master Richard are coming by the early train from King's Cross.'

The Tramp with a Visiting-card

The Comte de Morfieu, a paddle-steamer owned by a French company, is named after a Provençal of the fifteenth century. The passage of this single vessel constitutes what is known as the Marseille-Egée service. A service it cannot properly be called, but in a way the Morfieu is a convenience. Just when you have missed the regular steamer and resigned yourself to perhaps fifteen more hours on a very small and quite uninteresting island, the Morfieu, which observes no time-table, will often come puffing into view.

I was in just such a position in September, and for (I think) the fourth time in my experience this happened. I knew that salvation was nigh directly I saw a cloud of black smoke above the green-grey of a long headland. I was on board an hour later.

Nearly all the passengers — about a hundred, as we had a full load — were congregated on the port side, the wind coming mainly from starboard. I found a seat by squashing myself between two peasant women, who were, I thought, holding more than their share, and sat there in extreme misery; unable to read as my hands were too cold to hold a book; with no one to talk to, because those all round me were talking in languages which I know only as they are spoken in the various capitals.

By scanning the new horizon as far as the prominent persons of my two neighbours would permit, I presently discovered that I was not, as I thought, the only Englishman on board. About eight paces away, propping himself against the deck-rail with one arm, stood a man whose face, bearing, and clothes might all have been marked 'Made in London'. From his worn brown boots to his faded bowler hat he was shamefully shabby, but between his square chin and the place where his tie should have been he wore a splendid butterfly collar; a very dirty collar, true, but as stiff and uncomfortable as any barrister's. He was engaged in demonstrating some ingenious card tricks to a man whose back was towards me but the colour of whose skin indicated a Spaniard. The Englishman was trying to suggest that his friend would find it advantageous to put his interest in the tricks on a pecuniary basis. This the Spaniard could not or would not understand. He could hardly be blamed, as he was being addressed alternately in broad cockney and in excruciating French. 'Porkwar non compren?' the Englishman was asking repeatedly, and with growing exasperation.

It did not take him long to see me, and he came over at once.

'Nice to meet a fellow-countryman!' he remarked, 'no use for all these dagoes.'

I made a how-do-you-do noise.

'Are you at all interested in cards, sir?' he asked, coming to the point with laudable speed.

I stated that I did not play cards, that I hated all indoor games, and that I did not, to tell the truth, know the difference between a Jack and a spade. He looked glum.

'I could show you some clever tricks,' he suggested.

I intimated with considerable firmness that conjuring tricks of all kinds, and especially card-tricks, were anathema to me. In spite of this discouragement he evidently decided that a card-abhorring Englishman was preferable to a wooden-headed foreigner who couldn't understand his own language.

'I ought to introduce myself!' he said, and from his pocket he produced a card. 'You can keep it,' he remarked, handing it to me with some pride, 'I had a hundred of 'em done at Marsay.'

It was on the large side for a gentleman's card, being roughly equal in area to a postcard. My friend's name was printed right across the middle in huge, red block capitals. The name was 'Sir Henry Norton'.

I said, as gravely as possible, 'I'm delighted to meet you, Sir Henry.'

'Not at all!' he said briskly, and after the manner of true aristocracy he started to talk very rapidly in a man-to-man tone, showing clearly that the social differences which a title implied were not to come between us. I have seldom been put at my ease so vigorously. He told me about his many wanderings on the face of the globe, how he had seen strange things in India, and men lying in the streets of Port Said with knives in their gullets. Evidently he knew his Kipling.

As soon as I had a chance to interrupt the flow of reminiscence, I asked him how he came by his title. This, I think, pleased him. In his heart of hearts he had been longing to tell that story.

'King George has got a big heart and a long memory,' he said darkly, and paused to let the epigram sink in. 'Before the war,' he went on, 'I was just plain Henry Norton. Well, I did my bit, y'know, same as we all did, y'see, an' I saw a bit o' pretty heavy fighting. But I didn't get no medals to show the kids — not that I've got any kids. Of course, I didn't complain, I knew I'd done my bit, same as the rest. Some of us got the chinketies, some of us didn't. That's how things go, y'see. Matter o' luck, more or less, y'see. Well, I says to myself, never mind, I says. King George won't forget you, I says, he won't let you down. Well, I wasn't far wrong. See here, this is what I came across a few months back.'

He dived into his outer pocket again, and brought out a crumpled cutting from *The Times*. It was a New Year's Honours List; a red line led my eye down the 'Knights' section to the name 'Henry Norton, for special services to the nation during the Great War'.

'It's queer how things happen,' he said. 'Shouldn't be surprised if I get an invite to one of these garden parties they have at Buckingham Palace, one of these days.'

'It's not in the least unlikely,' I agreed.

I wonder whether he is still hoping for the opportunity of showing His Majesty a trick or two. I hope, at all events, that no one will disillusion him, for despite his witty profession I think he was simple enough honestly to believe in his title. Sir Harry Norton of Bedfordshire, who happens to be a member of my golf-club, and by whose permission I am able to publish this story, will certainly keep quiet about it.

A Prison in France

In a day when all men are interested in a thing called 'psychology' —
a bastard science, derived from an advanced physiology and an
imperfect understanding of elementary metaphysics — it is
important that I should state the exact circumstances of the
adventure which I here relate. I will therefore give such details as
occur to me to have any possibility of latent importance, in order
that my reader may have a precise understanding of what I will term
the 'cerebral' background of the adventure. I will then leave him to
seek for the complex impulses, the Freudian motives, the cross-
currents of subconscious desires, which go to explain my story; and
to discover in the end that there is no more to be revealed than what
his great-grandfather could have told him in a few simple sentences.

I was at Tours, or to be exact, I was at Tours by day and in a village
called Menanastres, some six miles to the north of it, at night. To rest
in this quiet place I deemed more suitable for a holiday than abiding
in the town itself, where I might have found my bedroom over-
looking a large garage; for I regarded this fortnight as a holiday, even
though the first four hours of each day were spent in forced confine-
ment in a stuffy library with six Frenchmen, a professor from
Gottingen, and a Swede.

This reunion of all the imbeciles, as I myself regarded it, was called
officially a *Grande Conférence Economique d'Eté*; its purpose was to
solve, by one gigantic salvo of concentrated argument, the problem
of population in France. I was a member of the circle by virtue of
having studied, for a dozen years or so, the cotton trade generally,
and, particularly, the problems of Manchester. My colleagues had
wished to co-opt someone who might be styled an economist
proper, as opposed to a eugenist who dabbled in economics;
moreover, a streak of cosmopolitanism suggested that it would be
well to have an Englishman to set off the Swede, whose claim to
distinction in the science of population rested on the fact that he had
successfully transposed the brains of two living dormice, and the
German, who was able to read *Das Kapital* in the original, though he
could make nothing of it. The Frenchmen had all been sociologists
practically from birth. They had read Adam Smith and Plato and

Marie Stopes throughout. Their unanimity upon the subject in hand was devastating. My only real usefulness was in interpreting the professor, who spoke no French, to the Frenchmen, who did not understand German. The Swede spoke no recognized language, but uttered occasional remarks in Esperanto, which the delegate from Gottingen very laboriously translated into English.

It may easily be imagined that I could have had no better rest cure than those daily sessions, when I sat in a deep chair with the warm sunshine falling through the high window to bathe my face, listening, only half awake, to the melodiously uttered discourse of my fellow sociologists. They spoke in turn, and at great length. Their voices rose at times with the hollow passion of the rhetorician who, with one eye on his watch, exactly times the beginning of his furious peroration. With a dramatic intent no less obvious they allowed their voices to fall, and this, when the sun was hot, occurred much more frequently. Their voices seemed always to be falling, flowing for a time in gentle undulations and then falling again. I would stir myself, now and then, to remind my colleagues that, in considering the production of wealth, it was necessary to remember certain laws which governed the relations of supply and demand. They listened with exquisitely polite attention, but could not altogether conceal a relief even greater than my own, when I sat down again and left the field clear for one of themselves. Then Monseiur R— of the Académie would say again how right Monsieur D— of the Sorbonne had been; that the population of France was declining; that the soil was remaining untilled; that the population of France must be made to increase again, but that the new France must come only from a certain section of the population actual; that this section was none other than the — (a word which I could never quite catch). Here a murmur of approval would go round the circle, belatedly caught up by the foreigners; Monsieur F— would rise to emphasize the importance of what Monsieur D— had said. And promptly at three o'clock we rose together, agreed with each other that the day's work had been successful and promising, and shook each other's hands. The thirty-six handshakes took a few minutes, but I was usually able to catch an autobus scheduled to leave the market place at three o'clock precisely. The labours for which I was receiving a generous 'expenses allowance' were then over until the following morning.

My autobus took me to a point on the main road from which I had a walk of two miles or so across the fields to Menanastres, a walk which served to rid my senses and almost my memory of the cobwebs of the Conférence and the exhaust fumes of the autobus. My snug little inn, which seemed to have taken on permanently the colour of the sun that was for ever shining upon it, was an unpretentious hostelry, or, more exactly, it had nothing about it but pretentiousness. Pierre Gonzare, after his brief first and last visit to Paris, had become fired with commercial zeal, and he advertised his establishment in a Tours newspaper as being equipped with *garage*, *bain chaud*, and *cuisine moderne*. The only one of these advanced conveniences which I discovered was the *bain*, and the water, though it may have been extremely *chaud*, never ventured to pass through the rusty tap. But the place suited me well enough. It was old. My room, which must have been reserved for special guests in the days when the aristocracy rested at country inns, was equipped with a huge oak bedstead and a feather mattress. The fare, if simple to the point of barbarism, was well cooked and served hot. The servant — there was only one — was a pattern of grave rusticity. The place had the air of having fallen asleep many years before, never to wake again, unless some explorer from the other side discovered and invaded it with a hideous paraphernalia of cameras and arc lamps.

It was here that, when the learned siesta of the day was over, I slept, and drank *vin ordinaire*, and read Trollope, and started off for long tramps which usually turned out to be lazy hours in woods, too enchanting to be passed by. I find it hard to believe that in those days, when I breathed fresh air and slept long and woke eager for my early morning walk, there existed something which may be accounted the prelude of my adventure. True, I was alone, except when I discoursed with Pierre upon the severity of the past winter; but I was not introspective. The fields, the sunshine, and Trollope were sufficient matter for my reposeful thoughts. The world was too new and appealing to allow my own soul to rival it as a subject of meditation. I was animal, and I was happy.

As to the evening itself — the evening which I shall never forget — I was spending it as I had spent previous evenings, sprawling on a sofa in my room; I had walked far that day, and had propped up my tired legs on two pillows taken from the bed, cushions being a refinement which Pierre had not noticed in Paris. I had had a fire lit, as a cold wind had come with the darkness and was penetrating the badly-fitted windows; it was, besides, a piece of self-indulgence which pleased me, for to light a fire on a chilly night in summer makes one feel that one is snatching the joys of two seasons. The servant had brought my candle, and in its flickering light I was reading a volume of Thomson, listening to the sing-song that the pages transmitted to my mind rather than paying any attention to the meaning of the words. I might have gone to bed early, but I preferred to exercise my eyes to deep weariness, enjoying my pipe the while, and then, stripping quickly, to plunge beneath the sheets and at once into oblivion.

I was surprised, a little annoyed, perhaps, when Pierre knocked heavily on the door and told me that a visitor wished to see me.

'A visitor! But who is this, Pierre?'

'I do not know, monsieur.'

'A gentleman?'

'Yes, m'sieur.'

I sighed, and said that the visitor had better be shown up. When he came I could not at once see who he was — my candle was not strong enough to light his face, and the only image I got was that of a tall figure, in a heavy motoring-coat, looming rather terrifyingly against the wall of the passage, which was made yellow by the rays of a little oil lamp.

A deep voice said '*Bon soir, monsieur!*' and then I knew who it was.

M. Le Feuvre (as I shall call him) was the moving spirit of the *Grande Conférence Economique*, the only one of the Frenchmen who stood out from his fellows by reason of a quickness and energy of temper, a certain impatience, that made him seem less academic than they. He was not so in reality. His doctrines were the same, they had been derived in the same way, and his addresses were no nearer to real life than theirs. But his force of manner, the relentlessness with which he pursued his thesis, made it come from his lips as a live thing rather than a skeleton; I could almost believe that, had any power been given him, he would have put his creed into practice; that he would have forced a world in love with the irrational to wed a pious and unlovely rationalism. By the grace of Heaven, however, M. Le Feuvre was not taken seriously by the *Chambre des Députés*. He prided himself on his culture, did M. Le Feuvre, and, indeed, I could never find any flaw in the logic of his aesthetics. At our first meeting he explained music to me until music became mere mathematics. He could discuss Milton and Goethe with equal brilliance. He told me what Shakespeare might have learnt from Hugo, why Swift was a cynic, and what it was which made the alexandrine the perfect vehicle for the expression of human emotion. I was alarmed by the extent of his learning and terrified by the mechanics of his artistic appreciation. He could say to a single canvas how much of Botticelli's work was good, how much was indifferent, and how much was definitely poor; and if he gained pleasure from any of Botticelli's pictures it was from the definitely poor ones, since these gave the most scope for his critical acumen. I have met no other man whose soul seemed so indisputably to be made of granite.

He came to me across the room, this giant of the Philistines, and greeted me with warmth. 'I have a little treat for you, monsieur,' he said. 'You will come, will you not?'

I hesitated for a moment. It was nice of the fellow to be so friendly, but what kind of treat could he offer me? Was some deplorable company giving a performance of Racine, hideously cut? Or must I make that seven-mile journey into Tours simply to eat veal and garlic at the newest restaurant while Le Feuvre, fork in one hand and toothpick in the other, talked sociology at me across the table?

'But how kind of monsieur!' I said, for there was no escape. 'May I ask what the treat is to be?'

'It is first — a little drive in my so smooth and swift automobile,' he answered mysteriously. 'And then — something which will greatly interest you.'

Cursing the hospitable instincts of the French, I put on my coat and followed him down the stairs. His automobile was indeed — as far as one could judge from appearances — both smooth and swift. It was long and low, very beautiful in line. I eyed it suspiciously, as it stood purring almost imperceptibly beneath the light of the swinging doorway lamp. It was like himself, that car, irresistible and without feeling. The contempt with which it ignored my beautiful inn, casting the glance of its huge cold eyes straight along the road, was hardly more chilling than its master's oblivious demeanour as he strode across the flags upon which travellers had stood three centuries before. As we passed out he allowed the door to swing and slam behind us. He half imagined, I believe, that it would be fitted with a compression-silencer.

We spoke little as we drove. Le Feuvre held his lips together in a smile, childishly enjoying the fact that he had a surprise in store for me. My silence he no doubt attributed to a curiosity so burning as to leave me bereft of speech; or perhaps he considered me just a stupid

Englishman and left it at that. But in reality I was silent from pure laziness. It was warm in the car — the machine must have been fitted with every kind of patent radiator — and I was comfortable. Since I could not be in bed, or drowsing over Thomson before my pleasant fire, this was at least a second-best, provided that I did not have to worry my wits into the alertness required for conversation with an eminent sociologist. I did not even wonder in what direction we were going. Wondering, indeed, would have been of little use. We had turned several times, whether right or left I had forgotten, and were now running at a furious speed down one of the long, straight roads that might have been anywhere in France or Spain. I sacrificed at the altar of sociability with occasional praise of the car — remarks which were bound to gratify the owner and which went so easily into French.

'It is most comfortable, your automobile!'

'Yes, it is not so bad.'

'And so silent.'

'You think so?'

'It must be very powerful.'

'Indeed, yes, it has all the power I require.'

It was not until we had travelled, according to my rough estimation, some fifteen miles, that my friend vouchsafed to enlighten me.

'Can you guess where I take you?' he asked suddenly.

I could not; I did not add that I had not even tried.

'It is to a prison.'

'To prison?'

'Ah, no, no, my friend! Do not alarm yourself. Not to prison. To *a* prison.'

So sleepy was I that it was some time before the meaning of this distinction dawned upon me.

'My ordinary friends,' he went on, 'I give them a little dinner and I take them to the theatre or to the motion-pictures. They have no *esprit*, those others. But you, you are a man of learning. I take you to something better, something that will be of interest. It is what you call an experiment, this prison of mine. I am the owner, you see. I am in complete charge of the prisoners.'

At this moment we left the main road, and after running for half an hour along a lane so deeply pitted that even Le Feuvre's thorough-bred could not entirely absorb the shocks before they reached us, we swung left again into a carriage drive. There was no lodge at the gate, nor any sign of a guard. Two minutes later our headlamps, sweeping round, gave me a momentary glimpse of a huge, stone château.

'A very old place, this!' was Le Feuvre's only comment as he brought the car to a standstill beneath a massive portico.

The door opened, as though automatically, as we stepped out of the car, and a man in uniform saluted as we passed inside. The door was carefully bolted behind us.

'Come upstairs,' said Le Feuvre, so briskly that for a moment I had the idea that the *Grande Conférence Economique* intended to reduce its membership. But he added, more pleasantly, 'You shall have a little drink. There is wine in my office.'

The interior of the château was like a museum; the staircase, made of stone and twenty feet wide at the bottom, divided to left and right, the arms leading up to a long corridor which extended both ways. The floor of that corridor was polished, and shone beneath suspended gas lamps. The walls were so tall that the ceiling was deep in shadow. Two guards were pacing up and down, one at each end, and their feet ringing on the boards sent the echoes travelling weirdly up and down the length of it. I felt that I would rather be in a common dungeon in the Newgate of the Middle Ages than in such a prison as this. The vastness and coldness horrified me. Something in the place confused my vision as mirrors will do, though I do not think that there were any mirrors; and I could not judge how far away were the doors at the ends. We paused at the top of the stairs and one of the guards, coming towards us, seemed to grow larger with absurd rapidity. He came quite close, so that I, still feeling as if I had found my way into the Louvre after hours, had an impulse to tip him. But he turned, and retreating, grew smaller as quickly as he had become enormous.

'They are unnecessary really,' said Le Feuvre (I was glad to hear him speak), 'but they give the place the correct air.'

He led me off to the left, and we seemed to walk for miles along the corridor, pursued by the echoes of our own footsteps.

'These are the prisoners' dormitories,' he remarked, pointing to doors on both sides. 'They are there all the time, for exercise is voluntary and nobody takes any. If I have done nothing else I have proved one thing — that man is a lazy animal. He will do nothing unless he is made to do it.'

We had reached the end of the corridor at last, and opening a door with a key he led me into an office, a small room so heavily loaded with the impedimenta of business that there was no room for any comfortable chairs. I sat down in a revolving desk-chair, feeling very uncomfortable, for a desk-chair makes a man look foolish who would be at his ease and sociable. Le Feuvre brought wine from a little cupboard on top of the office safe.

'You must understand,' he said, 'that this is in the nature rather of a clearing-house than of a prison in the ordinary sense; though there are some inmates whom we never clear.'

I did not care in the least whether it was a clearing-house, a lunatic asylum, or a post office.

'Indeed! That is most interesting!' I said. 'In our country we have no such clearing-houses.'

Le Feuvre ignored my remark.

'Yes,' he said slowly, 'there are some whom we do not clear. And those that I do not think it well to release — those are the ones that cry most to get out. They are the only ones who are not completely lazy. It is most troublesome.'

'It is a matter for your discretion entirely?' I asked.

'Yes. There are some that I think better kept here. They are not strong enough for the world outside — lame, some of them, and diseased; but most of them merely a little touched in the head. They are eccentric; they all think differently, and they want to pass on their mental disease and to paint pictures of things that should not be painted at all. I have a great deal of trouble with them, because they are always escaping, in spite of my precautions. But I will not make your mind sore with the sight of these strange ones. You shall see rather one who is about to be released. You will see what a promising fellow it is.'

In an adjoining room a telephone bell rang at that moment, and Le Feuvre went to answer it, passing through a door marked 'Private'. Hardly had this door closed behind him when another on the opposite side of the room opened, and a boy came in. He was dark-headed, well-built, and of good features, but he had nothing about him which would have distinguished him at once from a group of other French boys of the school-leaving age. What I myself noticed, as the light of a gas-burner threw his face into sharp perspective, was a certain simplicity of expression and a look of deep drowsiness.

He did not appear to see me at first, and when he did he stared closely at me for several seconds, blinking, as if his eyes were not yet accustomed to the light. Suddenly he gave a little cry.

'You have not come to take me away?' he asked, his lips trembling.

I could hear Le Feuvre's voice, as he hurled staccato sentences into the telephone in the next room. 'What is that? Ah, yes, she combats. She combats strongly. That is good. Ah! brave woman! True daughter of France!'

'Certainly not,' I told the boy. 'I am only a visitor to the prison.'

Le Feuvre came back, and the moment the boy saw him he fell to his knees.

'Monsieur!' he said, his voice sounding as if someone were gripping his throat, 'you will not send me away? You cannot, I am so happy here.'

A paternal gentleness came over Le Feuvre at once.

'Now, now, my little Georges, you must not weep. You have a great thing before you, a fine thing, to work for beautiful France.'

'I care nothing for France,' the boy replied. 'I want only to be restful here, where I am sure of always having enough to eat and to drink.'

A look of anger crossed Le Feuvre's face, but it was gone in a moment.

'Come now!' he said, still in the same gentle tone, 'you do not realize how much happiness there is in store for you. You know nothing of the world. How can you be afraid of that which you do not know at all? Our friend here, though he is a foreigner, will tell you something of the magnificence of France, which he loves almost as I do.'

I did not want to say anything, for at that moment I loathed Le Feuvre. But in the corridor outside I could hear the guard pacing — and, besides, I felt that to say something was the least I could do for Georges.

'Perhaps I myself do not understand France,' I said slowly, 'for we English are not of a temper that can understand it. But I know that it is very beautiful — so beautiful that it draws us away even from our own Yorkshire moors and our Cotswold hills and our majestic valley of the Thames. It has a warmth which we cannot find even in the lanes of Sussex, a richness of its own which equals even the richness of our chessboard landscapes. The long roads and the tiny inns, the simple peasants in their cottages, they stay where they are in

France, and we, who should possess such things, see them ever retreating before the rush of our own advance. There is a clearness in the air, a freshness in the dawn —'

The boy had listened attentively, though plainly without any understanding, as I had picked my way through words I did not know too well, trying, I believe, for the first time, to embody in language the feeling which was my France, and which would not allow itself to be embodied. But here he cut me short with another burst of passionate weeping.

'I do not know what you say,' he jerked out between his sobs, 'but I believe that you are only deceiving me. I know — I have heard — that it will only be fighting out there.'

'But, my dear boy,' said Le Feuvre, 'the days of fighting are over. We do not have wars now.'

The boy would not listen.

'You cannot be certain that there will be no wars. And if there are none, there will be other fighting, fighting for position, and perhaps for bread; fighting for something which is old and useless, or perhaps for life, which we do not want; fighting to please the old men who want this world of yours as it always has been, hard and miserable and full of fatigue.'

Le Feuvre's patience was ended, but he did not give his anger full rein. Only his benevolence fell from him, giving place to a terrible sternness. He seized the boy's wrist.

'See!' he said coldly. 'You are lazy. You must be made to do something. In time it will become less painful for you — you will realize that there is no joy but the joy of striving, no pleasure that has not been won by pain; if, when you have striven, you find that pleasure is still out of your grasp, you will strive again; you will fight and fight until you are overwhelmed, because you must obey a law which tells you to go forward. And you will not be alone, for there is a sweet fellowship in strife. there is a beauty in sharing defeat with your fellows. The wine may be sour, but you will drink because they drink it, drink it until the cup is empty, because then you will have shown your courage. Yes, courage, that is the thing which alone has beauty; we have made it beautiful, we that have lived for a thousand thousand years, I who live today, you who will live tomorrow. We cannot let our courage be defeated. Come now!'

A door opened — a door I had noticed before, opposite the one by which we had entered the room. It must have led to an outside staircase. Two men stood against the darkness outside, their figures stiff in the position of attention. Le Feuvre addressed them.

'Are you ready?'

'All is ready, m'sieu.'

The boy pulled away from Le Feuvre, but was sharply tugged back. Opening his mouth as wide as he could, he uttered one sharp cry, which seemed to be echoed by the black waste outside. Then, in silence, scarcely resisting, he was led away.

Le Feuvre turned to me, but his face was no longer clear. A mist hung in front of it, distorting the features, making it come and go, grow larger and smaller in swift succession, as the figures of the guards had done.

'That is number 12753,' he said. I heard his voice as coming from a great distance, but in a whisper only. 'I am sorry for him, I am sorry for all of them, those souls which hate to be born. But we cannot think of individual men. We must think of France.' His voice came nearer again, and, ceasing to be a whisper, grew shrill. 'France must have its men,' he cried. 'I do not care whether the souls fear the world or no.'

The room was swinging round, slowly, the furniture keeping its position but rising and falling a little. By following it round with my eyes I could still distinguish the open door through which the boy had been taken. I looked out after him, peering deep into the darkness to see where he had gone. But I saw nothing, only a murky void, until, straining my eyes again, I saw a candle which flickered in the wind, and seemed to go out, and then grew bright again.

When the *Conférence* assembled next morning M. Le Feuvre took me aside for a moment. He seemed greatly excited.

'My other colleagues know it already,' he whispered. 'I must tell you. The work is complete, yes, finished. Since we rose yesterday I do not sleep, no, not at all. I cease working hardly for meals. I am in my room. No one must disturb. I write and write, as the hands of the clock go round and round. And now it is complete, the draft of the motion which I bring before the *Chambre*. It is complete, and there is no loophole. When it is the law of France, France will prosper, for my motion provides that the people of France will increase, and go on increasing, until the fields are tilled again. You will like to see the draft, perhaps, yes? It is the fruit of my labour of many hours. Last

night I do not sleep . . .'
    I took the draft, though I had no wish to read it.

Elosindi's Christmas

I can remember how he looked, with the lamp shining on him; lying on his back, his eyes wide open and staring, one of his legs twisted horribly beneath him. I could have sworn, then, that his face was quite white, bloodless. It was only for a second or two that I saw him, but I remember it so clearly that I can see it now, with the dark group standing back to let me look. I can hear Kestin saying 'My god, Robert, you've done it this time!' And that was twenty-one years ago.

I suppose it was getting on for one when it happened. I remember Kestin looking at the clock in the card-room and saying 'D'you realize what the time is? Ten past midnight, Christmas Day. Look here, we must get back, I promised to put something in Sybil Irvine's stocking.' We had a beaker of port or something then to start the celebrations, and we worked our way gradually towards the terrace, and there was an argument as to whether Kestin or I should drive, and we tossed and I won. That's another thing I see very clearly, a five-abono piece lying heads up on the gravel.

I have mentioned the drink we had out of honesty; for even now the feeling remains that I have still to clear myself, that only by strict fidelity to the facts can I do so; but I am ready to swear that when we started I was dead sober. I won't answer for Kestin, but it usually takes more than he had had, and there were no signs.

They all stood with our host on the terrace of the Club to see us off, and said we must come again soon — knowing that it was supremely unlikely — and the foolish little red-haired man, I think his name was Lloyd, called out that if we knocked a tiger over it would serve as a Christmas dinner. Someone else, a girl, I fancy, shouted 'Be careful you don't . . .' but I lost the rest of what she said as I revved up in second. Perhaps, if I had heard it, it would have saved a lot of trouble. But we had promised Trevorley to be back on board by twelve, and I felt rather guilty.

The road from Lasa L'nong to Garrison Harbour was then the best, in fact the only good one in the peninsula. It led for a dozen miles along the top of the Abanindi Ridge, then zigzagged down in slopes of a mile or so, stiff enough to empty half your radiator on the upward climb, till it reached sea-level about a mile inland. From there, turning south, it ran parallel with the shore, straight as a broom-handle for four or five miles, then bending a little to the right to reach the harbour. From the ridge I could look far out to sea, and glancing left as we turned, I thought I could just discern the riding lights of the *Ethiopia*. In the deceptive clearness of the air she seemed but a mile or two away. Then, as we reached the first of the hairpin bends, the tsota palms rose up on either side and the whole view disappeared.

It seemed endless, as roads do seem when you are in a hurry, and each time it turned I thought we were reaching the level. When at last we had banked steeply, with brakes reeking, round the final bend and were clear of the trees, I let her right out and she charged towards the harbour like a cavalry horse released from temporary service on the limber. 'You'll remember,' Kestin said, 'that this — thing is hired.'

It was not till we were almost in Mbeme that I recognized it as a village. True, we had passed it on the way inland, and I remembered later how I had considered it an eyesore; a spatter of ramshackle huts on one side of the roadway, with the quarries behind scarring the blue-green slopes. It was a labour settlement, chicken-houses of a European type with local improvisations, stretched out — by the design, no doubt, of a Lancashire foreman — along the margin of the road and sprawling back towards the quarry workings. Yes, I had seen it that morning, but it had passed clean out of my mind, and when my headlamps first fell upon it I thought, honestly thought, that it was nothing but a clump of bush.

It was about that moment that Kestin bent forward to light his cigar; and he noticed, so he has always said, that we were doing thirty-seven. I am sure he was mistaken. The Darracq we had hired was not even new, and with half a gale behind her she would not have exceeded thirty-five on the level. Either the smoke was in his eyes, or his sight was dicky, or the speedometer was wrong. At any rate I slowed down, instinctively, for the acetylene lamps were none too strong and the sudden appearance of any object on so bare a road was enough to give me warning. The next thing I saw was a beam of yellow light falling across the laterite surface as a door opened.

Not more than twenty yards in front, and there Kestin is with me. I think I swerved a little, certainly I had my foot right off the accelerator and resting against the brake. But even so, I had no chance.

Kestin and I had exactly the same impression; that the dark shape positively hurled itself into the road. And, again, he agrees with me that in the moment when our lamps caught it it looked like a man's coat and trousers, fastened together but empty, the arms sprawling like those of a scarecrow. My foot went down hard, I reached for the handbrake but Kestin had it already. I felt a bump, not a very hard bump but it was as if a fist had struck me just above the heart. There was a cry which seemed to come from some way behind the car and which was lost at once in the scream of our tyres.

I had the reckless impulse to drive on hard, and perhaps I should not have conquered it if the handbrake, held by the ratchet, had not prevented me. Certainly my foot went back to the accelerator, and in that moment's cowardice I covered perhaps twenty yards before I stopped. We got out then and walked back.

Kestin said: 'This is going to be a very merry Christmas.'

There was a crowd in the road, it looked as if the whole village had assembled in the twinkling of an eye. They were quite silent, and when I came up to them they had a look which I can only describe as sheepish. For a moment I felt cool. I knew exactly what had happened. I was prepared to take charge of the situation. Then the crowd fell back a little and I saw what I have described to you. And a little more than I have described.

Only for a moment. The crowd closed again before I had got near to the man, and they took him up and carried him into the nearest hut. That was quite enough.

I sat down by the side of the road and Kestin asked me rather foolishly if I was going to do anything. I wondered for a moment if he grasped what had happened. But I said nothing, for my voice had faded out. I wanted to be sick, and couldn't.

I said at last: 'You'd better go in and see whether . . .'

There was really no need. We heard a scream, and I somehow knew that it came from the man's wife. Her screams went on, loud enough it seemed to me then, to carry to Lasà L'nong itself. And at once the voices of a dozen women had started in a death wail such as I had never heard and hope never to hear again, a noise of the jungle, high and bitter, trembling with a maniacal grief. The effect it produced on me was overwhelming. I wanted desperately to roar with laughter.

Kestin went in and stayed for perhaps a quarter of a minute. When he came out, I could see in the light from the window that his face was grey.

'Did you see him?' I asked.

He said, 'Only just — they were all round, there wasn't much light. But I'm afraid . . .'

No one molested us, but the men who were still in the roadway had us in their eye, and I could see that they would not have let us go.

'We must find the Msong Steshar,' Kestin said. He was practical as ever, but I noticed a dampness in his voice and I think that he was no less aware than I of the eyes darkly watching. 'We must find the Msong Steshar,' he repeated, 'and make a report to him. We can't do more than that.'

We found him, with the help of Kestin's few words of M'shee, in a cabin that stood by itself at the end of the village through which we had entered — a wrinkled old man in a European nightshirt with a little Kotta-English and a fund of courtesy, but he would do nothing to relieve our conscience. It was not his affair, he said, when with infinite difficulty we had explained the situation. 'If you had stolen something, or trespassed in the game-preserve up at Inyomar, I should be glad to help you to arrange for the customary fines. But knocking a man down, that's not my affair, you must see the sub-magistrate in Harbour Town. He lives over there, up the hill,' he added, sweeping the southern hemisphere with his long and bony arm. 'He is the man to report to, for assaults and woundings. He arranges for hangings, and all that.'

Little comforted, we went back towards the car. And before we had gone a dozen paces a woman stopped us.

'My son!' she said simply in English, 'you have killed my son.'

She went back into her miserable wooden house and inevitably we followed her. We stood all three about the single table, on which a kerosene lamp was burning, and in that curious, flickering light, we listened to her mourning. Her face in the yellow light, I can see it now, her face was what brought home to me the tragedy of what I had done. Before, I had been too shocked to realize the implications of the accident. My mind's voice had repeated, in horrible reiteration, 'A man's dead: I've killed him.' Now the fact broke in on me afresh in the terms of human sorrow. 'He was my son, my son Elosindi, he was my son.' I do not know how old she was, for the face of the Kotta ages early. But from the lines in the cheeks and forehead, the sharp protrusion of the bones, the dry and crinkly skin, I should have guessed her to be not less than seventy. She was handsome, as are all the Kottas, her eyes were large and bright, even the flat nose of her type did not ill become her. But the impression I first received, and that which rested with me, was her dignity. It was a humble face, too hardened by the flow of years to bend itself beneath emotion; only a single tear which shone upon her cheek-bone, and the mourning in her eyes, betrayed her sorrow. There was no anger in her face, and no reproach, only the tragedy of those who submit because they have always submitted.

I would have given everything I had to give her back her son.

Her speech was kin to her expression. And though she used her Kotta-English clumsily, there was nothing risible about her usage. She understood, she said, it was not the fault of the Inglissani. It was the fault of Elosindi, he was no doubt uncareful, he had never become accustomed to the furious engines that moved upon the roads. Only that he was a good son to her, he was all she had to lean on now that she herself was past working, and the most skilful quarryman from end to end of the coast. 'He was my only child,' she said, 'my only child. And the wife he leaves, who is sick and can do nothing, and his four children, how shall I nourish them?'

I had nothing to answer her, and, loathing myself, I listened while Kestin spoke to her with almost brutal firmness. He was sorry, he said, but it was altogether an accident, his friend the Inglissani who was driving the car could not possibly have avoided her son. He repeated 'Impossible, he could not avoid him, it was quite impossible.' None the less, he told her, the case would be judged by the proper authority. A report had been made already to the Msong Steshar, and we were now on our way to lay the facts before the sub-magistrate for Harbour Town. 'You can rely on him,' he said with finality, 'to see that justice is done.'

I saw for the first time a look of scorn in the old woman's face.

'There will be justice, no doubt,' she said. She knew that word. 'But who will feed my son's children? Will the magistrate feed his children?'

I murmured something, then, about *ex gratia* compensation. I even spoke wildly of an annuity. Even if she had understood such words it would have made no difference. There was a little smile, a pitiful smile, upon her lips. She did not believe a single word we said.

Instinctively I felt in my trouser pocket, and my fingers counted. I had just seventeen abonos, and half-a-crown English. I turned to Kestin, and remembered as I did so that he had been winning at whist all evening. I whispered, 'We must make a gesture, at least a gesture.'

He turned his back a moment and I heard the notes rustling. The old woman and I remained facing each other, silent and without expression. Kestin asked, in a businesslike voice which I hated: 'Will a hundred abonos help you?'

I saw a look of fierce indignation on her face, and I thought she would have turned on him. But she said, quite quietly, with only a shade of sarcasm:

'It is little to feed four children. When my son broke his arm in the quarry, and could earn nothing for three months, the Inglissani Mgasti gave me five hundred abonos.'

Kestin turned to me.

'What have you got?' he asked.

'Seventeen,' I said.

He took them, and opened his case again. We had just four hundred between us. He put the notes and coins on the table.

'That is all we have,' he said shortly.

'You are generous,' she said. 'You are kind, you are good Inglissani. But it will not feed his children.'

We walked back to the car then in silence. I told Kestin to drive — I had no more spirit — and he sat in the driver's seat, his hands by his sides, as pale as if it were he who had killed Elosindi.

I said, 'Aren't you going to start?'

He looked at me distantly, and asked: 'Do you think I'm perfectly sober? Do you now, honestly?'

I said: 'You're sober enough to drive. I can't.'

'But I'm serious,' he said. 'I thought I was sober, I was sure I was. But something's made me a bit queer. I saw — I thought I saw a ghost just now, as we came through the village.'

'A ghost . . . ?'

'I could have sworn that I saw that man, the man you killed, grinning at me through the window.'

It strengthened me to find that he had become hysterical.

'All right,' I said, 'you come round to this side. I'll drive.'

I don't know how long it took us, but we did at last find the sub-magistrate's bungalow. Kestin, growing sleepy, had begged me to be sensible and leave it till the morning, but I had the schoolboy sensation that I could not sleep until I had owned up. It seemed to me a matter of desperate urgency that I should place the whole matter before authority. I had to do something, take some action, to rid myself of the nightmare which had enwrapped me. I do not think we should ever have found the place but that one of the rooms was lighted. And so great had my eagerness become that I went straight on to the verandah, Kestin limply following, and knocked on the lighted window.

I heard a voice say, 'Satan's stomach!' and almost immediately the yellow curtain was thrown aside. The French window swung open, and the sub-magistrate stood before us, in a green kimono and green silk pyjamas, holding a twelve-bore in one hand and a book in the other. The book, I remember, was a volume of Gibbon's *Decline and Fall*.

We said 'Good evening!' and he answered, '—— your eyes!'

He was a very small man, with the figure of the White Queen. His face was thin, grey, and as dour as an art critic's. He spoke like a youth whose voice has not quite broken giving Company orders across a vast parade ground. He said:

'This is the fourth time I've just got to sleep and been woken by some tomfoolery. Have the goodness to turn out the lights of your machine. They'll scare my canary. Come inside. No, stay where you are. What do you want?'

Kestin did most of the talking for our side.

He said: 'We're sorry to bother you, sir, but we have something important to report.'

'Nonsense,' said the sub-magistrate. 'Nothing important happens on this coast. 'I've been here fourteen years, so I know.'

'We've had an accident,' Kestin pursued.

'An accident? With that machine, I suppose? I thought so. Of course you've had an accident, you all do. You go screaming up and down the new road in those silly things, making my life unbearable with your hootitoots and stinking oil and the dust you raise, never look where you're going, never put on your brakes, frighten my horses, and then you wonder you have an accident. No good coming complaining to me. The road's all right. Wha' d' dy' do? Bang a tree over? The trees all belong to the government. I'll have your hides tanned if you've bust one of them.'

'It's rather more serious than that,' Kestin said. 'We killed a man.'

(I blessed him for that 'we'.)

'It's cold here,' he said. 'All right for you fellows in your clothes, you don't seem to realize I'm undressed. You'd better come in. Are your boots clean?'

We went in, and he had the decency to give us cigarettes. There was a big double-bed in one corner and someone was snoring. He crossed the room and threw a towel over the pillow.

'Don't mind her!' he said. 'Now then, you say you've killed a man. What sort of man, black or white?'

I said 'black'. The way he asked the question tempted me to add 'Please'.

He snorted.

'D—d infernal carelessness. There won't be a native left on this — coast soon. You people don't seem to realize there's a labour-shortage. You're the sixth young fellow — well, you banged him down, you say, and you say you killed him. Are you sure you killed him? All right then. But I still can't see why you had to knock me up at this hour.'

He yawned and fetched a notebook from a drawer of the dressing-table.

'What's your name?' he asked Kestin.

'Kestin. Captain Arthur Kestin.'

'And yours?'

'Robert Hutchinson.'

'Where d'you live?'

'Well at present we're on the *Ethiopia*. She's moored in the bay, Gerald Trevorley's yacht.'

'That white boat.'

'Yes.'

He snapped his book with a gesture of finality.

I asked in a voice that I recognized as fatuous: 'Is that all?'

'Yes,' he said. 'I can't stay up all night, can I? Oh, one other thing, did you get the man's name? It wasn't Elosindi by any chance?'

Surprised, I said 'Yes?'

'It would be,' he said grimly. 'Yes, you would pick on him. The best quarryman on the coast. At least, so they're always telling me.'

I realized only then — I had been so stunned by his callous attitude — that so far I had said nothing to explain or excuse myself.

'There's a good deal more,' I began, 'that I have to say . . .'

'You can say it in Court,' he snapped. 'I positively must get some sleep now. The case will probably come up at Medua — I'm too busy for that sort of thing. I'll send the summons on board, one of my men can row out with it.'

Kestin asked bluntly: 'When?'

'When!' screamed the sub-magistrate. 'When? (It's all right, dear, that was only me, these gentlemen are just going.) Upon my soul, I call that pretty cool. You go hogging up and down the coast at ninety miles an hour . . .'

'. . . We were doing just twenty-five,' Kestin said quietly.

'— An hour, and you bang over valuable natives, and you get me up in the middle of the night to blather to me about it, and then you have the classic nerve to ask me, to ask me, precisely when the summons is to be delivered. Of course I've nothing in the world to worry about but you and your summonses. How would next Wednesday suit you after lunch with your coffee?'

Controlling my voice as well as I could, for I was furiously angry, I said: 'It happens to concern a great many other people besides myself. Mr Trevorley has a large party. His plans have been made very carefully. I'm dependent on him to get me home. I am the only person responsible for the accident — Captain Kestin was not driving — and I do not see why my friends should be inconvenienced simply because . . .'

'I can't help your friends,' he said. 'If you've behaved like a young fool, and they suffer, well, who's to blame? I can't summons you yet because I haven't got the right forms. It has to be on a blue form. I've only got pink forms by me — they're for natives. I can't summon a white man on a pink form. I've run out and I'll have to send to Medua for a new batch. And that's the fault of your other motoring friends.'

It was just then that I became convinced the man was mad. Kestin (as he afterwards told me) had made up his mind on that point some time before. In my bewilderment and modesty I had previously thought that the delirium might be partly on my side.

Kestin only yawned.

'I think we will wish you good-night,' he said, and opened the window.

The sub-magistrate laughed horribly. I have never heard another laugh so cracked and humourless.

'And how much night do you think I can . . . ?'

But we were outside and Kestin had shut the window.

'That's what comes,' Kestin said amiably, 'of following your suggestion. If you'd taken my advice and left Trevorley to . . .'

The window opened again, and the sub-magistrate bawled:

'Hi. Hudson! Cabstand! Come back!'

We turned round but we didn't budge. I was sick with misery and fatigue, I only wanted to get away.

'Did you pay any compensation?' he shouted.

As if my wretchedness were not enough I realized at that moment that we had done what every adolescent knows will put him right out of court. I did not answer, but Kestin, feeling no doubt the hole in his pocket, said dully: 'Yes.'

'Who to? Old Sikkita? The boy's mother?'

Again Kestin answered. 'Yes.'

'What did you give her?'

'Four hundred.'

'Then you're — lucky!' yelled the sub-magistrate. 'That son of hers has been banged over four times in the last fifteen months, and killed stone dead three times out of the four, and she's never taken less than a pony. I tell you you're —— lucky. Merry Christmas! —— your eyes! Good night!'

A Photograph of Mrs Austin

The experience I'm going to tell you about took place some time ago, but it was a curiously vivid one, so vivid that occasionally it still comes into my dreams.

It concerns a steamship called the *Joanna*. At least, that's what she was called when I knew her. She was launched at Greenock, somewhere about 1910, with the name of *Killin Lass*, and under that name she was used for several years in the Brazil trade, running between Liverpool and Santos. In the latter years of the war she was taken over by the Admiralty — for what purpose I don't know — and I think it was in 1920 that she was bought by Crowbitt & Pollyard, of Cardiff, who changed her name. I've heard it said that old Edward Crowbitt wouldn't have a ship with a Scottish name because he had once been worsted in a business duel by a man from Dundee. Be that as it may, the name was changed, and the *Joanna* was brought for refitment to a place on the south-west coast which I shall call Stallmouth. (For reasons which you'll understand, I don't want to give you the actual name.) From that time Stallmouth was her home port, and most of the regular crew had their homes there, including the master and the mate. She was used for miscellaneous cargoes, mostly on the Mediterranean routes.

You probably know that it's considered unlucky to change a ship's name. I myself think that all such superstitions are nonsense, but I'm bound to say that the *Joanna* did seem to become an unlucky ship. At the time I'm talking about I was working for a firm of brokers, and owing to an old family connection we had most of Crowbitt's insurance business, so I knew all about the *Joanna* from the time Crowbitt took her over. And really her misfortunes were almost a joke in the office — a bitter joke, I grant you.

On the very first voyage under her new colours she rammed a trawler — that was about four miles out of port. Fortunately there wasn't much damage. Then on her way home from Marseilles her steering gear went out of order; she had to be towed into Valencia and was held up there for nearly a fortnight. I think it was on the next voyage, or possibly the one after, that she shipped a big sea in the Bay which stove the hatch of No. 2 hold and drenched a lot of her cargo. It included several thousand pounds' worth of Italian silk goods, and they weren't much improved by the dousing. In the following year, at Port Said, she took on a coloured seaman who proved to have smallpox — five of the crew were infected and one of them died of it. And so it went on. Something seemed to happen on every single voyage, till the *Joanna* became a byword. It was a wonder to me that they could still collect a crew to sail in her. Actually there was a small group of men who stuck to her from the time Crowbitt bought the ship till the very end; I suppose they had some kind of sentimental affection for what was called locally 'that damned old steam-hearse'.

Then came the trip that was to prove her last. Early in April she sailed for Montreal, carrying machinery, and returned with a mixed cargo — mainly wheat and timber, with a small consignment of skins. The skins didn't occupy much space, but they were much the most valuable part — they were chiefly white fox and American marten. If I'd had any say in the matter, the *Joanna* would have been the very last ship I should have chosen for stuff like that. But of course Crowbitt & Pollyard didn't think that way — they'd have put the Crown Jewels in a coracle if they thought they could collect the freightage. I have an idea that the cargo was badly loaded, but we were never able to prove that. Actually she made a good passage till she was nearing the Irish coast.

There she came into very dirty weather, which followed her all the way home. And it was on the second night of that storm that old Dave Austin, the master, was lost.

It happened at midnight. He had been below, talking to the engineer, and before going up to take over the middle watch — the mate had kept the first watch — he went to look at some repairs which the carpenter had made in the forr'd hatch. As he turned to go back a tremendous sea drove against the port bow, throwing the ship on one side as if she'd been rammed by a cruiser and filling up the forr'd deck. That wave picked Austin up as an autumn wind picks up dry leaves. He was seen for just one moment, clutching at the stays, then he was gone.

That — as near as I can remember it — was the account given by Pittard, the mate, who was standing on the starboard wing of the bridge and happened to glance down just as the tragedy occurred. No one else saw it.

Of course, nothing could be done. In such a sea there was no question of stopping the ship. And that was the end of a very fine sailor.

It was not the last disaster of that voyage.

I no longer have a copy of the log entries, so I can only give you, in my own language, the facts as I remember them.

They continued to go through ferocious weather; in the heavy rolling the deck cargo got loose from its lashings, the hatch of No. 4 hold was broken and the water got through to the grain, with the inevitable result. On top of that the bunker hatch was damaged and water came into the stokehold. The ship took a heavy list to port. Then the main pump got choked. The hand pumps were set going but they were insufficient to cope with the water. By five o'clock on the next afternoon she was definitely sinking by the stern.

From all accounts, Pittard handled the ship very well, and at one time it seemed as if the worst danger was over — she was not taking any more water. Throughout the night he nursed her along through angry seas, keeping a resolute course for Stallmouth Bay; he must have been on the bridge altogether for something like forty hours without a break. During the night the wind fell a little, and in the morning he had his reward: the English coast was in clear sight, he had something less than twenty miles to cover.

There was water now in No. 3 hold and it was rising alarmingly; the speed was down to something like four knots; but Pittard thought he could do it, and do it under his own steam.

He *might* have done it — though I doubt it — if he hadn't made a gamble. When he passed Stallpoint Head — that was about two o'clock in the afternoon — the tide was just a little past the full. At the mouth of Stallmouth Bay there's a long sandbank, known as Foster's Bar, which stretches almost the whole way across to the eastern side. Normally a ship of the *Joanna's* draught can get over the bar quite comfortably at high tide; and rather than take the risk of coaxing a sinking ship round to the eastern opening — it meant an extra nine miles or so — Pittard decided to see if he could (as the expression is) leapfrog Foster. The third officer wanted at least to slow right down and heave the lead, but Pittard was strung up to recklessness. He was going to make a dash for it.

I think he somehow failed to realize just how far his stern had sunk. At any rate the attempt failed. The *Joanna's* stern ploughed into the bank and stuck there, wrenching off her screw. She was gripped as tight as a rat in a dog's teeth. As the tide went down she sank still deeper into the sand, till no tug could ever have budged her, and that seemed to be her last resting-place. The wind was getting up again, and it looked as if the ship would start to break up when the next big seas struck her. The crew were taken ashore in a coastguard's launch — their own boats had been either smashed or carried away — and they were heartily thankful to desert her.

The news came through to us in London next morning and I was sent off post haste to see if it was any use trying to salvage the cargo. I got the ten-thirty at Paddington and reached Stallmouth early in the afternoon. It was a Saturday, and Crowbitt's office was closed, but I found out where Pittard's cottage was and went round there. Pittard wasn't at home. A boy told me that he had gone to see Mrs Austin (the master's widow) to give her what comfort he could. I remember thinking how characteristic that was of the kindness of sailors.

My business couldn't wait, so I got the address and went on to Mrs Austin's house; it was a little Victorian villa on the sea side of Empress Augusta Terrace. Mrs Austin came to the door herself, and I have just a fleeting impression of her, as a young, pretty woman who seemed to be most unnaturally dressed in her heavy mourning. I said a few words to her — that came into my job a good deal and I always hated it — and then she took me into the parlour, where Pittard was sitting, and left me with him: he was a man on the under side of forty, half Irish, who looked like a lad grown out of his clothes; lank hair, a narrow bulging forehead, rather stupid eyes.

I say stupid, perhaps that is wrong. My first impression was that his eyes were tired and rather frightened.

I thought he probably felt that he was to blame for the loss of the *Joanna*, and I talked to him sympathetically about what he'd been through. He wasn't very responsive. He was looking away from me all the time I was speaking, all he said was: 'Ay, the *Joanna*, she was always a damned rotten ship!' But when I told him that I'd come to make an inspection he woke up and became slightly hostile. He said first of all that it would be quite impossible to get aboard her, that the ship was already breaking up and it would be very dangerous to bring a boat anywhere near. Then he said that I couldn't, in any case, board her without specific authority from the owners and I must wait till the office opened on Monday. That didn't suit my book at all. All kinds of things might happen before Monday — an enterprising fisherman might break into the saloon and help himself to anything of value he found there before I'd made my inventory. So I showed Pittard my authority — I'd taken the precaution to get it stamped by the Board of Trade before leaving London — and I said that if necessary I should wire for confirmation to Crowbitt's Cardiff office, which was bound to be open. In the end he had to give in.

We went down to the quay and got hold of a motor-boat used for lobster-fishing — the owner was just going to put down his pots on the other side of Stallpoint Head, and he agreed to take us to the *Joanna* on his way.

It was getting on for five o'clock now, the tide was going down, the wind had fallen almost to a dead calm. In the smoky sunlight you could see Foster's Bar appearing out of the water at the eastern end, the triangle of buoys beyond, and the ship itself, looking (as I saw her first) rather as if she were about to take off and fly. The fisherman had the same idea. He said, squinting at her one-eyed, 'She don't know whether she be goin' up to heaven or down 'tother place.' Pittard said nothing. He was sitting all by himself among the cages, with an unlit cigarette in the corner of his mouth, looking as scared and wretched as if he were going to be flogged.

I felt a certain sympathy with his nervousness (I'm using the mildest word) when we came alongside the ship. It's difficult to explain, but you know the odd, forlorn appearance of an old ship in dry dock waiting to be broken up. There's something — corpse-like about it. The *Joanna* was in the same period — breathing her last as you might say; she was deadly still — and yet she appeared to be water-borne. It was unnatural to see a ship so still in the water and at such an angle; it was rather as if you saw a dead man sitting up.

That feeling persisted when I got aboard; or I should say rather that it changed to an equally unpleasant one, a feeling that the ship was *shamming* death. I stood on the sloping deck looking up towards the bows. Still: she was quite, quite still; broken and deserted; and yet there was an old jacket that someone had left hanging on one of the davits, a cigarette carton lying on the deck, a mop leaning against the engine hatch, all the signs of a ship inhabited; you almost expected to see someone coming out of the saloon.

The fisherman said he would go and put down his pots and be back in an hour or so. Pittard didn't want him to go. He said to me in a surly way:

'It won't take you more'n a quarter of an hour, will it, just to look over the stuff? He may as well wait.'

I told him it would take *at least* an hour.

'He'd better lay by!' Pittard said. 'There's a mist coming up, he might not find us again.'

He was right about the mist. There was a low fine sea-mist creeping in from the south-east. But the fisherman only shrugged his shoulders and laughed. He was going to put down his pots, and that was that.

'Back in an hour!' he said.

I left Pittard sitting gloomily on the deck and got on with my job. The grain, of course, was a dead loss, and the timber in No. 3 hold didn't look any better for the soaking; it was Virginian red cedar, high-grade stuff meant for cabinet-making, and I could see that its value would be written down by something like thirty per cent even if it could be salvaged. I spent a long time in the No. 1 hold inspecting the cargo of skin; this seemed to be all right, but I examined every bale in turn and listed them — with my firm you had to be thorough. After that I went through the saloon and the quarters to note the fittings — occasionally one found stuff of some value even in an old packing-case like the *Joanna*. Finally I went up to the master's room, which was on the bridge-deck, aft of the chart-house.

And there, again, I had a rather curious sensation, for everything seemed to be exactly in place, as if Austin had just left it. There was a framed photograph of a woman, whom I recognized as Mrs Austin, lying on the floor; but nothing else seemed to have shifted. A watch hung over the berth, and I was very much surprised to find that it was still going.

But there was something still more curious about that cabin. I seemed to smell the smoke of tobacco in it. Not the stuffy, unpleasant smell that you find in a smoking-room first thing in the morning, but the smell of pipe-tobacco smoked quite recently.

When I came out I saw Pittard leaning against the starboard rail. I called out to him, 'I say, have you been in the master's room?'

He jumped as if a gun had gone off.

'I never been near it!' he said. 'I wouldn't go in there, not whatever you paid me!'

I said: 'Oh, I just wondered.'

I hadn't realized, till then, how long I'd been. It was going on for seven. And I realized now that the mist had thickened — you couldn't see the shore at all.

'I told you!' Pittard said. 'I told you we didn't ought to let him go.

He won't come back, he'll put in t'other side o' the head.'

He cupped his hands and began shouting into the fog, his voice angry and wild, 'Boat! Boat ahoy!' There was no reply, except the moan of a ship's siren far out in the channel, and the persistent clinking of a bell-buoy.

I said, 'Well, we shall have to stay till the fog lifts, that's all.'

'What!' he said, 'Stay in this ship all night?'

'Well, you can swim for it,' I said. 'It's about four miles, I suppose.'

'D'you realize she may turn over on her side, any moment?'

I told him that he knew best, but she seemed steady enough to me. In any case, since the boats were useless, we hadn't any choice. He had nothing to reply to that.

I left him, as he didn't seem sociable, and went into the saloon where I made myself as comfortable as you can be in a room that's tilted up to an angle of about thirty degrees. I found a tin of biscuits and a rather worn copy of the *Montreal Star*. The lamp was primed, and when it got too dark to read I lit it. When it was quite dark Pittard came to join me.

There was a set of dominoes in one of the lockers. I suggested a game, and we played for about an hour. But it wasn't a very good game, because Pittard didn't seem to be thinking about it at all – he was actually putting sixes to my fours and fives to sevens. He kept glancing over his shoulder, as if someone was standing behind him, until I myself began to feel as if someone else was in the room, watching us.

It was rather unpleasant: Pittard's nervousness, and the quietness of the still ship with the curtain of fog round it; the distant lowing of sirens. (*Imitation*) Like that:

About nine o'clock I said I was going to try and get some sleep. I thought I might as well use the master's room, since there was a good berth there.

'Unless you want it?' I said.

'Ye want it? Ye'll sleep in a dead man's berth?'

I said, rather sharply, that beds weren't usually put out of use just because a former occupant had died.

'All right!' he said. 'You can do as you like!'

I took a spare lamp I found in the locker and went up to the bridge deck. Again, when I went into the cabin I seemed to get a smell of fresh tobacco smoke, but I thought it must be pure imagination. I put the lamp on a chest beside the berth, took off my shoes and lay down, covering myself with a blanket — it was rather cold. I think I fell asleep quite quickly.

It must have been about three o'clock in the morning when I woke — it was still pitch dark. I had lain awake for perhaps three or four minutes, feeling a kind of uneasy loneliness, when I heard footsteps on the ladder which came up to the deck. I thought, of course, that it was Pittard coming up for something or other, but as the steps got nearer, coming along the deck outside, they sounded as if they belonged to a much heavier man; ponderous, deliberate.

Whoever it was stopped outside and seemed to hesitate for a few minutes. Then the handle turned, the door opened slowly and someone or something came in. I couldn't see anything, I could only smell him, a stale smell of whisky and tobacco.

Curiously it took me a little time to get my tongue loose. Then I said: 'Hullo, Pittard, what do you want?'

There was no answer.

But his knee was pressing against the side of the berth, I seemed to feel his eyes looking at me.

I put out my hand, slowly, for the box of matches that I'd placed on the chest. I felt for them, felt all along the top of the chest. At last my fingers touched the box and I made a grab to get it and my hand touched something else, something soft and cold, icy cold. I struck one match, it flickered and went out, I struck another, and keeping my eyes lowered I stretched out and lit the lamp. Then, only then, I looked up to see who it was.

He had moved to the other side of the cabin and had his back to me: an elderly man with very broad shoulders, wearing a sea-captain's cap and a dark blue jersey. I particularly remember that there was a big tear across the shoulders of the jersey. And the other thing I remember is that his clothes were soaking wet.

I was going to say something, but my voice wouldn't come. I just lay and watched him and listened to his breathing, heavy and uneven, like the breathing of a man who has run a long way. He was hunting for something, his hands exploring the locker as a blind man's hands do. I watched those long, white, bony hands, their curious, convulsive movements.

Presently the hands came to the photograph, the photograph of Austin's wife, and turned it over, and held it and stroked it. Then the photograph was slipped into an outer pocket, and the man stood still, and then he turned a little and I thought he was going to face me. I called out then, 'No! No! I don't want to see your face!'

He didn't seem to hear me. He turned again and went slowly towards the door. And now I had a queer, driving curiosity to see his face; there was a mirror above the washing-cabinet and I looked to see his face as he passed it. But I didn't see it, I didn't see anything in the mirror.

He went outside and moved towards the ladder, with the same deliberate steps that had brought him. I felt that I had to follow. I took up the lamp and went after him.

By the time I got down to the deck below he was half way towards the door of the saloon. He didn't seem to need any light, he went on steadily as if his feet could find the way by themselves, his body leant back to correct the slope of the deck, and swaying a little, as a sailor's always does. I remember that as if it had gone on for a long time, that broad, dark figure at the edge of my lamp's light, advancing deliberately towards the saloon, swaying a little.

When he reached the door of the saloon I stopped, about ten feet away from him. He opened the door and then stood still, with one foot on the step. The light of my lamp didn't penetrate into the saloon, it only showed me, dimly, the man's big figure, still as a statue now, against the darkness. I don't know how long he stood there — a minute, perhaps. Then his hand turned just a little, and then I heard his voice, a low and phlegmy voice: 'I see you, Pittard.'

I thought I heard something like a cry, a cry or a gasp. I'm not sure of that. I remember moments of silence, tense, binding silence, and then the man with the tear in his jersey going on into the saloon, disappearing there. Presently his voice came again.

'*You* thought you'd have her, Pittard. *You* thought I wouldn't find you. *You* were wrong, Pittard.'

I didn't mean to move, I didn't want to move, but my legs took me forward, took me right in there. I saw Pittard then, I didn't see the man who'd come for him, I just saw Pittard crouching on the floor, Pittard's white, sweating face, his eyes, his eyes staring at something beside my shoulder. . . .

'Listen, Pittard! I'm not coming up behind your back, like you did. You're going to see what I'm going to do.'

Pittard didn't move, only his eyes moved, watching the hands as they came nearer. He was trying to speak, struggling, struggling to get breath, his mouth was open, his lips were wobbling like a broken spring. I wanted to help him but something held me fast. And now I thought he was done for, the last sign of resistance had gone out of his face, he was nothing but a bundle of helpless terror. The hands, the hands, I saw them travelling towards his throat, I saw him shrinking, further, further, the muscles of his neck tautening —

'PUT OUT THAT LIGHT — PUT OUT THAT —'

(*Sound of crash*)

Darkness. The lamp had dropped from my hands. I turned and stumbled out, slamming the door behind me. I ran, blindly, barged against the bridge-deck ladder, leapt up it as if all the fiends were after me, made for the cabin, threw myself inside and locked the door.

Silence then. The ship silent again, nothing but the bell-buoy clanging and the distant sirens.

With the coming of daylight the fog lifted.

The cabin, with the light coming in through the port, was just as it had been before, the lamp standing on the chest, the matches beside it: except for one thing: the photograph was gone, I couldn't see it anywhere.

I went down to see Pittard and asked him how he had slept. He said that he had slept badly, he had dreamed unpleasantly. That was all, he didn't seem inclined to talk.

About eight o'clock the fisherman came out for us. He had some story that he'd been all up and down the Bar the night before but couldn't find the ship.

Pittard said nothing at all as we went ashore. He sat by himself as he had done coming out, and now he had the white, dazed look of a man who has been many hours without sleep; the look of a man whose senses bring him nothing that has any meaning.

There was a crowd of Sunday-morning loiterers on the quay, and the harbour constable was among them. The moment he landed, Pittard shambled across to him.

He said: 'You can take me up, Dick. I won't give you no trouble.'

The man laughed.

'Take you up, Charlie! What you bin up to?'

Pittard stared at him.

'You know! Dave Austin. Him goin' overboard . . . *I did it!*'

Outsiders: Two Sketches

The Mysterious Army

I saw Tom Abbot yesterday; yesterday morning on Nelson Quay.
He sort-of looked, and I looked, and I went on, but he came back and
stopped. You see, I'd given him a grin without thinking. You forget
sometimes, and seeing a chap you know you give him a grin before
you've thought about it. He came back and said 'Why it's —, isn't it?'

It wasn't any good pretending, having given him a grin like that.

I said, 'Yes, that's me.'

'How are things with you?' he said.

'Oh, just the same,' I said, meaning he could think what he liked.

He told me he was here for three days. 'That's my ship,' he said.
He pointed to a collier, come in that morning, I'd seen her hitch-up.

'Are you on that?' I said.

'Yes,' he said, 'I'm cook.'

'You've taken to sailoring, then?'

'Yes,' he said. 'I tell you what,' he said, 'come along over there and
we'll have one. Sake of old times.'

'I'm sorry, Tom,' I said, 'I'd like to, but I've got to get on.'

'What!' he said, 'you've not gone teetotal in your old age?'

'No,' I said, 'but I've got to be getting on, I'm late. So long!' I said.

'I'll see you again?' he said, but I didn't say anything; I just walked
on.

I suppose there's a sort of fate that makes you run into some chaps.
That was the third time I'd come up against him. First was at Wipers.
We had a good time there, till I stopped one, always up to
something, Tom was, Tom Thumb we called him, he wasn't much
bigger than a kid, face like a monkey, always thinking of something.
But he'd do anything for you, we all liked the little b—. Next time
was in twenty-five, thereabouts, well, back in the old days anyway. I
was up seeing the Arsenal, it was a big crowd that day, and there he
was standing right in front of me. I could hardly believe it, seeing
him like that, just the same, waving and shouting, hat all on one side
of his head, face just like a monkey. He took me back to his place
afterwards, he was working at an eat-shop in Highgate somewhere

then, we had a good evening, all the old jokes, it was like old times.

Funny, meeting him again on the quay like that. Of course I wouldn't have stopped him, only I gave him a grin before I'd thought. You do that, seeing a chap you haven't seen for a long time. With the fellows you see every day you know what to do and they know what to do. If they're like you are that's all right, you stand a bit together. And if they're the other sort they say 'Morning' and just go on, that's all they can do, they don't mean anything by that, you don't want anything else. Yes, that's all I want, no questions, no anything else, just 'Morning' and pass on. It's better like that. Running into Tom it was different. He didn't know, how could he know? He wasn't dressed all that smart himself. So there wasn't anything I could do but say I had to hurry.

What I don't like is — I may run into him again. He may just catch me when I'm not hurrying. And then it'll look as if I ought to say 'Look here, Tom, you come round to my place.' And that's what I don't want, I don't want him to see my place. Of course, there are other streets I can walk in. But it's always worth being on the quay, in case you catch the eye of the right man at the right time. And there's always something to see there, one of the boats unloading or something. There's the recreation ground, but that's depressing, all kids and tulips.

The trouble is, now it's summer, you get the days so long. I get up early, I always have done since when I had to, it's a habit you get. Besides, what's the good of lying in bed? Six, I'm up, most days, and about by seven. And it gets dark nine, say. That's — how much? — twelve, fifteen hours. That's a long time. And all that time I've got to keep away from the quay, else sure enough I'll see Tom. 'Hullo,' he'll say, if I begin to hurry, 'are you frightened of me or what?' And if I tell him I'm late again, what'll he say then?

If he says anything to me next time I'll tell him to take his —— face away and bury it. I want to be left alone, I don't want chaps coming round asking me questions. He'll be gone in three days, and that'll be all right, but until then if I go on the quay I've got to be hurrying so as he won't stop me. I don't want to tell him anything, seeing I used to be the same as he is. I don't belong to his sort, so it's no good his coming round me. He's a decent little chap, Tom is, always was, do anything for you, that little chap would, the sort of little chap you wouldn't mind your sister marrying. No, I don't think there's anyone I used to know in the old days that I was fonder of than Tom.

And he's just the same, little face like a monkey, smiling all day long, you can see just to look at him the decent sort he is. But it's different now. When you're unemployed you can't give a fellow a drink for the one he gives you. That's part of it, but it's like that all the way, you're different, you don't belong. I'm not grumbling, mind you. All I want is to be left alone. I don't want that fellow Tom saying 'Hard luck. Is there anything I can do?' Because there isn't. I can stand most things but I can't stand that. If he said that I think I'd punch his face in. I don't want any 'Hard lucks', I just want to get where people who aren't my sort don't see me. He's a nice little chap, Tom, but I wish to God he'd get out of this town.

Luck

One Row is the same as another in that part of the town, and he did not realize he was in his own till he heard Susan shouting at him. He had come to wander as his legs took him, not looking much, even when he crossed the main road; if a car was coming, well, the fellow must put his brakes on.

He turned slowly, when he heard Susan's voice; all his movements had become slow; and saw her coming down the Row towards him, a pile of underclothes under one arm and a child, rump forward, head hanging down behind, beneath the other; she always carried her children like that till they reached the toddling stage.

She said: 'I seen Ted. They want a carpenter up Thomson's, Ted saw the notice.'

He replied, staring towards her knees, 'A carpenter?'

'Surely!' Her voice was coloured faintly with excitement, and she did not often get excited. 'Ted's gone after you, he'll be lookin all over.'

'Always mixin up with some'n else's business, Ted.'

'Well, you'd better look sharp,' she said. 'That notice been up an hour by this time.'

'The town's full o' carpenters,' he said reluctantly.

'But not such as they use at Thomson's. They want a neat hand there. You got a neater pair o' hands than most, so you always told me.'

'I told you a lot,' he said.

Then, nodding to dismiss her, he went off, and into Arkley Street. The gate of King's yard was open, he went inside and across to the shop, where King was working.

'Lend me one o' your planes, Reg,' he said. 'Ta! Can I use this bit o' wood, it's nothin but knots? Ta!'

He pushed the deal across the bench, swung the handle of the vice, and jerked it tight; picked up the tool in his huge hand and began to plane. He thought, for a moment, that the feel of it hadn't altered. But it wasn't running straight: it was his wrist, stiff, it began to hurt almost at once.

'D'y' ever sharpen y' ruddy tools, Reg?'

'There's nothin wrong with them ruddy planes,' King said.

'Y' mean it's my ruddy fist?'

'Can't say.'

'S'long, Reg.'

He went as far as the corner, hesitated, and then turned uphill. He walked at policeman's pace, shoulders slouched, hands in trouser-pockets. When he reached the entrance to Thomson's yard he paused again, screwing his face doubtfully, and spat. Presently, with the air of a bored cattle-dealer doing the round of the market, he went inside. Over to his left, at the door of the joining shop, there was a queue roughly formed, backs against the wall. Still with a look of indifference he strolled near enough to see the card stuck sloping on the window. CARPENTERS And then, looking quickly away as if he were not concerned with it, he went over to the wall and propped his back against it, a few feet away from the man standing last. He stood there with a blank face, looking from him. When one of the men called to him 'How goes, Archie?' he said without turning his head, 'All right.'

Somebody called to the man three places up: 'What are you doin here, Charlie? You ain't a ruddy carpenter.'

'No harm in tryin y' ruddy luck.'

'Come to that, there ain't none of us ain't ruddy carpenters, not like what you'd call a carpenter.'

That's right, he thought, there's none of them ain't ruddy carpenters.

'Except Archie there,' the first man said, 'he's a neat hand, Archie there is. He may not be much to look at, but he does know how to handle a ruddy saw.'

'That's right, Sam. You and me, we might just as well go off home, now Archie's come. It's his ticket, this one is. What you say, Archie?'

'I say y' can hold y' ruddy mug.'

Ignoring him, his friend said at large: 'Well, they want several, so they tell me. An' it's goin to last a bit, for those as get it. Gov'ment contrac', so they tell me.'

'Well, here's three cheers for the ruddy gov'ment, whoever gets it. First time I known the gov'ment been any ruddy use to anyone.'

The door opened and the first man went in.

Well, that was right, Archie thought, what Davis had said. A neat hand, he'd always been, down at Holford's, there wasn't anyone who'd say different. And he remembered, Davis did, though it was four years back — no, five now — Holford's shutting up. Unless Davis was only kidding — Davis had been on the varnishing floor at Holford's, he wouldn't have known. Still, there was no denying, he'd been a neat hand in his day. In his day. Forty-four now. That wasn't all that ruddy old. The third man was in now, the first two had come out and pulled a face and gone away. Well, that was how it should be — call themselves ruddy carpenters! But they were getting through quick, here was the third man out again. Who would it be, doing the picking?

He remembered then. The foreman of the shop at Thomson's was Spot Peggit, a young fellow. Why, he was at school with one of my lads, he thought. He could remember young Peggit coming round with Andy, him showing him how to use a keyhole saw. Had an uncle in Thomson's, young Peggit had, and now he'd got foreman. So now he'd got to go to young Peggit and say 'See here, Mr Peggit, I'd like to have that job you got, I need it bad. Me got neat hands? Well, I'd like to show you, Mr Peggit, if you can spare the time.'

Suddenly he thought, 'Peggit or no Peggit, I won't get it. It doesn't come my way.' He'd been this round so often, line up, wait half the morning, Sorry, Full up now. And if you did get in, half a week, a month maybe, then, Sorry, the orders aren't coming in, We got too many carpenters. He didn't get on. It was all right, down at Holford's, that was a proper job till they shut up. He could do it as well as the next man then, better, he'd always thought, 'Archie's got a neat pair of hands,' they'd always said. But now, he couldn't remember the feel of it, they'd come round and look at him and say, 'Look here, you with the funny nose, how long 've you been handling a ruddy saw?' You got like that, you came to a time when your back turned, and then it wasn't any good. What was the use of going after a job when you knew you weren't any ruddy good?

He was next now. They'd only taken one of the six who'd gone in. 'It's no ruddy use,' he said aloud, and slouched out of the yard.

He didn't go home till after dark. Susan met him at the door.

'You got it?'

'No.'

He went past her into the back room and put his cap on the mantelpiece. She called after him, above the screeching of the children: 'Did y' try?'

He said 'No,' and again, sulkily, 'No, I didn't.'

Putting her lips together, she said thinly: 'You're lazy, Arch. That's what you are, you're bone lazy.'

So that was what she thought! He was quite startled, she had never said anything like that before. And now there wouldn't be another chance like the one at Thomson's, he knew there wouldn't. Lazy? Well, he could have told her something. But it wasn't any good explaining, you couldn't explain. He got his cap again and went out into the Row.

Excursion to Norway

The distance in a straight line from Vaagsö to London is around one thousand miles. It was in London that the Vaagsö raid was mainly planned, the chief reason being that the three services are accustomed to meet there. When the time comes to put an Allied force upon the mainland of Europe, the success of the operation will depend first of all on the precise interlocking of movements by sailors, soldiers, and airmen; people brought up by different schools, who eye one another with a mutual, smiling superiority, as the Rugbeian eyes the Marlburian, as a man ploughing the land looks upon his friend tending a machine.

So, through last November and nearly to Christmas, Lieutenant Commander Peerforce, who hates all towns, was working some fourteen hours a day on the top floor of a house in Cricklewood. At the same time a man well known to him, Captain Geoffrey Mellier, RA, was inhabiting with continuous unhappiness the navigating officer's quarters in the light cruiser *Hazlitt*, in a draughty and fogbound bay in North Wales. The connecting links began, 'Sir, I have the honour . . .' and some had little pencil notes at the bottom: 'Dear Maurice, could you, do you think, persuade your friends in Whitehall to crack along a little faster . . .'

The house in Cricklewood was shabby-genteel, wanting paint on the front door and new panes in the bottom windows. The top-floor windows looked upon a galaxy of the underclothes of north-west London. The business managed in the four small rooms might have suggested a wholesale grocery concern: ledgers, stores lists, files of indent forms, typewriters chattering. But the place wore a naval tidiness: a Royal Marine stood sentry at the top of the ruinous stairs. For perhaps five hours in every twenty-four Peerforce was on the telephone. ('But I must have another hundred and fifty jerseys for the soldiers. Yes, it's inclined to be cold at sea, even soldiers require jerseys. What? All right, then, I'll get through to Phillips and get his authorization for a charge note to go through to Western Command Paymaster. No, old boy, I don't really care one hoot in hell how you do it, but I've just damn well got to have those jerseys in Aberffraw by the 18th.')

For perhaps an hour at a time, late at night, the telephone was silent, and he could really get down to the job, with the charts and oblique photographs and another fill of tobacco . . . 'From the intersection QS the oil tanks on Maaloy should be in the line of visibility after 7½ minutes' steaming; allow 8 minutes; so if *Gurkha* was on QS at T.43, *Pathan* should sight tanks at T.58. The snag there was that Finchwater apparently couldn't take on Task F in less than nine minutes from Task E, which was fixed now for T.53 . . .' That must be reworked somehow. He took the telephone again. 'Give me extension 9. I want to speak to Squadron Leader Finchwater . . . I'm fearfully sorry, but this thing doesn't work out. You've got the large-scale thing there? Now look — you see Sconce Point? And you see Hamstead Ledge? Well now, my distance between those is 7½ minutes, say 8 minutes . . . What? No, old boy, I don't go about in Spitfires or whatever you call your crazy contraptions . . .' Vaagsö; it looked delicious in the obliques. The kind of place that Pauline would like for a holiday, and he could get some fishing there. But in those December days Vaagsö remained unreal, a focus merely, an enchanting formula. Some snag would crop up, and Exercise Uganda would be scrapped *in toto*, like Exercise Angola and Exercise Congo; all this labour on detail gone to blazes.

In the *Hazlitt*, Mellier was bothering in the back of his mind about Michael's tonsils. The doctor thought they would have to come out, Christine thought he wasn't up to an operation with the effect of the September whooping cough still lasting; and somehow Christine seemed to have guessed a little about 'Uganda'. Nothing in the world would make Mellier try to dodge it, but he wished it would happen and be done with.

In Cumberland, the 96th Commando was at rest after covering the Langdale course of forty-two miles in twenty-six hours; and Private Ebbury, comparatively new to the Commando, was writing a letter in the Keswick YMCA: 'Sir, I have to speak again about my war profishensy pay which I have owing from para 2 order of my old regiment last Jan or Feb and which I never got, and I pick up 7/6 from June to Aug, and no one wants to fight for the old country more than me, but I don't see how you fight for the old country on 7/6 a bloody week, so hoping you will oblige, sir.'

2

On December 19 the Rear Admiral at Aberffraw had a signal which read, when translated, 'Meteorological office states 27th most likely date for favourable conditions Vaagsö'. A message went to Peerforce, 'Report station immediately'. Peerforce thought, 'So it really is happening, and I'm really going to be in it.' He telephoned Dobell's flat. Dobell said, 'Yes, I've had the same one. Curse of it is I've got a party on — I mean a party of my own. Going to be a bit difficult to find my toothbrush and so forth. You won't mind my being *slightly* blotto? Not *really* blotto . . .'

Back at Downshire Avenue, hunting for his binoculars, Peerforce thought, 'It cannot be true. They would find some way to dodge me out of it. It will only be a rehearsal, I'm not really going to Vaagsö, it can't be true.' The binoculars couldn't be found, and he worried about them all the way to Aberffraw: eleven hours of comfortless dozing, the lines jammed up with Christmas traffic, twelve passengers in Peerforce's carriage, Dobell incessantly grumbling. 'It's not that I have any objection to war *per se*. But I cannot see why it has to get all muddled up with my parties. One thing at a time is what I say. Allow me to finish my party, gentlemen, and I shall then interest myself keenly in your war. Allow me to extricate myself from my friends and I shall be delighted to intricate myself in your railway carriage.' Pauline would probably find the binoculars, Peerforce thought, and they might just get through in time. A shocking thing to go to Vaagsö without binoculars. The train provided no food. 'You see, it's the Christmas season, sir,' the guard explained. Dobell said, 'A picturesque custom among the British: at every Christmas-tide a certain number of officers are roped together and starved to death in railway trains.'

Aberffraw was dark like the grave, the houses in a corpse-like stillness. A Welsh voice breaking into song was washed away by a gusty wind, which blew fine rain and locomotive smoke across the quay. The long train on siding 5 had no lights in the carriages: in that intensity of darkness you realized rather than saw the blobs of men who were forming on the cinder track; in a moment's lull of the wind you heard the chunk of someone's rifle-butt against the carriage, a voice almost whispering 'Troop Five'. Against the wall of the customs shed you could just see the crocodiles of men as they passed from that darkness to the other darkness where the ships lay. The gasps of the shunting-engine hid the noise of the sea.

The Brigade Major and Mellier shared a cabin: throughout the morning of Christmas Day they were sick alternately, and sometimes sick in unison. 'I suppose the blasted nautics are enjoying this,' the Brigade Major said. The orderly who came in with messages stood by respectfully while the Brigade Major vomited. Between his spasms, Mellier was trying desperately to write to Christine again about Michael's operation, meaning to get the letter posted at Bridget Sound. As the starboard side rose from every roll, he saw the sea like a gray scarf coming out of a mangle, twisted and torn. In the afternoon he fought himself out of his bunk and struggled down to see the men. The men, of course, had guessed, though no one had told them. 'It's a proper show this time?' and Mellier said, 'I'll tell you later on. Where? My dear Spud, I haven't the faintest notion.' An Irishman groaning on the floor turned over and said, 'Honolulu, it would be.' 'That's right,' Mellier said, 'Honolulu. We're starting a war there,' and a man stopped vomiting to laugh, and they all said, 'Honolulu it is,' laughing. A gray, small man, whose army age was twenty-nine, was carefully ironing his battle-dress trousers. Private Ebbury, yellow with nausea, came over to Mellier: 'Excuse me, sir, I'd like a word with you if I might, sir, it's about my war proficiency pay. I never had . . .' 'You'll all get used to this presently,' Mellier said. 'You've only got to pretend you're on the swing-boats at a fair.' Then he rushed away and was sick again.

There was no sensation when the ships came into Bridget Sound: it happened once a week or once a month that warships put in to fuel there. The *Gurkha*, with decks slightly awry from the buffeting, made fast at Union Wharf, and the party standing by from Stafford's Yard set to instantly to bandage her. At dinner the Rear-Admiral talked of Avignon and Vaucluse wines.

The operational conference was at half past ten. 'I must call your particular attention, gentlemen, to paragraph 7 in the method section of Operation Order No. 1. There will be some damage to purely Norwegian property — that can't be helped. But as far as possible you are to take note of all damage of that kind, giving the owner's name when you can. You must emphasize that loyal Norwegians will be treated with the greatest consideration. You, Mr Field-Warwick, have to destroy the herring-oil factory in the north side of Ulversund by gunfire. You will be very careful to keep your fire short of the bungalows in the hill beyond.' Field-Warwick wrote on his pad, 'Preserve bungalows', and said, 'Very good, sir'. Afterwards, in the *Pathan*'s wardroom, Mellier said to Peerforce, 'I suppose it won't turn out to be just another rehearsal?' And Peerforce said, 'No, I think we really go there this time. Sickening, losing my damned binoculars.'

Next day was Boxing Day, and at four in the afternoon the expedition sailed. The wind held, the passage was rough, and they damned the meteorological office. The soldiers were inclined to blame the nautics, considering an influence on weather to be some part of the seaman's craft. The Brigade Major was anxious, wondering if his troops would get there in shape for fighting, since the best of warriors is not so good when his belly is swivelling, as they say, upon the navel. Mellier had found his sea-legs and was trying to learn the last amendment to the operation order by heart — relieved that he had got his letter posted; relieved, in a way, that he had kept the rules and not told Christine what was on.

Between decks, the common feeling was a little changed, the torment of seasickness relieved by expectancy: as a theatre queue standing for hours in the rain will brighten when the actors start to arrive. And the meteorological people proved, after all, that they had the weather under control. For though the cold remained, intensified, the gale fell dead and the sea to the flatness of pavement. The clouds had gone. The sky looked tangible, superbly rich in its depth and ablaze with stars. A little unreal the brilliance of these stars; unreal the first shape of Norway, the distant, snow-draped hills cut as if from paper and laid against the darkness. Still less believable that this was battleground. They saw, with some surprise, that the lighthouses of Hovdenoes and Bergsholmenes were working. So nothing had leaked. At 08.49 hours the *Pathan* passed into the fjord. She was precisely sixty seconds late. No longer a rehearsal, but the show itself; and still, to Mellier, it lacked reality, a battlefield so silent yet, an operation so precise.

3

At Z.12 the first assault ships pulled to port, steering for the bulge of Matrog, the destroyer nursemaid steaming in their wake. The *Hazlitt* held her course, the rest in line ahead, their intervals exact, till the *Gurkha* swung sharply nor'ard for the shelter of Maaloy. The minute lost had been made up: the *Studland* had dropped astern; at precisely 09.11 hours she released her assault landing-craft. A minute to go and the lads above should be starting up the orchestra. A minute went and the voice of thirty kestrels filled the sky.

'Pretty good for Finchwater,' Peerforce said. You could feel on the *Hazlitt*'s bridge the force of the bombs exploding on Maaloy: as if the ship was clutched by that ferocity of sound, and shook a little to get free. Uneasy, for he liked the solid earth to fight on, the Brigade Major kept one eye on his watch. It was nice, he thought, the Air Force timing; the Air Force was a good show after all, he might put his son there. Another minute and the *Hazlitt*'s guns began to speak, treading across the air bombardment as if that were mere silence. Like all things that the Navy does, the barrage was tidy, precise in time and space; to the eye a window display of golden sausages, to the ear a vast contusion. Far over, high and angry flames showed that the oil tanks had gone up, and a show of fireworks leftward must come from the ammunition store. Those were the Air Force jobs, the Brigade Major remembered, and he jotted the time approvingly. The assault landing-craft were lost beneath the smoke. A red Very light leaped from the haze, and three more followed. So quickly that it seemed to be simultaneous, the destroyers pitched a row of flares far up into the sky. The guns had stopped already, and before the last of the star shells burst, the crunch of bombs had ceased; the RAF made no mistake about their cues. You caught sight, over to the north, of a Hampden banking steeply, you heard her with her sisters come screaming along the line of shore. The smoke bombs fell, a row of bulbs planted by a titanic gardener, and the separate puffs were joined in a cloudy sash. Like toys packed up, the Hampdens were gone, no one knew how or where.

'Soup, sir,' the Brigade Major's batman roared into the silence; and 'Flags,' the Rear-Admiral said testily, 'Request that person to moderate his tone.'

Iota landing group, with the Lokke factory on the mainland as its objective, was put ashore in a narrow creek. Compared with practices on the English coast the landing was a simple affair, the rocks not hard to negotiate, no wire worth mentioning. 'Like getting off a taxi' someone said. The group commander, Lieutenant Stow Treddart, left his men narrowly dispersed in a vegetable garden and the adjoining timber-yard, and went forward to reconnoitre, taking only a runner. Neither came back. A man called

Olland, normally a land agent's clerk in Newbury, could see the chimneys of the factory from where he stood behind a stack of deals. He was colder than he had ever been in his life, and wanting desperately to urinate: for he happened to be a man whom noise alarms (he had just discovered this) as many children are scared by Christmas crackers. The barrage on Maaloy had stopped, there were no more of the shattering crunches — only from somewhere behind him the whipcrack of rifle fire and something which might be light machine-guns. In an odd way he was sorry the row over there had stopped, since that had been someone else's war and the next might come his way. Death was something a chap could put up with, but not with a noise like that if it came quite close.

Between Olland and the factory the timber houses were spread unevenly, like recruits on their first parade, with no fenced gardens: a careless town built wandering towards the hills. The nearest sound was of a dog barking; the smell of bread from one of the houses covered the smell of brine and fishery. The corporal, rather out of breath, said, 'The sarge has taken over — we go this way,' and started off in cat-darts towards the sea. Olland went after him. They used the drill for this, combined as the forwards are in football — Bob Collett and Dyson over on the right, Wee Peter left, with Olland and May beyond him. You had to look both ways at once, keeping the houses scanned, never letting Wee Peter get out of sight: with an eye to your feet, where boats and the clobber of fishermen could trip you at every stride, and one for the rear to be sure that Huggins was in his place there. That was all there was to it, except to shift like a bat out of hell. He began to like the cold, as the warmth of exertion came up to meet it, though the coldness of the air he breathed was like sandpaper along his throat and chest; he enjoyed the working of ship-cramped limbs, the sense of his body's skill which he had got from High Pyke and Skiddaw. A little frightened still, he was glad to hear Mac's familiar grunts, Mac's blasphemy as he tripped on a rubber fender; he was reassured by the shape of Wee Peter's huge behind and the grenades he always carried there. Seawards the guns had started again, but that was the other fellow's war.

Some way ahead, a plait of fuliginous smoke had sprouted where the Mortens factory should be — so the Kappa group had done their stuff already. Something had stung him in the forearm: he was surprised to see blood running down the back of his hand. The corporal was swinging left and the section closing in. He turned and vaulted over a chicken-shed and cut the shortest way up the road with Mac puffing behind and, from the strange nature of the Scots, occasionally laughing.

4

The German armed trawler *Fahn* had scampered away with her brood, the steamships *Regmar*, *Norman*, and *Eduard Fritzen*, and had beached them near the head of the sound. There happened, then, to be the noise of hell from the *Hazlitt*'s guns, in deliberate duel with the Rugsundo battery. But Peerforce was not a man much disturbed by sound, and as he sat in the boarding-craft he was making notes in his neat, small writing: 'I was ordered to board and search *Regmar* and *Norman* before sinking them; 11.06 hrs. boarding craft put off . . . 11.09 hrs. first boarding-party with Lieut. F. Dobell, RNVR; boarding-party with seven ratings under my own command boarded *Norman*. Both ships found abandoned except for one officer on bridge of *Regmar*, dead. Stores and ammunition found in *Regmar*, some removed as Appendix D to be attached. Papers of both ships removed. Some sniping occurred from crews which had taken positions on the hill. One rating wounded in left foot, one in jaw. We returned fire from *Norman*. 11.19 hrs. I ordered Lieut. Dobell to proceed ashore and capture party responsible for sniping. 11.31 hrs. Lieut. Dobell returned with six prisoners . . . 11.48 hrs. above-mentioned ships sunk by gunfire.'

In this affair Dobell was slightly wounded, a part of his left ear being blown away. He was an auctioneer in civil life, his training in land warfare had been negligible, and his methods were not according to the book. A lane led up from the shore towards a farm in the hill; up this lane Dobell trudged, vaguely flourishing his pistol and shouting in English, 'Come here, you b—s, blast you, come over here.' These particular Germans knew less about land warfare than he did, and half a dozen of them came.

The Brigade Major wrote upon his message pads. This morning was full of aggravations. The No. 18 wireless sets were giving trouble (he made a note, 'Recommend spare battery with every set'); the last shell from Ragsundo had pitched unpleasantly close, bringing a spray of splinters up to the bridge; and no one knew what had happened to Mellier. Still, there was some convenience in having a cruiser for one's battle headquarters, and the uproar kept out all the little sounds that made most of life so tiresome. The sun appeared, and the hills became a glory of magenta. The Brigade Major smiled.

Close to the telegraph office, which was now on fire, Olland leaned against a wall. Mysteriously, he had lost his way among the houses; he thought the street going left would lead to the factory but he couldn't be sure. He was very tired, the tiredness chiefly in his legs and brain; it came, he supposed, from the Norwegian air, for the exertions of that morning had been child's play. It angered him to find himself so feeble, and he wondered how he would ever clean his battle-dress, filthy all down one leg with this perishing blood. A minute's rest and he would get on again, trying the left-hand road. The sound of rifle and sub-machine-gun fire was distinctly from that direction. This road was narrow and cobbled, and had the fresh marks of scrapping in it: a handcart overturned, with bits of equipment flung about, and a body — one of ours, he thought — with its face on a doorstep. Further along, a wounded German sat against the wall, with his back this way, firing unsteadily but patiently through a gap in the houses. The smoke confused you, gathering and dissolving, creeping along the eaves. An Englishman with his helmet gone arrived through the smoke behind; his face was bloody and soberly anxious, the face of a man doing figures who can't get the answer right. 'You belong to Iota?' this man asked. (It was Captain Mellier, Olland saw now.) 'Have you any idea where your chaps have got to?' As a kind of answer, the fire on the left increased; a Bren was letting fly by the sound of it, and fairly close grenades were popping. A man blackened with smoke ran by, shouting, 'Through that way, sir!' and Mellier followed, with Olland after him. There were more behind: the cockney Ebbury and Charlie Rose, Swindles and Spud and the redheaded corporal from Potters Bar. They ran together and silenced the German and arrived in the brewery square.

The demolition party with its bag of tricks was squatting behind a weighhouse, the sapper sergeant in gentle reproof eyeing his watch. The factory gates were forty yards away, and the bodies of Mac and Dyson showed what happened when you tried to get there by brute force and bloody ignorance. From the gate of the brewery, where a score of men were crouched, Mellier looked round and saw how the pattern stood. Intelligent, he thought, the way the Germans used their limited fire-power. They had rifles in the factory itself (they were sniping now) and (from the pepper-marks on the brewery wall) perhaps a light machine-gun.

Captain Mellier moved out a little way and guessed where the machine-gun was: beyond the church, the flat roof of a place that looked like a custom-house. A bullet chipped the cobbles beside his feet, he went back into shelter calling, 'Corporal Wield . . . You will take the rest of your section, with Murphy and Rose. You see the yellow house, the second one, with the thingummy on its roof? That's where you're to wait till I give the signal — You're clear on that? — Then straight in with grenades. Don't stop for drinks or anything. Now, Hodson, you see where that cart is over there ? . . .' ('The surgeon's fee might be ten quid, say three quid for . . . say fifteen quid all told. Christine's people might be good for a fiver, and anyway it had to be done. Poor Mike — would it scare him when they put the mask over his head?') 'You're in a bloody mess,' he said to Olland, and Olland grinning said, 'Bloody's the word, sir.' He looked about for something to clean his trousers with; Wee Peter would never cease to rag him for getting his trousers mucked like that. But the nearest likely place was the first of the yellow houses, and that was where the spasmodic bullets fell. He crept to the weighhouse and sat down among the sappers, shutting his eyes. A Bren was in action somewhere near, and it felt like knuckles inside his forehead.

Olland passes in and out of sleep like a train through a few yards of tunnel. It is the pop of Mellier's Very pistol which has wakened him and now the act is on. From his former place by the brewery gate he can see far along the seaward wall, can just discern the figures of Corporal Taper's party as they dart across toward the farther gate. A random shot from one of Hodson's men is enough to provoke the factory light machine-gun; two rifles join in from the factory windows, and Hodson's rifles reply. But as yet no noise from the left. The men waiting in the scanty shelter of the trees are very still. Mellier is kneeling there, with his head turned sideways, his face patient but a little vexed — the face of a schoolmaster waiting for a simple question to be answered, faintly absurd, with the eyebrows sooty and moustache soaked in blood. 'What's the blokes waiting for?' the corporal asks. The sergeant says, 'Ay, yon Saxons, they're bloody idle;' and then the racket starts on the left, grenades and yelling and 303; and Wield's fun-and-games are under way.

5

To a point the improvised plan worked smoothly enough. The Germans in the factory had done well, managing their fire with discretion and economy, but the arrival of Taper's party from the rear disturbed their steadiness. The light machine-gun stopped altogether (perhaps from a jam, perhaps from a grenade lobbed neatly through the side window) and the rifle fire became erratic. What happened on the left is less clear. Mellier believed that the German machine-gun was out of action; that was what the sounds told him; and certainly Wield's assault went in, for in Chatterley's report he says that he afterwards saw the bodies of two machine-gunners lying close to Wield's own. The fact remains that when Mellier's party sprinted to the factory gates the machine-gun opened up for a final burst, laying a cone from the factory gate to the other side of the square. When Olland saw Mellier running forward he felt quite fit again, and went hell-for-leather after him. When the machine-gun opened, Mellier went over like a rabbit, and Olland went past him, running flat out, supremely happy and a moment afterwards dead. Mellier got up again and went on doubled up, hugging his stomach. A man called Felworth got through the gate first, with Ebbury second, then Mellier and the rest behind. The sappers with their machinery followed sedately, the youngest of the party taking pains to keep in step.

The Brigade Major, whose helmet had been removed into the sea by the last explosion, had a typewritten list of the infantry tasks on the back of his message pad: 'offices of the German command, w/t station, searchlight station, coast defence guns (4), car and lorry garage, lighthouse mechanism . . .' As the messages came in he ticked them off. Nothing yet from Treddart, whose pigeon was the Lokke factory; he looked through his binoculars again, but all the smoke was confusing and the brewery got in the way. Also, the *Hazlitt* was eternally in gentle motion; another nautical custom he supposed, and a guest could hardly interfere. A tongue of light sprang from the way he looked, followed by a triple explosion like the bark of an old farmyard dog; and where the flash had once come from, the black smoke bulged to the shape of a chestnut-tree. He murmured, 'Good boy, Treddart' (not knowing Treddart had been dead for an hour), and put a tick against the Lokke factory. . . .

They noticed at Bridget Sound, waking to find the warships back, that the *Hazlitt* had been patched close to the water-line, that the *Gurkha*'s upper parts were all askew. 'All done by seagulls,' they were told by Peerforce; 'the beasts come very fierce this year.'

The soldiers lounged in the thin sunshine all along Crippett's Yard, smoking, and some asleep. Along by the gates the colour sergeant was fussing over his stores checks, and the children ran happily among the soldiers, sniffing the curious odour they had brought and begging for sweets.

In the Queen's Hotel, Peerforce found his binoculars, sent on from London. He asked what had happened to Mellier. 'One in the tummy and one in the left leg,' the Brigade Major told him. 'The Doc thinks he may get away with it — but the leg won't be any good.' 'I wish you'd see him, sir,' someone said. 'He's worrying frightfully. He got his first task through on time, but the Lokke show was frightfully late.' A sergeant came: 'Begging your pardon, Mr Chatterley, sir, I'd be glad if you could see that bloke Ebbury. Just to put the fear of God into him, if you wouldn't mind, sir. He does nothing but moan about his back pay.' 'I'll leave you this to pay for the drinks,' the Brigade Major said. 'I must go and talk horse-sense to Mellier . . . Oh, and Maurice, you've heard, I suppose, that you're going back to Cricklewood?' 'Cricklewood? My God.' 'But this time it's something really interesting. You've heard of a place called this?' He wrote on a piece of paper 'Madagascar' and threw it in the fire. 'Yes, Africa, or thereabouts . . . It'll want a good deal of donkey's work; the programme-timing at Vaagsö was not nearly good enough . . . I must go and see Mellier, and get this blasted bandage changed.'

Exhibit 'A'

In the army you meet the pleasantest men alive and you lose them; as soon as your friendship is established they get posted away and are never seen again. The other kind — the ones who waste everyone's time on courses with verbose and fatuous questions, the bullies, the bores, the bad hats — always come round again in the swirl. It was therefore no surprise when, after two years' merciful separation, I found 8064119 Dubb, W. taking care, according to his lights, of the Trans-Iranian Railway.

We had left Ahwaz in the evening. The rear coach in which I travelled had been loaded higgledy-piggledy with warlike stores and other goods having, I suppose, some relation to the war — telephone switchboards, typewriters, boxes of coffee and (Heaven knows why) women's shoes — leaving only two carriages for passengers. One of these I shared with three friendly people of most agreeable manners, a little Hindu captain from Mysore, a lieutenant from Kansas, gigantic in person and good-humour, and the elderly Iranian Minister for Regional Settlements; the captain's servant was in the other one, with a lance-naik of the Indore Infantry and some Persian civilians. Somewhere near midnight my uneasy dreams were permeated by the notion that we had stopped and started to drift backwards, and I woke fully to find that we were standing still.

On that line at that period nothing a train did could be called unusual. The others were snoring; I happened to be in the worst stage of sandfly fever, which is a piffling disease but does not seem so when you have it, and there was no evident reason for me to move: but when nothing had happened for about forty minutes I was sufficiently puzzled by the stillness to stir myself and get down on the track. At the forward end of our coach my torch revealed a broken coupling; there was no sight or sound of the rest of the train.

In the brake-van at the rear I found a smell of opium and a Persian brakesman asleep on the floor; from the polite but rather discursive speech he made me before going to sleep again I gathered that the Deity had personally broken the coupling and that appropriate action would be taken by the railway authority in due course. When I returned to the carriage the opinion of my fellow-passengers, sitting in total darkness, seemed to be roughly the same. Captain Sivaji remarked that all Persians were lazy rascals. What, the lieutenant asked, could you expect in this sort of a goddam country: why, in Kansas they'd have had a relief engine back and hitched on to us half an hour ago — not that couplings ever did break in Kansas. It was God's will, but a very great misfortune, the civilian said in his fragmentary but graceful English: it was absolutely essential for him to get to Tehran by next evening, and he hoped that the railway authorities would realize this. Did I know anyone among the railway authorities, he circuitously inquired, who would accept a small honorarium for hurrying the coach towards Tehran? These jerks, the lieutenant continued, could do what they liked with their goddam railroad, but if they didn't deliver the carcase of Lieutenant Oswald D. Oldenveld at Tehran some time before next sundown there would be all hell to pay and then some. Presently I heard him sleeping again and Sivaji followed him. The Minister stayed awake, uttering little cries of agitation and despair. My own inclination was to curl up in my corner and rely on someone discovering, not too far up the line, that the train was a coach and a brake-van short. But at that time the Royal Engineers had only just started to take over the virtual operation of the railway; native railwaymen might regard the loss of a coach or two as immaterial; my reasons for wanting to get on with the journey were urgent enough to make me climb down once more and I started to walk along the line.

I went some distance, more than a mile, perhaps, always thinking that I should come upon some post in another hundred yards. It was the enterprise of a fool — Heaven knows how far I might have walked — but I was rather light-headed from fever, and there is a Providence which cares for fools. At the time it seemed quite natural when the cutting opened and I distinguished a small stone building beside the track. It showed no evidence of life, but a faint light leaked from the door of a ramshackle hut behind. I thumped on this and went inside.

The hurricane lamp burning dimly on a table showed immediately the evidence of British habitation: an SMLE rifle lying half-stripped on a trestle-table, webbing equipment on the drip-stove, familiar pin-ups. The stale air had English cigarette-smoke in it. But the bundle I tripped over cursed me in clear Italian and a second, when I prodded it with my toe, rolled over to reveal the face of a Kurd. 'British here?' I asked this man, and in time he got himself erect and went over to a third cocoon which I had not noticed. This, very slowly and with a wealth of oaths, unwound itself; became by degrees a man standing at something approximating attention; displayed, as I turned up the lamp and brought it nearer, features of dreadful familiarity.

I said just now that Fate looks after fools. Yes, but in a way of her own. Open-handed, she had cut short a crazy pilgrimage of what might have been twenty miles and given me a Station. (Station? I didn't know, I don't know now.) She had supplied the outfit with what I most needed at that time and place, a man of my own speech. And then, with a sickening turn of humour, she had let that man be Dubb.

A very sleepy, a much surprised, a feebly grinning Dubb. *The* Dubb, once bane of an overworked CSM's existence and of mine, the CO's recurring nightmare, a permanent blot upon a good battalion's reputation, immortal and incorrigible, the dim and dirty, the effeminate and sloppy, the one and only Dubb. Unchanged: with uneven strands of thick, straw-coloured hair falling about his eyes and neck, a golden stubble on what passed for his chin, the butt of a cigarette lodged on his right ear, his flabby lips parted in apologetic and canine acquiescence: the same bow-legged stance, his over-long, thin arms hanging as limply as old. Feeling the sensations of nightmare I uttered the time-honoured imbecility, 'Hullo, Dubb, what brings you here?' and got the answer it deserved:

'Well you see, sir, I got taken on a draft, that was when you was gone on leave, sir. Come on one of them troopships — feedin's somethin awful on them, sir. Make y' a cup of tea, sir?'

Yes, I could do with that.

He called laconically, 'Abdul! Char! Bucky-upoh!' and the Kurd went into action with a spirit stove. 'Got put on a sort of a railway job,' he added to me.

From the War Office downwards some organization had been required to remove 8064119 Private Dubb, W. from a camp near Bridlington to where he stood now; to collect and equip the man, handle his documents, provide him with the trains, the ship, the convoy, the food he disapproved of. Of this Dubb knew nothing. He had been there, and now he was here. That was all. And it seemed to me a pity.

'Listen,' I said, 'if you're a railwayman nowadays you may be able to do something for me. I've lost a train.'

He clicked his tongue. 'Time and again I've missed trains myself, sir.'

'Not missed it — lost it. The train's gone on and left my coach behind — down the line there. Coupling broken.'

He clicked his tongue again. 'What train would that be, sir?'

'Well, it left Ahwaz at 8.24.'

'But there isn't a train at that time, sir.'

'Whether there is or isn't, there was. And it must have passed through here about an hour ago.'

'I didn't see no *train*, sir,' he said, as if I were inquiring about a herd of giraffes in top hats and crinolines.

'Whether you saw it or not I want to get it back,' I told him. 'Or rather I want to get a locomotive. Can you get on to Dorud or somewhere and tell them what's happened?'

He thought it most unlikely that he could get on to Dorud. But there was, he confessed, some sort of a telephone in the office ('only it's a Persian job, if you see what I mean') which was meant to connect him with Dusaband. ('Only the serjeant there, he don't much like being called up at this hour.') I dismissed the serjeant's sensibilities, and Dubb, till then in shirt and pants, produced a grimy bush shirt and drill slacks from under his bedding and put them on, adding a battered topee: the temperature at that hour and altitude must have been below freezing-point, but there had been a Command Order that summer dress was to be worn from the first of that month, and this particular order Dubb had chosen to carry out. I noticed with horror that the arm of the crumpled shirt was dignified by a lance-corporal's stripe. We took the lamp and crossed over to the stone building, where an aged Persian in some kind of railway uniform was snoring on the office desk.

'Did you see a train go through, Ammid?' Dubb asked him.

The Persian made the noises of one disturbed in sleep.

'He says he didn't see no train either,' Dubb told me reproachfully.

'Get on with the job!' I said.

He knelt on a form and addressed himself to an apparatus of the kind one's son makes after reading *The Boy's Own Book of Indoor Games and Hobbies*. I cleared a part of the table behind him to sit on, and while he laboured the memory of his transgressions passed before me like a documentary film: while on Active Service being absent without leave, losing by neglect one respirator, anti-gas, damaging through neglect one rifle, neglecting to clean his billet, being late on parade, appearing on parade 'in a filthy condition, sir'. And ah, God, if CSM Barnett could have seen the 'office' we were in now! In my experience the British soldier on a lonely job becomes exceptionally tidy; isolation somehow promotes self-esteem and a care for the small decencies of living. To this, as to every other rule, Dubb was the exception. Railway schedules mixed up with *Picture Posts*, Company Detail and letters from home, boots and pull-throughs and disintegrating socks were scattered about the room in a chaos suggesting the tenancy of orang-utans.

'Goin to have a bit of a tidy-up tomorrer,' he remarked, as if he felt my thoughts through the back of his neck. 'Only you can't seem to get no cleaning stuff.' (In what past life had I heard those words?) He went on cranking the machinery. 'Ullo!' he repeated wearily, 'Ullo . . . ullo . . . ullo . . .' He pushed the topee still further back, lit the cigarette stub and got into a more comfortable position. I recalled that in civvy street he had been a baker's roundsman and as he sat now I could picture him half asleep in his van: how often, I wondered, had he set out in the morning without the bread and been obliged to go back for it? 'Something wrong with the wire, I shouldn't wonder. There is, more often than not. *Ullo . . . ullo . . .*'

The door towards the line opened. My friends had grown bored or anxious, perhaps they had found the carriage too cold, and here they were, Sivaji's bearer and the lance-naik as well, all rubbing their frozen hands and muttering and blinking. A few flakes of snow followed them into the room. 'Is this where we get any action?' Oldenveld wanted to know. There was action from the Kurd, who had brought in the tea; he disappeared and returned smiling with the Italian prisoner, the kettle, two mugs, five NAAFI cups and a couple of mess-tins: not in the War Office itself had I seen so much tea being slopped about. For another ten minutes, but with less visible optimism than the priests of Baal, Dubb went on cranking and ullo-ing.

The Minister for Regional Settlements approached me with diplomacy: I fancy he had a 500-rial note crunched in his hand and with the smallest encouragement would have slipped it into mine.

'You will make him understand, if you please, that my business is impotent? There is vitality for me to reach at Tehran. Please, yes!'

'That's what he's telling them,' I said.

I had rather lost interest. While the rest were frozen I was swimming, and things in the crowded room were starting to float and bob. 'Action!' Oldenveld was saying again and again. 'I don't *want* any more char, I want action!' while the Kurd and the Italian stood in line with the Persian railwayman, holding fresh cups and equably smiling.

'Dubb!' I said. 'Is there any back door to this place? I mean, is there any road to it, any vehicle, donkeys?'

It took him a few moments to get out of the trance in which his own voice had wrapped him.

'There's nothing only the truck the old wog got, along by the quarry. You never seen such a thing. Had it for a contractin job, makin the railway. Dirty? Strewth! Fallin to bits. The wog aint clean himself, neither.'

'I don't mind about the wog. Where could he take us if he could take us anywhere?'

'Well, there's nothing like what you'd call a road. A track, you might call it. Get washed away whenever the floods come. Join up with the Ammydam road in the end — if it keep goin at all, see what I mean. Sometimes it do and sometimes it don't. I could see the bloke for you, sir, only he's not a bloke that goes in for night work. Might be eighty by the looks of him. Not much more left of him than there is of the truck.'

'Rout him out!' I said. 'Tell him the Prime Minister of Persia requires him to report instantly with truck. But first put on your greatcoat — it's snowing.'

'Well, if you don't mind, sir, I cleaned the buttons on Sunday, sir. I wouldn't like to have them out in the snow, if it's all the same to you, sir.'

'All right. Only buck up!'

Sivaji, who was shivering all over, poor fellow, furiously ordered his bearer to shut the door which Dubb had left wide open and then, turning to Oldenveld, resumed the gentle and cultured voice in which he had discoursed to me on Shelley and Keats from Ahwaz to Andimeshk. 'You see, it is always the same. The Persians are a poor race, but they build for themselves a great railway-line and it works. The English come, the Persians are pushed out of the way — and then nothing works. The train breaks in half. The signalling apparatus will not function any more. What do the English do? Nothing. "That," they say, "is the affair of the Persians," ' (he turns one sympathetic eye upon the Minister) "— what are native peoples for but to remedy the results of our own inefficiency!" Of course I'm not talking about any gentleman present,' he added courteously. 'Once the English were a strong race; they were cruel and treacherous, but they were virile, self-reliant. Do you find such Englishmen now?'

Of the article he referred to only two samples were in the vicinity: one had sandfly fever and the other was Dubb. I decided not to join in the discussion.

'Now these,' my friend continued, turning his head, 'what have the English done, what will the English ever do for them?'

Guiltily following his glance, I found there were three more souls in the room than I had realized — I had not seen them come in, or particularly noticed them on the train: three children, Bakhtiari by the look of them; barefoot, each clothed in what we should call a nightgown, dark grey with many seasons' dirt, and probably nothing else. Children? Two were toddlers; the third was perhaps fifteen, but there was not the slightest doubt about her condition and it looked to me as if her time was close. While her sisters hung whimpering to her skirts she was talking in a scared, persistent fashion to the porter, who presently made a decorous approach to the Minister. The Minister turned to me.

'You will excuse, please, the man says the female says she must reach to her grandmother in Tehran. The grandmother will be appalling with anxious, and there is high vitality for medico treating in Tehran. For me also there is largest vitality to reach to Tehran.'

'Poor little bees!' Oldenveld said.

'It is of no interest to the English,' Sivaji commented very gently, with just a quarter of one eye on me, 'whether the little girl gets to Tehran or whether she dies.'

I was saved from the duty of answering the Minister by the sound of three ear-splitting explosions. They were followed by a noise like that of a reaper-and-binder, of several reaper-and-binders working together, which grew until the little building shook with it and then petered into silence. Dubb reappeared.

'Very sorry, sir, couldn't make the ole bloke hear me. Had to do a bit of scroungin — borrowed his truck. Thought you might like to go down to the Ammadam road, sir — might pick up a convoy down there.'

I told him I was not up to driving on a mountain track I didn't know, at night and with this bug on me.

'Drive you m'self, if it's all the same to you, sir. Antonio, here, he can mind this joint. There aint nothing in it now the phone's packed up, he's only got to keep a tally on the trains, an there won't be none of them, most likely. Only take an hour, sir.'

I put the matter to the others: they could stay where they were and wait for something to happen, or they could take a chance on reaching the main road and picking up some kind of transport which might get them on to Hamadan. They went outside and surveyed the truck, an affair of Detroit origin and some 30-cwt capacity, with local improvements: it was perhaps fifteen years of age, and looked as if a tap from a hammer would cause it to fall into quite small bits. Was this soldier an efficient driver, the Minister inquired. This soldier had won prizes for driving, I assured him. Was the road perfectly safe? Perhaps a little rough by Tehran standards, I said. They were still debating while Dubb coaxed the engine into a new convulsion, and then they decided to go.

'Got one of the side lamps goin,' Dubb told me with satisfaction. 'Manage with that, I reckon. Headlamps been pinched — blokes round these parts got no notion of right and wrong, sir.' Then, 'Oy!' he suddenly said.

The Minister had taken the spare seat in the driver's cab. Dubb said 'Oy!' once again and made a gesture with his thumb. The Minister sadly but without protest moved himself to the back. In a casual fashion Dubb picked up the Persian girl, placed her in the comparatively comfortable seat, dumped the toddlers on and about her and wrapped the whole bundle in an army blanket. 'Do best hold on at the corners — the truck aint what she was,' he advised the passengers at large; then re-lit his cigarette, spat, pushed his topee further back, took his seat and let in the clutch.

My recollection of that journey is fragmentary and dreamlike. As the truck, leaping and plunging, hurled us about like dice in a box I had glimpses of a cliff-face coming straight at my eyes, of vertical drops which seemed to start directly below our wheels. Sometimes I found myself on top of Sivaji, who crouched face-downwards on the floorboards, sometimes my head knocked against his bearer's or against the sharp shoulder of Oldenveld, who was gasping 'Gorror — *mighty* — would *you* say — gorror-mighty!' Huddled and bouncing like a ping-pong ball, the Minister too seemed to be in prayer. Occasionally I caught sight of Dubb's head turned towards me and through the shattering din I once or twice caught his voice: 'Road want something done to it . . . bit of a close one, that was!'

When this confused experience had lasted through most of eternity the truck gave a sharper twist than any which had gone before, nose-dived, sprang up again and went into a starboard list which brought Sivaji on top of me and my own face within inches of the ground. Like that, it came to rest.

'Sorry about that, sir,' I heard Dubb say. 'Weren't really fit for the road, this truck, brakes are U-S. Better climb out the other side, sir. Bit of a drop there is, this side.'

That was correct: beyond the side-board of the truck there was a foot or less of slatey rock; beyond that the Hamadan road, 150 feet below.

'Pity we couldn't quite make it, sir,' Dubb said.

Yet we seemed, in a fashion, to be under a lucky star; for when we had done the remaining half-mile of hairpin bends on foot and reached the main road there were lights approaching: a convoy of ten-tonner Mack-Diesels, a dozen or perhaps twenty of them, grinding steadily through the narrow pass. That was as far as our luck went. Oldenveld stood as far out in the road as he dared, bellowing at one after the other; we waved, we pleaded, we imprecated. In the light I flashed from my torch I had glimpses of the faces of Indian drivers, dutiful, impassive. Not one of them would stop.

We sat down on the boulders which lined the road, and presently that shapeless, toneless voice of Dubb's was in my ears again: 'Very hard to make anything stop — they think it's tribal blokes trying to hold 'em up, the way they do, sir. Not without we was to put something big in the road, a bit o' rock like that you're sittin on now.'

The rock weighed, at a guess, four and a half tons. I said: 'You can, if you like. Not me.'

A little later he was climbing up the cliff, taking a short cut back to the truck. He had, I supposed, forgotten his cigarettes or his pay-book.

'What a country!' Oldenveld had started again. 'Trains run when they like or don't if they don't like. Break in half and no notice taken, no complaints and no action. Look at this road, now: back where I come from . . .'

'My country,' said the Minister, 'is one of high misfortunes. We have an industrious that is second to nobody in the world. We have an aspiration of the highest and up to date, we work, we struggle, we labour. Always the foreigner come to put down and destroy. Today I have business of the highest vitality. I ask only for the train or the auto to take me to Tehran. In the train I have the part which does not go. In the auto is the driver which does not stop.'

By way of example, a second convoy went by.

At least the snow had passed, leaving the sky clear. Around us, as the light broke, there grew a scene more fabulous than any I had witnessed in four continents: a giants' chamber of receding and overtopping walls hewn out in every shape that the most diverse body of sculptors might conceive, in boldly slanting planes, in fluted bastions, gothic verticals, extravagant arabesques; and as these turned variously from black to smoky grey, from grey to silver and reddish brown, a vast steeple of snow which overlooked them all was catching from the hidden sun a film of delicate mauve which passed to vermilion, to deep rose, to the subtlest green and then to flaming gold. Exhausted as I was, I drank from this stupendous and tranquil mystery of light an enchantment which lasts till now. I said sleepily to the Minister:

'If it has nothing else, your country would at least possess a beauty which defies all comparison.'

'It is capital that we do not possess,' he answered without looking up. 'Without capital a nation can do nothing. And without a vehicle I cannot reach at Tehran.'

'The Indian driver does not stop,' Sivaji was saying — and I thought again how beautiful his soft and delicately modulated voice was — 'because the soul of India has been submerged. When Indians are free, there will be none, I say not one, who will ever pass by a needy traveller.' And a few minutes later he was saying, 'This is what the English philosophers themselves have preached, the great law of charity towards those in distress; preached, but never practised — because the soul of the English themselves has been atrophied by the lust for power and wealth.'

'Just one little little morsel of action,' Oldenveld murmured, half asleep, 'give me for the love of old Abe one tiny particle of action!'

In the steadily lightening scene a new and more abrupt change took place. The truck which had brought us, just visible from where we sat, had looked like a permanent part of it: at the very lip of the precipice she had lain on her side, reposefully, like those who have died honourable deaths. But now she stirred, hesitated for a moment as a nervous diver does, and then in a series of strangely agile somersaults plunged down on the road. A boss of granite which she struck in her descent came after her like Mary's lamb; and when the cloud of dust had settled, the roadway, which for all its roughness had been clear of major obstacles, was neatly barred across by six or seven tons of twisted steel and rock. Presently Dubb was at my side.

'Sorry about all them boulders, sir. Never thought all that stuff would come down — I just tipped the old truck over with the jack and I thought she'd fall by herself. Still it make a road-block all right, don't it sir?'

'Yes,' I said, 'it makes a road-block. It makes a road block which it will need twenty or thirty men to shift. Putting it another way, you've blocked the road for perhaps three days. I am supposed to be in Qum in a few hours' time, this gentleman, who is a member of the Iranian Government, has the most urgent business in Tehran, so has the American officer, and the Captain here. All those important appointments have been finally knocked on the head. And apart from throwing the whole Aid to Russia convoy programme out of gear that's all the difference your little act has made.'

'It's these kids what's bothering me,' Dubb said with a trace of unhappiness, nodding towards the three Persian children, who lay on the roadside huddled together and asleep. 'That big one, she's in a bad way. Should've reported sick days ago, if you ask me. Still,' he said more cheerfully, 'those lorry blokes won't go past without stopping any more.'

If there was any difficulty in following his reasoning it was removed by the appearance of a truck which came swaying and bouncing towards us at 35, lurched round the bend and stopped at the barrier in a long, zigzag skid. It was a truck similar to the one which now lay in wreckage on the road, and not — to the casual eye — in much better repair; and on it, somehow, were heaped not fewer than forty people, very old men, cripples, women with babes in arms, children of all ages, as well as chickens, goats, and at least one donkey foal. ('Come from Curbeller, most likely,' was Dubb's comment. 'Go there for their religion. Rum, if you ask me.') These slowly, and with no trace of annoyance, disentangled themselves from the truck and fell into groups at the roadside, where some stood amiably gossiping and some lay down to sleep. Our next visitor was of a rather different cast.

His vehicle was probably of the same horsepower, but with seats for only four: an American saloon with the bows of a submarine and headlamps like aero engines, immense, immaculate, and stinking of cash; and the uniform of its single passenger — the pressed and spotless tunic with its splendid epaulettes and several rows of decorations, the burnished high boots — made one feel as Dubb might have felt if he had been granted the power of feeling, a ragamuffin of the seediest type. Hardly less point-device was the driver, who left the car with its nose to the tail of the pilgrims' truck and came to me.

'Colonel Ustusov wishes to speak to you, Major.'

'Although I am rather troubled with fever I should be most happy to see the Colonel.'

'He wishes you to come to his auto.'

'I await the Colonel with the greatest eagerness,' I said.

In the end he came: a Colonel in fairly unreliable humour: and with the others grouped about us we held converse through the interpretation of the driver, whose shaky American was helped out by rapid and admirable French. Rapid, but hardly rapid enough; for although our talk lasted for some forty minutes, and Ustusov kept the bowling almost entirely to himself, that length of time hardly sufficed for all that he apparently needed to say. Like the others, Ustusov had business in Tehran; but this was business compared with which the business of the others was mere foolery; in brief (and he was by no means brief) the successful prosecution of the war depended entirely on the early if not the immediate arrival of Colonel Ustusov in the capital. He was being held up by incompetent management of the roadway. The British were responsible for the roadway. I was the only British officer present, and I was therefore responsible for removing the obstacle to his passage: my failure to have done so already was characteristic of a British incompetence and deliberate obstructionism with which Ustusov was painfully familiar. The whole matter was going to be reported to the Colonel's GOC, to the British GOC North Persia Area, to the British Embassy. The report would unquestionably be transmitted to Moscow and from there, with observations at the highest level, to London . . . With the sun already high enough to be a burden, the fever running at high voltage through all the veins between my stomach and temples, I was unequal to these civilities, or even to keeping fully awake. I offered the man, from time to time, a cigarette; I spoke of my profound admiration for the army he represented; and I remarked, in the end, that if he could find a force of a hundred able-bodied workmen for removing the obstruction I should be happy to give the necessary orders. 'Only,' I said and the driver translated, 'to the best of my knowledge and belief there are not as many as six men of that kind within a hundred miles of us, unless they be Lurish tribesmen who would shortly settle the matter for us both by removing the tyres of your car and then cutting all our throats.'

And there I was extremely wrong. Where the road showed again half a mile ahead and at a higher level I saw what I took to be a mirage of a kind common enough in those parts and particularly at that hour of the day: the semblance of a long, straggling line of men coming towards us on foot. But Dubb was never an ingredient of mirage, and the foremost of this party, as it approached, was unmistakably Dubb: behind him, ragged, acquiescent, smiling with all the seductive charm of their race, the male population (I should have said) not of one village but of two or three, with the usual cohort of children trailing after them like the tail of a kite.

It was a moment not without drama: even Ustusov was smitten with silence. But Dubb himself was unequal to the central role. Unkempt and repulsively dirty, hands in pockets, a cigarette stuck to his underlip, he was wandering along with an invertebrate, civilian slouch that violated the whole, long, proud tradition of the British army. When he reached the barrier he merely stopped and caught the aged man who came just behind him by the arm; made two gestures, one with his thumb at the debris, one with his chin towards the ravine which lay below the road; and with that, washing his hands of the whole affair, sauntered on to stand with his back to the Colonel and continue his talk with me.

'Blokes what used to work on making the railway. Told me this was a government job "Shah makee muchee trouble," I said — that's right, aint it, sir — these blokes do have a shah?' Then, musingly, 'Hard on them kids, all this, aint it sir!'

It was at this point, when Ustusov had not yet recovered his rhetorical powers, that I saw no further advantage in struggling against the weariness which fever and a sleepless night had laid upon me. I got down beside the boulder on which I had been sitting, made a pillow of my greatcoat and let my eyes fall shut.

When I woke, perhaps an hour later, I saw Ustusov holding a conversation of gestures and polyglot phrases with the men who had shared my carriage. His driver had returned to the car. It was not hard to guess that my friends were trying for seats; I noticed that the Minister was fingering his notecase in an idle fashion and I thought I could detect between his face and the Colonel's profile an incipient understanding. That was no affair of mine, and it seemed a little improbable that Ustusov liked me well enough to choose me as a passenger. I slipped away quietly and went up the road to the block.

A miracle had been achieved there. The ruined truck appeared to have been sheared in half, a part of it was down in the ravine and already there was a passage some four feet broad. With the shifting of one giant boulder, on which a score of men were shoving and sweating now, the space would be wide enough at least for Ustusov's car to get past. I looked about for Dubb and found him talking to the Colonel's driver.

'. . . Tehran, British hospital,' I heard him say with the loud and pedantic emphasis that the ignorant use for the insane. '*British* hospital, savvy? Then — drive HQ and wait for Colonel. Got savvy? Colonel — say — you — go — quick. No stop. Muchee speed — Colonel's orders — savvy?'

The grunts and excited cries of the improvised labour force were increasing in volume: with some cunning they were using a member from the truck's chassis as a lever, they had the boulder rocking and then toppling. It turned half a somersault, they shoved the truck's tailboard in to prevent it falling back, and with the fury that Persian labourers can show on their best days a dozen of them hurled themselves against it. It rocked and toppled again, they swarmed upon it afresh, in four seconds more it had completed the second somersault with half its base projecting over the outside edge of the berm. With a certain dignity, a sense of occasion, the elderly foreman walked up to it alone and pushed it with his hands.

'Mind, muchee quickee!' I heard Dubb say, and then all sound was hidden by the boulder's crash into the ravine. Ustusov's car shot forward, scattering the workmen from the six-foot gap they had so stalwartly cleared. The seat beside the driver was empty; but when I glanced into the rear compartment I just caught sight of the puzzled faces of three small Persian girls. Hearing the first of Ustusov's yells emerge from the engine's roar, and wishing, for reasons purely of prestige, to avoid the spectacle of an Allied officer tearing a British soldier limb from limb, I allowed myself to disappear among the crowd.

Twenty minutes later, when I returned circumspectly to the spot, the gap had been widened by another two feet; the driver of the pilgrims' truck was cranking his engine and the pilgrims were laboriously piling themselves on board. I glanced about for any recognizable remains of Dubb and saw him standing beside the driver's cab, displaying a weak and foolish grin as he shoved a 100-rial note in the pocket of his bush-shirt. The spare seat in the cab was occupied by the Minister. I called out 'Dubb, come here!' but evidently he failed to hear me. He ambled round to the back of the truck, where I saw a hand come out with another 100-rial note: immediately above the hand, and packed like the heart of a lettuce in a tight cluster of dark and grimy faces, the defeated, resigned and reluctantly graceful face of an Allied colonel.

As the truck rattled away Dubb continued the desultory conversation with me which seemed to have gone on all through my lifetime.

'Couldn't have you in with all them wogs, sir — dirty lot, they are, you don't know what you might pick up. There'll be the ELS truck coming up in less than half an hour now, proper driver an all, you'll be all right an hotsy-totsy on that, sir. Bit of a squeeze to get em on that truck,' he said reflectively. 'Easy enough, them three Indians, it was the Yank what took up all the room.' He broke off to shout at the working-party, who after their latest effort had fallen into somnolent chatter. 'Oy! Shah say Work — muchee quickee! Make all road hotsy-totsy for Major Sahib!' And then to me again, 'Well, if you don't mind sir, oughter be gettin back now. That Antonio might be gettin all mixed up on the job, them Eye-ties don't have no idea how to organize. Get the wogs on at tidyin the billet — have to keep at em, you know sir, blokes what've got no notion of civilization. Honky-tonk, sir!'

With the ghastly topee slung on his arm he gave me that deplorable jerk of thumb to cheek which was the best salute we had ever managed to teach him; once more relit his cigarette and, leaving me to think what I should say to DAD Claims about this business, shuffled off, bareheaded in the now ferocious sun, five-feet-three-inches of ineradicable contempt for the King's Regulations, to begin the twenty-mile tramp back to the place where he supervised His Britannic Majesty's affairs.

Crossroads

'But chérie, I can't tell you how marvellous it is — I can hardly believe it — seeing you safe and sound!' said the elder of the two women on the sofa in the sun-lounge of the Quatre-Cantons Hotel. 'What you must have been through! Such courage! Really you are a marvel!'

'A marvel?' said the sulky-mouthed young man who smelt faintly of jasmine. 'She is a classic example of the fact that fortune favours the feather-brained.'

The younger of the women, the one at whom all the other guests were covertly staring, said in her pretty French: 'To say the least, I call that ungrateful! I did do all I could.'

'She first leaves her dressing-case in the flat, and I have to go back for it,' the young man continued. 'She then loses all the tickets and starts a first-class row at the barrier. Next she indulges in a quite reckless love-affair with an aged Deputy. After that she talks politics in a loud, clear voice with an obvious agent sitting in a corner of the compartment —'

'A love-affair?' put in the elder woman. 'Darling, you are naughty!'

'But Thérèse, it was all such fun! You should have seen the place we actually started from, quite at the world's end. The people! Such absolute darlings, and I think they really wanted to be helpful, but not bright — no, really, not, not very bright! (That sheep-faced old man who sold us the wine — darling, will you ever forget him!) How it did stink, that *estaminet* of his! And do you know, I left my scarf there — wasn't it stupid of me! But just at that point we were rather rushed (weren't we, darling?) with other people wanting to slip in and bag our seats. Such a duckie scarf! But really it was all so terribly amusing — those people, so painfully like the cattle they spend their time with — and the dreadful pictures stuck up on the walls of that shack — I can see it all now . . .'

'With an aero the mechanism is full of delicacy, like the whims of a virgin,' the miller repeated. 'A man who is drunk cannot operate all the levers.'

'To steer such a machine above the mountains requires courage,' said the proprietor of the café. 'This gentleman the pilot here is Polish by the look of him. The Poles, in spite of everything, have great courage when they have taken a little wine. Wine calls out the noble thoughts which lie buried in a man's heart. If he steers his machine into the side of the mountain he should be thinking noble thoughts, then his soul will already be near to heaven.'

Nodding sagely, the constable emptied his glass.

'All the same, he can't start without an Air-Worthiness Certificate, properly stamped. I've got it all here — no, I left it in my other coat — it's all in Section 16 of the Regulations.'

'The Regulations don't operate. With a new government there'll be new regulations. You can't operate on the old regulations.'

'It's all in Section 16 of the Regulations,' the constable repeated, 'or Section 19, I forget which. *Permis de Séjour*, Permit to Leave, Passengers Carried, Currency, Air-Worthiness Certificate. No one is allowed to mount up into heaven unless all the papers are in order.'

'Another glass, Mr Constable?'

'No one can mount up when it's dark,' said the miller, who knew everything. 'In less than half an hour it will be as black as the inside of my black stallion Premysl. The field is full of ditches, the machine will gallop to make its leap, the little wheels will tumble and the wings will be torn off like the dress of a bride.'

'No one can mount,' grumbled the village auto-engineer, who had come in once again, covered in black grease, to report to the pilot, 'so long as three cylinders are as dead as butcher's meat. Two hours,' he shouted in the sleeping pilot's ear, 'not a minute under! What d'you think — Michael's groin! — dead as mutton, three of 'em, constipation in the ports, whole job got to come down again, foofsk!'

'Ja, yes!' said the pilot, only half waking. 'Famous, excellent! Half an hour, forty winks, then I'll make some tests.'

'No one is to leave without the proper regulations,' the constable said drowsily. 'There will be a motor from Brzeletten with all the new regulations. Soon, I expect. Tomorrow or the next day. Yes, please one more. Your health, sir — most grateful!'

The proprietor refilled his glass. He said, 'Nothing can come from Brzeletten. The road's under water — three kilometres — ask the miller there.'

But the miller was less positive. 'Wenceslas said he would get

through with his big motor. I told him, "You'll be stranded, my
friend, you'll get yourself drowned," but he said "I'll get through to
Brzeletten all the same, and back this evening." He's quite reckless,
Wenceslas.' Then, 'Listen!'

The proprietor turned down the radio, they all heard distinctly the
rattle of Wenceslas's ancient Chevrolet and the squeal of its brakes as
it slithered to a standstill in the mud outside.

'That means,' said the miller perspicaciously, 'that he has been to
Brzeletten and got back again, or else that he was turned back by the
floods and couldn't get there at all.'

They knew the right answer a moment later, when Wenceslas
himself, a little grey kernel of flesh and whisker enveloped in sodden
hat and draggled coats and giant suitcases, barged in through the
ramshackle door which led to the yard. 'Twice,' he said, 'I have
risked a horrible death and the loss of my motor as well. In here!' he
called over his shoulder. 'Here is the pilot of the aero, that's all I can
do, I have twice put my life in God's hands, two hundred korunas
would not be too much for such a service as that.'

Everyone turned to stare at the first of Wenceslas's passengers,
who, dishevelled and tired, stood and looked about him with an
expression of nervous exasperation; a man who might have lived the
whole of his thirty years in artificial light, a dress designer perhaps,
perhaps an instrumentalist in some orchestra. 'Which is the pilot?
. . . Be careful of those things! . . . . There's some more baggage in
the car.'

And then the hush which had fallen night after night upon the
Ladislas Theatre took hold of the crowded café as if at a word of
command.

For there, like a Velasquez on a rubbish heap, was Anna
Chelnikovna herself; with her lustrous chestnut hair in the famous
Chelnikovna wave, with the ear-rings that a king was said to have
given her; darkly and simply dressed, but wearing the grey
travelling-coat with such an air that it only increased her slenderness;
tired, and yet so vital that even her weariness was like a veil that
accentuates the loveliness beneath. She stood perfectly still, with a
look of faint perplexity, as she always did upon her entrances (as if
the crashing wave of applause were a mysterious noise coming from
a long way off). Looking to right and left she smiled, and everyone in
the room could feel that this soft, confiding smile which half the
painters of Europe had tried to capture was intended only for him.

'Thank you, oh thank you, Mr Driver! No, please — please, don't move, anyone! I'm not wet really, only a splash on my sleeve. What fun it was — such a journey! Yes, my secretary will settle with you. Oh, Boris, would you be a precious — my gloves, I think I must have left them in the car. I'm such a fool, always leaving things. Now please, please don't anyone bother about me!'

But every one of them, of course, was bothering. The only decent chair — the one the proprietor used himself — was whipped over the counter in a jiffy and placed close to the stove. The miller was beside her with wine and a glass of tea, someone gave her a cigarette, the constable himself broke loose from his coma to light it, standing with his feet at attention as in his old infantry days. They were whispering all round the room: Yes, it was Anna herself, the great Anna, the one whose photograph they had all seen in the papers, whom two or three of them had watched from the gallery of the Ladislas! The greatest artist of her time, and a woman of romance besides; one who had got through three husbands, it was said, and quite lately a man of ancient family had blown his brains out to prove the strength of his devotion. And yet, as they saw her now, she was plainly not that sort of woman at all. With all the elegance of her dress, she was simple and human like themselves, she was joking with the miller exactly as if she were a baker's wife, winking at little Ferencz, warming her hands in the way that peasants do; with just the needful modesty she was pulling off her wet stockings as freely as a cottage woman in her own kitchen. 'How nice this is! Do please forgive my feet — I stepped right in a puddle. In Praha they say I ought to have a nurse!' In the radiance of her freindliness the inquisitive, converging stares were turning into smiles and laughter. Only the three men in city clothes who had arrived that afternoon were untouched by the general good humour. They continued to stand in a close triangle, talking in undertones, forever lighting cigarettes.

It was they whom the secretary approached, a little furtively.

'Excuse me, gentlemen — I understand that you've taken places on the plane?'

The oldest of the three, the narrow and bald one, turned his head. 'Plane?'

'This plane that's going to Zurich. That's the pilot, I gather, that fellow sleeping over there.'

The man with dark glasses said, 'Zurich? I didn't know. I was told it was doing little circular trips — a sort of travelling circus — just a thrill for the country people.'

'Listen,' the secretary said very quietly, 'Madame here — you know who she is — Madame has a very important engagement to fulfil in Geneva —'

The bald man faintly smiled. 'So many people have engagements nowadays. But there are, of course, the regular lines.'

'— I'm told there are five places on the plane and that you've taken three of them. Listen: Madame is ready to pay a very large sum for two of those places. Any currency you like — Swiss francs, or American dollars if you'd rather. Two thousand dollars for each place. Now that's a business offer — I take it you are men of business —'

'In a modest way,' said the man with glasses, who owned three newspapers, 'yes. But — let me be just as frank as you have been — I question whether they accept even American money in the nether regions. That's why I'd just as soon be in Zurich, even with my pockets empty.'

'I think Madame might go to three thousand. Six thousand for the two places.'

'I doubt,' said the bald man courteously, 'if there is much one can buy in political prisons, even with three thousand dollars.'

From the group round the stove came another outburst of joyful laughter. They were drinking, at Anna's expense, the health of the constable; the constable was responding with a speech about his army days, about duty and the homeland, which meandered on and on.

'Tell me,' Anna whispered to the proprietor, 'who is that boy over there, the one beside the old woman — he looks so interesting and so sad.'

'That? Oh, that's Janos Hanka — that's his mother, she used to live near here. They're waiting to go on the aero.'

'What — that old lady? Is she going flying?'

'Well, Janos, you see, he can't leave her behind. She lives for him.'

'But why is he going — Janos?'

'Well, you see, he's a barber, Janos. That's his trade.'

'But people in this country have to get their hair cut! Even in a small village like this —'

Against the ferocious competition of the radio the constable was droning on about the honour and hardships of the police service. The miller explained: 'Yes, that Janos — I knew his grandfather — he's a clever boy, remarkable, he keeps a grasshopper in his tongue. That's why he's done so well — up at Pardubice. Magnificent tips. He got a job at Pardubice, you see — his uncle Karel had something to do with it. Quick as a kingfisher. He could always tell which party the customer belonged to. "Austrian style?" he'd say, "straight beside the ears?" he'd say, and before the customer said "Yes" or "No" he'd have sized him up. Then he'd have the jokes ready — a new lot every fortnight — one set for Christian Democrats, one for the Slavophiles — they used to laugh so much he had to hold them by the nose to get his scissors at them.'

'But he's not making jokes now.'

'No, Honourable. No, just once he made the wrong jokes. A Russian gentleman — Janos mistook him for a businessman from Plzen. Everyone makes mistakes sometimes. And they took down his name. So now he is on his way to Zurich — two seats in the aero. It's cost him all his savings, I should say.'

'So! Poor fellow!' Anna said.

The secretary was at her side. He whispered, 'Anna, it's hopeless. Those three, they wouldn't part with their places for all the money in the national bank.'

'But surely the pilot could fit two more in?'

'He says he'd never get it off the ground with the extra load. Not even with one more. And anyway there's not an inch of room.'

'Not even for me? *Eh bien!*' Anna said with a gentle gaiety, 'we must settle down here — we can't possibly go back to Brzeletten tonight — we must be satisfied with Mr Proprietor's wine and Mr Miller's philosophy.' She turned to Ferencz, 'Ferencz, can you work the radio — can you find some music? I'm tired of all these speeches. No, not yours, Mr Constable, yours was delicious. You know, Boris, I like this place, I feel happy here.'

'Yes, and life in prison will be the greatest fun in the world!' the secretary murmured. 'Anna, are you never serious! I told you it was lunacy coming here — just a rumour of an independent aeroplane!'

'My darling, how dull they are, the people who take life seriously! Well done, little Ferencz!' The boy had found a programme of Liszt, she began to hum the tune and then to sing. Presently everyone was singing. 'Don't worry, Boris,' she said, 'Don't spoil it all by worrying. I feel so gay tonight, my heart is full of light and warmth, I want to make everyone happy.'

The rain had started again, sizzling mournfully on the iron roof, successive clouds from the sputtering stove so thickened the grey smoke of cigarettes that the light from a single kerosene flame above the counter scarcely reached the far end of the room. It was cold. From knot-holes in the slatted walls damp tongues of draught found their way down people's necks and up their trouser-legs; only the smell of the place, wood rotted with spilt wine, soiled clothes, butts smouldering in the unwashed spittoons, convinced the secretary that he was not still out of doors. Yet none of the villagers seemed to think of going home. Their eyes shone, farm-hands and herdsmen who had passed the age for laughter laughed like children at a carnival feast. Anna was seated on the counter now, the miller had his arm about her, Wenceslas held her hand in both of his and the three of them drummed with their feet to the jaunty music trickling from the radio. 'Fill them up, Ferencz — Boris there will give you the money!' They started to sing again, even the city men sang.

A grey woman with an army blanket over her head pushed her way through to the constable, who lay on his back by the stove. 'A message, Lorenz! Stefan took it from the telegraph — urgent, he says.' 'In a minute, my love, in a minute!' He laughed and wiped his forehead. 'Look at Anna Chelnikovna there — Anna herself! Like one of God's angels come down, and just the same as us. Marvellous!' he took the paper from her hand and stuffed it in the top of his holster; his eyes closed again, he sang a few bars rallentando, sighed happily and once more fell asleep.

'The pills,' Mother Hanka said for the tenth time, 'you've got the pills?' Even her lips hardly moved; for more than three hours she had sat on the narrow bench like a statue carved in cheese, worn hands upon her lap, her wrinkled face perfectly still, only her dark-rimmed, frightened eyes moving restlessly towards either door that opened. 'The doctor said it was easy — that's right, isn't it? No pain. The doctor said you just go to sleep. Didn't he, Janos? He did say that?'

Without turning his head the youth Janos replaced the shawl which had slipped a little from his mother's shoulders. 'We shan't need them now,' he said tonelessly. 'It's all right now we've got the seats.'

'But the aero may not start.'

'It'll start all right.'

'It'll frighten me,' she said in a small, pitiful voice, 'going right up, with nothing underneath. The pills — that would be easier. No pain — that's what the doctor said — you just fall asleep.'

'Quiet, motherling!' he said, between severity and tenderness. 'You think too much, you ought to rest.'

Like her, he sat as in a trance, but no longer paralysed by fear.

Three years before, to pass an idle evening in Praha, he had bought a balcony ticket for *Ruy Blas*: a fresh experience — he had seen only trivial pieces before — and the sight of Anna Chelnikovna as the Queen, passing slowly across the stage at the end of the first Act, had come to him like vision to a man born blind. Denying himself all other luxuries, he had watched her in a score of roles since then; but she had remained, for him, the Queen: divinity in human form, beauty and splendour brought to earth, a lasting presence in his mind which turned the long, grey hours in Scholtka's saloon to one heroic dream. Here, chilled by the torment of delay, his thoughts had still been turning to the voice and features which idealized all he was leaving behind, the music of his own tongue, the ancient glories of his race, the warmth and tenderness of the Bohemian countryside: and the sudden appearance of Anna herself, so near that he could almost distinguish the initials embroidered on the scarf she wore — Anna herself, vision become reality, holiness brought close enough to be touched and smelt — had almost stunned his reason. The terror of the last few days (for himself, for the mother he so fondly cherished); the bewilderment of a desperate journey; the load of anxiety for the future: all were lost in his wonderment at this miracle of circumstance, this undreamed-of answer to unspoken prayer. He forgot the coldness of this room, the cramp in his back and the emptiness of his belly; no longer heard the little ceaseless moans that his mother gave or the rustic chatter about him; saw nothing but Anna's face, the tiredness of the eyes which he fancied were turned now and then towards him, the radiance of her smile. The party was dispersing at last, with boisterous farewells; the engineer came in with a new report, the constable's wife returned and tried once more to rouse him, fresh gusts swept coldly through the room as the doors continually swung. But of all this traffic Janos saw and felt nothing. Anna — Anna herself — Anna was here.

Then, as in his dreams, he saw her coming towards him: Anna, coming to him, Anna herself, coming so close that he could have touched her hand.

And now her voice, the rich voice that so easily filled the Ladislas, softened to a sweet familiarity as she bent and spoke in his mother's ear:

'You are going to Zurich? On the plane?'

'My son —' she answered feebly, '— my son here, he arranges everything.'

Anna turned, she smiled to Janos as if to an old friend, sat down beside him. 'You will forgive me? I shouldn't be interfering. I only wondered whether you know of anywhere to take your mother when you get to Zurich. I mean — it's a large place, you'll feel strange there.'

Janos muttered: 'Yes. Yes, gracious lady. Yes, I'll have to find some place.'

'I was going to say, if you find yourself in any difficulty, I have an old friend there who would care for you both until you've made some further plans. She wouldn't want any money, she's very well off, and so kind. It's the Comtesse Saint-Serquigny. Look, I've written her name and address here on the back of my own card. If you give her the card, and just say you are friends of mine, that's all she will need.'

Janos took the card. He stammered, 'I — gracious lady — I don't know what to say, I can't, I could never thank you —'

She drowned his confusion in a smile so intimately friendly that it won an answering, shy smile from him. She said with gentleness, with utter simplicity: 'It's nothing! You know, it will be a happiness to me, in the hard time I've got to face now, to think of your mother being cared for by my friend — to feel that I've done one little thing for someone's happiness. It will be so good to know that at least two people like you and your gracious mother here — people who stand for what is best in our dear country — to know they are happy and safe. You see, I know what you've been through in these last few days. I've been through something like it myself.'

'But you,' Janos whispered, 'you, gracious lady, you are going back to Praha?'

Smiling again, she made for her hands a forlorn gesture of resignation. 'Yes — or wherever they choose to send me.' She was looking at his face with a certain shyness, as if she were half-afraid to bore him with her confidence. 'Yes, I came here just on the chance that I might get a place on the plane. You see, my life in Praha is finished — I've given some pleasure to people who loved the drama, but with the new regime they won't want me any more. I thought there was still something for me to do — for my country, I mean. I thought that if I went abroad, instead of going to prison here, I could use my art to show the world a little of our cultural heritage. Perhaps it was only vanity —'

'No!' he said fervently, 'no, gracious lady, no!'

'At any rate, the fates have ruled against it. Tomorrow I shall go back to Praha, and the rest will be in the hands of God.'

Janos stared at his knees. Such sadness and such courage, in those eyes, were more than he could face. He found himself saying, 'It's only for my mother — she's getting old, you see. It wouldn't matter about me. Only if they took me away —'

'Of course!' And then she whispered, 'How much I should love to care for your mother myself — if only I were free!'

Except for the constable, still snoring by the stove, the regular customers had all gone home. The proprietor had fallen asleep with his head on the counter. In the other corner the city men, huddled in their travelling-coats, were playing cards with the secretary, and their sleepy voices alone broke the monotonous noise of rain dripping from the roof into the puddles outside. 'And forty . . . And fifty . . . No stake! . . .' The engineer came in once more, shaking himself like a wet fowl. 'It goes now,' he announced, 'the ignition. God and the holy angels know how.' He would test as soon as it was light, the pilot mumbled, only half awake. Still sitting up, with her back against the wall, Mother Hanka seemed to be asleep. The eyes of Janos himself fell shut, and when they opened again he found that Anna's head was reposing on his lap; her hair falling over his knees, her breathing quiet as a sleeping child's, her sad, tired face relaxed in the innocence of sleep; as if, he thought, the Blessed Virgin herself had come to me, to me, to comfort her distress.

An hour passed, and her eyes opened. She smiled, as if to an old and trusted friend.

'Such lovely dreams! How good you are, to make a pillow for me, how kind!'

'Gracious lady,' he whispered, 'will you please — just one thing, I have just one thing to ask you. At Zurich — when you get to Zurich — to care for my mother. The place you spoke of, I'm sure she'll be all right there. With you to look after her. I'll follow if I can, there may be some way of getting across. Yes, yes gracious lady, I want you to have my place.'

'I don't understand,' his mother repeated.

'It's all right,' he said, 'it's perfectly all right. I shall put you into your place in the aero, and then Madame Anna will look after you — there's no one in the world as kind as she is. The journey won't be long, probably you'll sleep, and then at the other end Madame will take you to a lovely house. I'll come there as soon as I can.'

She said stupidly, mournfully, 'I don't understand.'

They picked their way across the filth in the yard and out to the lane. In the first, misted light the others, a little way ahead, looked like an eastern caravan with overloaded saddle-bags. With one arm taking most of his mother's weight, a holdall stuffed with her possessions in the other hand, Janos, undersized, eighteen hours from his last meal, stumbled manfully along the pot-holed road, past the dark shapes of the limekilns, the sawmill, the farrier's shop.

The plane, parked under the trees in a corner of the fog-wrapped meadow, might have been some farming implement long out of use; the engineer was wearily swinging the starboard screw, to which the engine never responded with more than an angry sneeze. The pilot, yawning, lit another cigarette. 'God does not will!' the engineer explained. 'In any case, the machine would only destroy itself, a day like this.' The intending travellers stood about like the figures of a toy Noah's Ark. 'Perhaps, after all, it would be quicker to walk,' murmured Anna to Boris.

'Sometimes, Anna, I find your wit rather a bore,' the secretary said.

Panting, Janos joined the rest and edged his way shyly to Anna's side.

'If you please — if you will excuse me, gracious lady. My mother's so worried, she doesn't understand. Perhaps — in your gracious kindness — perhaps you would explain to her, explain that you yourself will have her in your care —.'

'But Janos, of course!' She turned, with the friendliest of her smiles relit, and moved towards the old woman, who stood like a lump of basalt fallen from a cliff; then stopped. 'Oh — Boris — my scarf, I must have left it in that café place —'

'Then it must stay there!' he answered shortly.

'But Boris, the little man gave it me — *le petit autrichien*. I value it more than anything in the world.'

'More than —?'

Janos, in a moment, said 'I — Madame — so small a service —'

She turned swiftly and seemed to give him, with her radiant smile, the whole of herself. 'Oh — oh Janos, you are so very sweet!'

Janos ran. Because the entrance to the field would have taken him forty yards out of the way he climbed through the wire fence, tearing his clothes. Forgetting all his tiredness, the weakness of hunger, he ran like an athlete, taking the puddles as they came, splashing himself with liquid mud from head to foot, past the farrier's, past the limekilns, stumbling, falling on his face, dashing on again. The scarf was there, on the floor close to where she had been sitting; pale blue, no larger than a handkerchief, with 'AC' beautifully embroidered in one corner and 'AH' in the other, an exquisite thing. He picked it up by the hem and placed it carefully inside his coat; pushed the proprietor out of his way and ran back to the lane.

There the constable, with a piece of paper in his hand, came forward and stopped him.

'This aero,' the constable said, 'someone was talking about an aero. In the café there. You were one of them — that's what they told me — you were going to mount up in it.'

'But not now, Mr Constable. Only —'

'Wait!' The constable had him by the arm. 'It's a new Regulation, it came by the telegraph — my wife ought to have told me. From Brzeletten, from headquarters. Nothing at all to leave — no aero to leave the ground. Absolutely definite. Nothing to leave the ground at all, not even if it's a plough or a hay-cart. Headquarters Regulation.'

Somehow, the engineer had triumphed. From the meadow, half a kilometre away, a succession of explosions was followed by a steady roar which, almost at once, was doubled in volume.

'What's that?' the constable demanded.

'Perhaps a motor-bicycle.'

But the constable had already started to run.

Exhausted as he was, Janos was still a match for a pot-bellied old man who had been drinking most of the night. In a few paces he had overhauled him, he had some thirty yards to spare when he reached the entrance to the field. The aged gate was wide open, lolling from its bottom hinge; he lifted it out of the mud and had it fixed across the gap, a feeble but temporarily effective barrier, a moment or two before the constable arrived. The plane was still in the same place below the trees, its engines roaring in turn; but as Janos stood against the gate it began to move, came in a duck's waddle towards him, turned clumsily to face the greatest length of the meadow and halted again, grumbling and trembling like a fly on a window-pane. In the voice of his soldiering days the constable was shouting.

'Open this gate!'

'Gate? I don't understand.'

No longer confused, spurred by fury to the vigour of his earlier years, the constable seized the top bar of the gate and started to climb. One foot came over Janos's side. Janos seized it and jerked it upwards. The constable lost balance and fell on his back in the mud.

Now the plane was like a timid bather entering a chilly sea. It crept forward, it made a little rush, hesitated, plunged forward again. Still a lame, ungainly thing, it yawed and lurched across the hummocky ground, now slithering sideways, now rearing sharply as a clumsily ridden horse does, but gradually gaining speed, till it seemed that the ground flattened before the rush of its wheels. Then it was a fluid shape against the mist, lifting slowly and diminishing, then it was only a falling noise, and then, above the cloud-bank, a bird in effortless flight towards the grey emerging hills. Janos kissed and waved his hand. Smiling, he walked to where the plane had stood below the trees.

There the auto-engineer was relighting a cigarette which one of the travellers had thrown half-smoked on the ground. 'My father put the tyres on carriages,' he said complacently, 'and I send them up into the sky.' The other figure, the one leaning against the fence, should have been that of Boris the secretary; but long before he reached them Janos had seen that it did not belong to a tall young man.

'Mother!' His voice was tight with shock and anger. 'Mother, why didn't you go?'

'The lady,' she answered feebly, '— I didn't quite understand — the lady thought it wasn't right, she thought I ought to stay with you. The gentleman got in the machine instead.' And since he made no reply she went on falteringly, 'The pills, Janos, there's still the pills. I told you, I said that would be the easiest way.'

He took one of the two pills from his pocket and put it in her hand. 'We'll get some water, back at the café,' was all he said.

But his anger subsided as they returned together to the gate. She was, after all, an old woman, country-bred, who had never had a schooling like his own; how natural, in the stress of this hour, that her rudimentary wits should have failed altogether, that she should wholly have mistaken what Anna said to her! On the way back to the village the constable was holding him tightly by one wrist screwed behind his back, but he was scarcely aware of that; he was thinking how he had still a little time to feast on the resurgent happiness within his heart. 'Yes, with water,' he repeated absently to his mother, who was limping along behind. 'Yes, with water, the doctor said.' With his free hand he got out the scarf and held it against his face, where its softness and its smell quickened his memory of the night, of Anna's head upon his thighs. What, compared with that hour's holiness, could life have offered a man like him? 'Yes, motherling, yes, the doctor said it was all quite easy.' And as they stumbled on towards the police office, muddy and dishevelled, watched curiously from cottage windows, the face of the barber, Janos, grey with hunger and lack of sleep, still shone with a mysterious smile.

All in the Day

Whenever people are arguing about who won the War, my thoughts, for some reason, go to a man who was known to me as Taylor 08. Not that he was doing much about the War at the time when I knew him — that happened later, when he was in Italy and I in Baghdad.

I became aware of his separate existence on a route march, when 'B' Company was ascending a steep hill east of Marlow. (In the autumn of 1940, having new men to toughen quickly, we were doing longish marches in Field Service Order every Tuesday and Friday.) The first thing I noticed was a steel helmet of which the crown came level with the shoulders of the man in front. Beneath this helmet, when I stooped a little, I saw the thin and pasty face of a boy who looked about nineteen. He was bathed in sweat; and he was smiling to himself, with his teeth together, as men do when in pain.

I marched beside him for a little way.

'Are you all right?' I asked.

'OK, thanky', sir!'

He didn't look it. At every pace his diminutive legs had to travel about nine inches further than nature intended, and I guessed from my own experience that the heavy ammunition boots were a torture to him: he was, I discovered, a gas-fitter's mate, just three weeks in uniform.

'You can stick it out, anyway?'

'Cor, easy, sir!' He wriggled his rifle loose from one shoulder and slung it on the other, heaved at his equipment and spat out the pip of an imaginary orange. 'Nice walk in the country and the Army pays yer — money for jam, sir!'

But the state of his feet, when I saw them after the march, was gruesome. I told him to report sick and get them some attention.

Shortly before one o'clock, next day, Brewer the CSM came to the office tent with the familiar expression of one who is being put upon.

'Taylor 08 asking for interview. I've told him the time for interviews is after Company Office. These young recruits, you know, sir —'

On this question, however, I always took a line of my own. I said firmly, 'I'll see him!'

The Taylor who was indignantly marched in to me was a different man from the one of the day before. The impudent swagger, the guts, had gone. This was a homesick child.

'How are the feet?' I asked him.

He didn't seem to hear me. Without speaking, he laid on my table a telegram.

I scarcely needed to read it: in those September days every morning brought half a dozen telegrams which were always much the same. BOMBED OUT LAST NIGHT, this one said, PLEASE COME IMMEDIATE LOVE LIZ.

I said: 'I'm sorry about this, I'm most terribly sorry!' and I went on with a piece which I had almost got by heart; he mustn't worry too much, the authorities had everything under control, they would find somewhere for his wife to live.

He waited till I came to the end, and then he said, 'I got to go, sir! I can borrow the fare. Be on parade temorrer, sir — I only want 'alf a day.'

This was Brewer's cue. His face already looked as if it had been pickled in cement. His voice came on like a jerky record on the gramophone: 'Can't be done, sir! Command Order, sir — London area out of bounds to all personnel not on duty.'

To the haggard child before me this made no sense at all. He looked at me as if I were a dog refusing to perform some simple trick from sheer stupidity.

'See how it is, sir, the wife, sir, she's got no head on her for business an' all. Three kids, we've got, sir.'

I explained again, as patiently as I was able: the order had been made for the general good . . . thoroughly competent people would be doing everything possible for his wife and children . . . and so on. He, in his turn, started to restate the situation as it appeared to him. Without the assistance of Brewer we might have been arguing the thing all afternoon.

'You heard what the Comp'ny Commander said!' Brewer suddenly fired. 'Salute! Right — turn! Quick march!'

That was that.

'It's hard on these fellows,' I said when Taylor was out of earshot. 'Less than forty miles from their wives!'

Brewer performed the action I always thought of as 'sniffing at attention'. He said venomously, 'It's these perishin' women, if you ask me, sir. "Please come immediate!" What does she think he's joined — the League of 'Ealth an' Beauty?'

So I did not ask the Company Clerk to get me Taylor's home address till Brewer was out of the way.

I was summoned to London myself next morning: someone in Public Relations at the War Office. The interview was over before lunch, and I thought I might see for myself how Taylor's wife was getting on.

This, when the bus put me down at Lion Cross, did not appear so simple an undertaking. To the left of the main road an area of some ten acres looked rather like a West Indian township after the passage of a hurricane. Pitlock Street, the one I was searching for, was luckier than most of its neighbours — it still existed; but all the houses on one side had been pushed over into the roadway. Here the authorities were certainly at work — police, rescue squads, ambulances. But it did not seem good sense to ask these tired and frantically labouring people if they could tell me the whereabouts of Mrs Taylor of Number 23.

'The police station,' an old woman suggested. She was sitting on a pile of rubble, wearing a man's overcoat over a flannel nightgown and contentedly smoking a cigarette. 'They do say they've got all the names there. The station in Longmore Road, I mean.'

But as things turned out I did not have to go so far. Nearby, in Gaylor Street (I think it was), the rubble had been shovelled aside to make a passage just wide enough for vehicles to get through to the main road. Along this passage, as I reached it, came a small and very wobbly cart, so heaped with odds and ends that it looked like toppling over at every yard: there was an aged sofa, upside down, and several chairs; an ormulu clock, a bulging trunk, an array of kitchen tools and ornaments; in the midst of all this, a pair of toddlers sitting with their legs over the side and happily sharing a bag of sweets. In front (where the donkey should have been), a girl who might have been no more than seventeen was tugging manfully, with a third child of perhaps four years holding on to her skirt; while a pace ahead of her, in his undervest and battledress trousers, head down, shoulders thrusting against a length of chain between the shafts, was Taylor 08.

He caught sight of me before I could turn away; and for me it was a difficult moment. But not for him. With native wisdom, he evidently knew there were subjects which it was a waste of time to discuss. He faintly grinned. 'Had a bit o' luck, sir! Bloke I know over Turnham Green, I called to mind he had this barrer.' And then he laughed. 'Thought I'd take a loan of it — it's no use to Bert any more, he got himself blowed up. My nippers!' he added laconically, jerking his head. 'And this is Liz.'

I took the girl's place in the shafts — it seemed to be what manners demanded — while she continued to shove at the side. We went on, in that order, to the tram-lines, and across by a route which Taylor knew to the Harrow Road.

'Yes, it was a bit o' luck, taking it all round, sir,' he said, as we sweated through Willesden. ''Course, we lost a lot o' stuff — beautiful eidydown we lost, wedding present from Mum and Dad. But we got quite a bit of it. Tidy job o' work, it was.' (This I could see. His own and his wife's faces were mostly brick dust.) 'Nippers all right, too. Charlie, there, he thinks it's an extra bit o' holiday, don't you, Charlie!'

'But where are you making for?' I asked.

'Out Wembley. Got an ole auntie that way, she'll give Liz a doss, I reckon — a few days, anyway.'

'But you know,' I said, with belated severity, 'if you'd left the whole thing to the proper people they'd have moved your family to some really safe place in the country.'

Plainly he thought that foolish. He said, with an inflexion which made me think of J. D. Rockefeller, 'Yes — and what would've 'appened to all my property? Aw — they'll be right enough! Safe as 'ouses — Wembley.'

'And I think I ought to remind you,' I continued with some diffidence, 'that you're going to find yourself on a charge tomorrow. Absent without leave. That means loss of pay, and other things besides.'

He turned his head to give me a confidential glance. 'Them Jerries,' he said, 'they're beginnin' to get on the awkward side of me!'

At dusk, after some six hours' hauling, we reached the aunt's road, and there I thought it well to leave them. To be honest, I don't think my legs or shoulders would have lasted another half-mile, that sweltering day.

'Very kind, I'm sure, Mister!' the girl said when I took my leave.

At which her husband reproved her: 'Oy, Liz, you say "sir" when it's an officer!' That much hold the army had gained on Private Taylor.

He had the eldest child on his shoulders now; the other two were asleep, curled up amid the crockery. 'Well, sir,' he added, with just a trace of shyness, 'I'll be seeing yer!' And I watched the mobile junk-shop creaking on, shakily but at a steady pace, till a bend in the road put it out of sight.

I asked Brewer next morning, 'Anyone for Company Office, Sergeant-Major?'

'No charges this morning, sir.'

'Is Taylor 08 back?'

'Taylor 08, sir?'

He seemed surprised.

'There's nothing from the Guard Room, sir. I'll ask the Platoon Sergeant — 11 Platoon, that is. Dyson — find Sergeant Jacks an' bring him here. An' get a move on!'

Jacks came, and stood at attention.

'Taylor 08, was he on parade yesterday?' Brewer demanded fiercely.

There was just an instant's pause; glancing sideways, I saw a look pass between sergeant and sergeant-major: an army look, delicately turned, packed tight with understanding.

'On parade all day, sir!' Jacks said smartly.

Brewer, turning his stony face towards mine, showed the expression of sterling honesty which is achieved only in a lifetime of artistic lying.

'Then that would be all right, sir?'

I said it would.

Later that day we were marching up a hill still steeper than the one near Marlow. I caught sight of a man who seemed to be half buried by his helmet; one whose tiny legs, matching their stride to that of the man in front, worked very lamely but with a slogging resolution. I came up beside him.

'How are the feet doing now?'

The grin which appeared was gone so quickly that I wondered afterwards if I had only imagined it.

'Feet, sir? Fine, sir! Nice walk in the country an' the army pays yer! Money for jam!' said Taylor 08.

A Common Tongue

'What did you say that dump was?' Mr Konnixel asked wearily, accelerating to sixty-five mph. 'Perry-gwex.'

'No, that was Angoulême. Périgueux comes next.'

'What happens there?'

'The Cathedral of St Front. Byzantine. Copied from St Mark's, Venice. And the church of St Etienne. Eleventh century.'

'But we've just done St Mark's, Venice. No cut in seeing another one just the same.'

'Well, Périgueux is on the list your wife sent you.'

Mr Konnixel (President, Universal Squelchy Lubricants) nodded glumly, accelerating again. 'If it's on Lou's list, I take it in! What was that you said about that cock-eyed church at that last place? Byzantine-Romanesque? What a sales-tag! Make a memo — remind me to put that in the next mail to Lou. Eu-rope,' said Mr Konnixel (Vice-President, Cosy Old Time Parlour Stores Corporation) for at least the hundredth time, 'is just one big bellyache to Harry Lincoln Konnixel.'

The road bent sharply and a rudimentary village collected on its banks. Mr Konnixel dutifully slowed down to fifty. Marcel Lepaon, pushing his barrow into the main road, did not slow down, because the village — after all — was his.

'This place called something?' Mr Konnixel demanded.

'Bosseux le Nèpe.'

'No matter! Cathedral?'

'Not one.'

'Praise be to — Oh, my gosh!'

The brakes of the car were miraculous. As my forehead was jerked against the windshield I got a picture like a still taken from a film — of a long, two-wheeled barrow, of an elderly peasant looking straight in front of him and wearing a small, reflective smile. This picture turned over sideways and disappeared. I think my head was between the steering-wheel and Mr Konnixel's chest when the long scream of the tyres ended in a noise like a tidal wave falling on shingle.

'This,' I heard Mr Konnixel say with a note of acerbity, 'is where you start right in with your parly-voo!'

My senses waveringly returned to action as I stumbled out of the car, and I saw that in the unequal clash of forces we had not had things all our own way: our nearside wing looked like the face of a boxer who has taken heavy punishment. But the barrow had ceased to exist. One wheel, perambulating on its own, had come to rest some sixty yards farther along the road, and the rest — most of it under the car — was firewood. Spread fanwise over a surprising area of the road was a litter of apples and tomatoes, lightly dressed with the contents of perhaps a hundred eggs.

The peasant, unharmed, had scarcely moved; his expression alone had changed, from one of gentle optimism to incredulity. I had the impression that he was expecting the sequence of events to be put into reverse, the barrow to be restored undamaged to his hands. And he was as silent as a statue.

Not for long, however. While I was still groping for a conversational opening, he found one. Speaking without heat or flurry, he said — as nearly as I can remember — 'You — you are a madman and a wild beast. You are a kind of an imbecile. To drive your machine like that, it's the work of a criminal. To murder innocent people, to destroy their property, to you that means nothing at all.'

Mr Konnixel had his head out of the driver's window, and long before the speech was over he had become tired of listening.

'What is this hobo saying?' he wanted to know.

'He maintains that you were driving too fast.'

'Well, ask him why he didn't look where he was going! Ask him if he's blind or just plain dumb.'

'My employer — the driver of the car,' I said to the peasant, 'insists that you were pushing your barrow without due care and attention.'

'In this country,' he answered, 'we have some laws. In America it is doubtless permissible for those millionaires there to drive their machines at two hundred kilometres into the labourers' property, for example. Here we have a police force, and people who do that sort of thing are put in prison.'

'He says' — I told Mr Konnixel — 'that he's going to have you summoned and jailed.'

'Oh, for Pete's sake. Say, what does he want for that ten-cent perambulator he was pushing around?'

I turned to the peasant again.

'My employer is willing to overlook your carelessness and from sheer generosity to contribute something towards the replacement of your ancient barrow.'

The old man's expression changed. He looked swiftly at the wreckage in the road, at the car, at Mr Konnixel's race-club cap.

'It was a vehicle of exceptional construction,' he said with precision. 'to replace it will cost 50,000 francs. And the other property 20,000 francs. Then there's the damage I've suffered in the nerves. Altogether it will be 75,000 francs.'

I relayed this quotation to Mr Konnixel. Mr Konnixel, immediately getting out of the car, said: 'So this jerk calculates the good God sent him a sucker, huh!'

In France, where intelligence reigns, you are never far from refreshment. Mr Konnixel, imperially surveying the scene, caught sight of the Café Bar Dubosc less than thirty yards away. He looked hard at the peasant, made a hitching gesture with his thumb, and marched deliberately into the bar. The peasant followed, with me behind. Almost in one movement the owner of the bar, who had been watching us from his doorway, flicked the dust from three chairs and set them at the one small table.

Mr Konnixel (Director, Amalgamated Hard-as-Iron Steel Utensils) gave me his hat, sat firmly down, and beckoned the peasant to the opposite chair. I, having ordered three large cognacs, which I thought might have their use, took my place in between.

'Tell him,' Mr Konnixel ordered, 'that my name is Harry L. Konnixel, aged sixty-three, and a business man.'

I told him. The peasant, removing his beret, replied that he was Marcel Lepaon. He also was a man of business. This morning he had been on his way to the market to dispose of six — no twelve — dozen eggs of exceptional quality, together with other valuable produce of his own holding.

'Okay, okay!' said Mr Konnixel equably. 'I don't want the history of his life; we can take that as read. Tell him I'll give him 5,000 francs for his ten-cent go-cart and 2,000 more for the produce.'

'Mr Konnixel,' I said to Lepaon, 'offers you 7,000 francs in compensation.'

Lepaon stood up. 'Very well! I call the police!'

Mr Konnixel said, 'Wait a minute — wait a minute! Tell him, Hushesson, if he wants to play the law game with me I'll hire the best lawyer in all France.'

I did so.

'It would be cheaper, for example,' said Lepaon swiftly, 'to pay me my 70,000 francs.'

'I'll give him 10,000,' said Konnixel.

Lepaon sat down.

'I will accept 65,000 francs.'

Passing these communications back and forth, I noticed with interest how much my two clients (if I may so call them) were alike. True, my employer's clothes were more expensive than those of Lepaon, his skin more subservient to razor and soap. But they were roughly of equal age and equal build — both spare and knobbly men — and the hair of both was grey and thin. They sat, now, leaning back from the table, each with his hands folded on his stomach, each with the air of a chess-player who already commands the board. Between utterances their thin lips snapped together as if worked by powerful springs, and beneath their narrow, deeply furrowed foreheads the knowing, sceptical eyes of each man never shifted from the other's.

'I'll see him buried and gone to hell before I pay him one cent over 15,000.'

'I make this gentleman my final offer. Unless he pays me 60,000 francs I go at once to the police.'

It was scarcely necessary for me to go on interpreting. However little he knew of the French language, some special sense seemed to inform Konnixel of the meaning of '*soixante mille francs*'. If the words 'fifteen thousand' meant nothing precise to Lepaon, he could yet smell the figure and find the smell too thin. All I had to do was to translate, as occasion offered, a few of the more interesting embroideries of the debate.

'. . . My employer wishes you to know that in his country a man who tried to sell eggs at half a dollar each would presently find himself in a madhouse . . . M. Lepaon says that eggs are extremely scarce in France. He expected to sell this produce at particularly favourable prices. He is in urgent need of money to provide the *dot* — the dowry — for his daughter Isabelle, who is a good girl but as skinny as a starved hen . . .'

For a moment Mr Konnixel's concentration relaxed. The little crowd which had collected at the scene of the crash was now reassembled in the café-bar watching the duel with the partisan but scrupulous connoisseurship which the English exercise at Old Trafford. Among them, close to our table, was a pale young woman of perhaps twenty-five, and a flick of Lepaon's eyes informed me that this was Isabelle. Undoubtedly she was thin and perhaps an invalid. But in the instant when my employer and I glanced up at her I thought her face was like the work of Fra Angelico. What Konnixel thought I could not tell.

'Dough for his daughter?' he said acidly. 'I'll say he does! Everybody wants dough!'

'I am willing,' said Lepaon, 'to make a special concession. I will release M. l'Americain for 57,000 francs.'

'This hobo,' said Mr Konnixel, 'exaggerates my sense of humour. When I say 20,000 francs I *mean* 20,000 francs.'

'50,000 — that is my last offer!'

'Say — listen — 21,000 francs are going to buy you most of the eggs in France!'

Now and then Mr Konnixel struck the table. More than once M. Lepaon with a definitive shrug of his shoulders got up and moved towards the telephone which was fixed to the back wall of the bar. And twice the proprietor refilled our glasses with the air of a professional second in a boxing-ring.

Without an audience the duellists might have flagged at an early stage. But I saw that M. Lepaon, however little his eyes moved, was continuously aware of the crowd behind him, increasingly conscious of his prestige. He no longer fought for himself alone. The dignity of Bosseux le Nèpe was involved. With his wits matched against the rich American's he was David opposing Goliath, he was Maréchal Foch and the tiger Clemenceau, he held in his virile hands the glory and honour of France.

And Konnixel? Collected, dour, watchful Konnixel stood brave and solitary against the thousand angry spears of Bosseux le Nèpe; hard-pressed, Konnixel fought to save his francs as Horatius battled for the bridge.

'I tell you, Mr Lepaon, I am *not* the Rockefeller Trust! Not one cent over 25,000 do you get out of me!'

'Monsieur, to offer less than 50,000 francs is the act of a practical joker!'

But it had to end. I was half-way through my translation of one of Lepaon's more ambitious speeches when Mr Konnixel, glancing at his wrist-watch, broke in to ask me, 'What time did I say we'd make that next place?' And when I told him, eleven-thirty, he said laconically, 'OK — 30,000!'

'Trente mille,' I said to Lepaon.

It was as if a code word had been uttered which the combatants had long since agreed between themselves. Lepaon, without a moment's hesitation, said quietly, 'It will do.'

Both men stood up. From a roll of thousand-franc notes — he carried them in hundreds — Konnixel plucked off thirty and laid them on the table. Lepaon swiftly counted them, nodded, and put them in his belt. With dignity the two men bowed and shook hands. From the audience came a murmur which sounded to me like applause.

On the way back to the car Konnixel pulled me close to him and with incredible swiftness transferred two more bundles of thousand-franc notes from his pocket to mine. He whispered, 'Give those to Isabelle — tell her it's for her dough!'

I executed this commission and rejoined him in the car. We shot away like a bomb from a three-inch mortar.

'I guess I had the best of *that* guy!' my employer said complacently, when we were clear of the village. 'Thought he could make a sucker out of Harry L. Konnixel, huh!' He was silent for a few kilometres: I never saw a man so happy. 'You know, Hushesson,' he said presently, accelerating to eighty-five mph, 'I *like* Eu-rope!'

A Question of Value

Everyone who visited the charming Seth-Pollocks took more than a casual glance at the picture they called 'The Peasant Girl' which hung beside the chimney-piece in their delicious drawing-room. For although it was a small canvas (only fifteen inches by twenty) and begrimed by many years in the soot of London and other cities it had kept its magic.

'It's the girl's face,' some of the visitors said, 'the expression in her eyes!'

'The colour!' others exclaimed. 'The rose and the mauve in her shawl; I've never seen anything like it in any other picture.'

'And the background is so marvellous!'

'The way he's posed her head!' said the knowing ones. 'You can tell from that alone that it was painted by a master.'

But kind, cosy little Janet Seth-Pollock, who herself possessed a creditable skill in oils, would have none of that.

'To tell you the truth, it's a very ordinary picture,' she always said, in the firm tone that comes naturally to the mothers of adolescent children, 'Before the First War you could have bought dozens like it for three or four hundred francs at little shops in Montmartre. Only, I *like* it. I do think it's very, very beautiful, and it's just perfect for that piece of wall. Whenever I feel at all depressed I just sit and look at that girl, and that smile of hers cheers me up in about two minutes. That's why I wouldn't part with it for a hundred pounds,' Janet always said.

Naturally, her husband talked about the picture in a slightly different way.

'You like it?' he said to his friends. 'Well, so do I, rather. No value, of course. To tell you the absolute truth I got it for thirty bob in a junk-shop in the Waterloo Road. But I do think the colour's good — and the treatment of the neck's rather pleasant, don't you think? Actually a friend of mine thought it *might* be a Vercoutère. But then,' said Mark Seth-Pollock with the faint, self-deriding smile which was part of his charm, 'people always do say these things!'

In truth, that was what Mark believed with nine-tenths of his brain. With the other tenth he thought that, by one of life's marvellous chances, he really had bought a Vercoutère for thirty shillings. For men are fools of the optimistic kind.

None the less he was startled — dramatically, splendidly startled — by the behaviour of Austin Bearwool, when Bearwool came to see him privately about the purchase of some house property in Leeds. Bearwool, who could never do business sitting down, was standing in the middle of the Seth-Pollock drawing-room, expatiating with his usual cultured gloom upon the recent decline in property values, when the picture caught his eye. He stopped, in the middle of a sentence, as if he had been struck by lightning.

'Wait a minute!' he said. 'Wait — a — minute!'

For a few moments he stared at 'The Peasant Girl' like a man transfixed. Then he moved closer. Then back. Then very close.

'Seth-Pollock,' he demanded, 'where did you get this thing?'

Mark told him. 'Do you think it's good? I know you're interested in pictures.'

'I am interested,' said Bearwool slowly, 'in this particular picture.'

'Holkis thinks it's a bit like Vercoutère's style.'

'For once,' Bearwool said impressively, 'Holkis was talking something like sense.'

Then Janet came in.

'Darling,' Mark said, in a voice which he believed was entirely free from excitement, 'Mr Bearwool thinks this might *possibly* be a Vercoutère after all.'

'Oh, nonsense, Mr Bearwool! Years ago I used to turn out that sort of thing myself. Of course my pictures didn't *look* like old masters because the paint was clean. I'm afraid lunch is going to be five minutes late — Ethel's having some technical trouble with the gravy. Darling, give Mr Bearwool another cigarette.'

But Bearwool was in no mood for smoking.

'Tell me, Mrs Seth-Pollock,' he said severely, 'do you read the *Collectors' Quarterly*?'

'Well — not every day.'

'Then perhaps you don't know the story of La Moissonneuse? Vercoutère did it in his middle — his finest — period. About eighty years after his death — just when his work was coming into fashion with collectors — the Marquess de Sansôme bought it for the equivalent of £250. Or *thought* he did. Years later, when the picture had been sold to Erhart the American banker for a much larger sum, it was found that Sansôme had been palmed off with a clever copy.'

'How did they know?' Mark asked.

'By the girl's thumb! It's a very queer thing — Vercoutère had a certain idiosyncrasy in painting the human hand, it appears in every known portrait he ever did. He *always* made the thumb of the left hand unnaturally long in proportion to the fingers. No one knows why — some critics think that his own left thumb may have been very long, and that he painted thumbs that way so as to pretend to himself that it wasn't a deformity. Anyway, the long left thumb is a sort of signature to a genuine Vercoutère.'

'Then that settles it!' Janet said cheerfully. She was standing close to 'The Peasant Girl'. 'This thumb's in perfect proportion.'

'My dear Mrs Seth-Pollock, you — as a painter — can hardly have failed to notice one thing about that picture! Look, stand here! Now, can't you see that the part of the canvas where the left hand is has been faked up? The surface is quite different. The thing must have got damaged at some time — stained with damp, probably — and some competent artist was set to paint it over and put in a new hand. I should say it was done less than fifty years ago. If you cleaned away that work you'd probably find the original hand underneath — and that might be very, very interesting.'

Mark asked, 'Would the cleaning be an expensive job?'

'Well, fairly expensive. It would need an expert. But when you think that Hugo Erhart, junior, has advertised an offer of fifty thousand almighty dollars for the genuine Moissonneuse . . .'

'But darling,' Janet said when Bearwool had gone, 'do we really *need* all that money?'

'*Need*! My dear, who *couldn't* do with fifty thousand dollars?'

'I mean, we've got this absolutely darling house, and a very nice car —'

'— which rattles abominably and eats up oil —'

'And we've got Ethel, and the children are all at quite respectable schools.'

'My darling girl,' Mark said, running his finger down the Ws in the telephone directory, 'I do feel perfectly delighted that you are satisfied with the few poor comforts which I've been able to provide for you. But to talk of fifty thousand dollars as if it were neither here nor there —!'

'But darling, 'The Peasant Girl' *was* a birthday present to me. And I do rather love her!'

Mark, however, had found the number he was looking for and his attention was already occupied by the telephone. '. . . Mr Wallright? My name's Seth-Pollock. My friend Mr Bearwool has recommended me to ask you if you can help me. I have an old picture which needs a certain amount of restoration; it's rather nice work, and Mr Bearwool thinks it's worth very expert treatment . . . What? . . . Oh, I'm sorry, that's a pity . . . Well, thank you, yes, I expect I'll call you again then . . .' Ringing off, he turned to Janet gloomily. 'He's leaving London tonight — special job in Edinburgh, several weeks!'

'Oh,' she said loyally, 'what perfectly sickening luck! Look, I wonder if I could find someone myself . . .'

The someone she found — after telephoning a friend of her Slade days — was Mr Hawkills. She expected a grave and elderly man, like the doctor in advertisements, but the one who came was in his early twenties, broad-shouldered, flannel-trousered, with the smiling confidence of a recent Cambridge degree.

'I hate to call any job simple,' he told her, 'but this one looks to me like a push-over. You can see with your naked eye that this bit of over-painting isn't twenty years old. All the rest of the canvas looks in very sound condition, so I can't see there's likely to be any very great complications. Of course, I'll go carefully — I'll start with a very weak solution of acetone in rectified turpentine.'

'It's a lovely picture, isn't it!' Janet said.

'Yes — yes, I suppose it is. To tell you the honest truth, I'm not much of a judge of art. I look at pictures more from the chemist's angle, if you know what I mean. But I do assure you,' he added quickly, 'I won't do anything to hurt the original pigment. I really can promise you a perfectly scientific job.'

'What more,' said Janet, 'can I ask than that!'

The confidence of Mr Hawkills was not unjustified. A week later he brought the picture back and proudly unwrapped it before her.

'It was really quite easy going,' he confessed, '— as I thought it would be. The new pigment just tumbled away. Of course, I did it very carefully, all the same — if you try to work fast on this sort of thing, it's terribly easy to pick up some of the original paint. Now you see *why* it was painted over? That long triangular mark on the hand — the thing must have been dropped sometime when it was being moved about, it may have hit the corner of a table or something. So some fellow filled in the crack, and painted the filling over, and he thought that looked rather a mess, so he went the whole hog and painted a new hand.'

'I see.'

'So now you've got the thing exactly as it was originally painted. The only trouble, as you can see, is that in the bit I've restored the paint's clean and the rest of it, of course, isn't. I could go over the whole canvas and clean it up, then you'd have it uniform. Only that wasn't the job you gave me.'

'No, of course it wasn't! Well, I shall have to ask my husband if he really wants that done as well. Really, I do congratulate you. I think you've done a *very* skilful job.'

To be praised by a woman is always agreeable. To be praised by Janet Seth-Pollock was ecstasy. With Janet's cheque in his pocket, her kind words in his ears, her smile bathing him like the Italian sun, Mr Hawkills did not notice that she was sending him away at half-past four in the afternoon without thinking of offering him tea.

It was not till he had gone that she examined the picture with any concentration. But concentration was unnecessary. Anyone would have seen at a glance that in the restored left hand the thumb was unnaturally long.

It was Ethel's day out, and Mark, who was dining with business friends, would not be back before eleven. Janet was therefore at leisure. She went without hurry to the cupboard in her bedroom where she stored the things one keeps away from children, souvenirs of her girlhood, old, beloved books, a manual called *La Technique du Peintre-Faussaire*. The satchel where she kept her oils was on the upper shelf, untouched for more than a year. An old delight returned to her with the smell of the pigment; and soon she felt again the sensuous pleasure which a skilled craftsman gets from his tools, as she came to handle her brushes, her old palette-knife.

'Look, I'm afraid I've been rather indiscreet,' Bearwool said to Mark on the telephone. 'I dropped a hint — it was only a hint — to a fellow in·my club that a man I knew might *possibly* be in possession of La Moissonneuse. And the fool's been chattering, I'm afraid.'

'Oh?'

'Yes, and I'm afraid the rumour's leaked through into American collecting circles. And the result is that Hugo Erhart's agent is on his way over now — in the *Queen Mary* . . . Look, I do hope you'll at least let him have a look at it.'

'He can come over and look at it all day,' said Mark, a little frostily. 'I do hope he enjoys it. I personally think it's a very beautiful picture. Now that the over-painting's been cleaned off there's only one thing wrong with it.'

'You mean —?'

'The girl's left thumb is in perfect proportion to the rest of the hand.'

But Janet that afternoon was entertaining an old school friend in her delicious drawing-room.

'To tell you the truth, it's a very ordinary picture,' she was saying. 'Only I adore it. I do think it's very, very lovely, and it's just perfect for that piece of wall.'

The End of Innocence

The school porter, no respecter of junior masters, simply put his head round the door and said, 'Mr Saunders wants Collinson'.

'Collinson!' The master called mechanically, 'Housemaster'.

The boy, Hugh Collinson, abandoning the books spread on his desk, got up and left the room. He went down the corridor, across Founder's Court, and through the pillared lobby known as the Forum. Here, on the games board, the teams for this afternoon's two matches had been posted, with his own name sixth among the forwards in the Second Fifteen. These lists he had seen already. The small card pinned by itself in the top right-hand corner had been there since the previous Saturday, but he paused to stare at it as a girl will stare at an engagement ring in a jeweller's window. 'J. D. Maskin is awarded his 2nd XV Colours.' In those few words was the hope and almost the promise of Paradise. For it was not impossible — it was even likely — that in a few hours' time the card would be replaced by another, where instead of 'J. D. Maskin' the name would be 'H. Collinson'.

The wind which blew about these buildings came at him like a damp lash as he turned the corner by the fives courts; the morning mist of late November still lay morosely across the scarred turf of Upper Field, and along the asphalt path which led to Saunders's the leafless trees dripped maliciously on his bare head and neck. But a mind glowing with the thought of coming splendour was impervious to the stock discomforts of a winter term. He had entered the house and even reached the door of his housemaster's study before he was attacked with a faint anxiety: why this urgent summons? Something to do with work, or had he carelessly broken one of the minor rules?

The blow fell swiftly.

'Oh, yes, Collinson, there's a wire from your father. He's coming down.'

'Coming down, sir? When, sir?'

'Today. He wants you to have lunch with him in the town.'

'Lunch? What time, sir?'

'Time?' Mr Saunders picked up the telegram again. 'His train gets in at 2.15. That's going to be rather a late lunch for you. But I expect Miss Brier will give you something to keep you going.'

The boy stood still, as if incredulous.

'Only — the match, sir. It means I can't play.'

'Yes, you must let O'Connor know. Yes, it's bad luck, it's a pity. But I doubt if it's going to be much of a game, anyway. Torrington are pretty weak this year, they won't be sending much of a side.'

O'Connor, the Captain of Football, had his study in the Science Block. When he heard Hugh's news he was not well pleased.

'That'll mean putting Turner in,' he said, 'or Scollard. Scollard's got no weight and Turner's got no wind. Really, can't you train your parent not to do this sort of thing?'

'He's never done it before.'

'Did he not know there would be a match on?'

'He should have — it was in my Sunday letter. I'm awfully sorry, O'Connor.'

'Perhaps,' O'Connor persisted, 'he's one of these otherwise admirable people who think that rugger doesn't matter?'

'Well, he was tried himself for Cambridge.'

'I beg his pardon. This must be a sudden brainstorm. OK — that's all.'

But Hugh, twisting out of the door, was halted by a surge of despair. He said, turning back: 'O'Connor, I really am most fearfully sorry. I mean, I've been longing for this match all week. I've wanted to play in it more than any other this term.'

With the bored, impatient eyes of a large employer, O'Connor looked up from his work again. 'How so?'

(But he knew. He was nearly nineteen.)

'Well, it's the last Second Fifteen match, for one thing.'

'Indeed?' O'Connor reached for the fixture list. 'Correct, dear boy, correct! And it should have been your last public appearance this term. A solemn thought! Food for further meditation.'

Those final words of O'Connor's, like sparks pricked from the ash of a dead fire, went on recurring in Hugh's brain throughout the three-mile walk to the station. According to rule, Colours were awarded after a match only to one who had played in it; but there had been one instance — in Hugh's first term — when a regular player in the First Fifteen, missing the final match through injury, had been given his First Colours afterwards as if he had played. Would

O'Connor recall that precedent? Could it possibly have been in his mind when he talked of 'further meditation'?

The hoardings where the trams began, the long row of dismal houses reaching to the gasworks — his eyes received these images like a film imperfeclty sensitized. O'Connor was said by people further up the school to be a reasonable human being. Had there been something in his face — some fellow-feeling?

The train was late. Waiting on the platform, he tried to summon some filial sentiment, but it was hard for him, absorbed in one department of his life, to think of someone who belonged to another. He had for his father the unemotional affection which soldiers feel towards a sound commander: the man was what a father should be, upright and reliable, one who would never embarrass you in public by pretentious behaviour or in private by sentimentality. Like their pleasant home at Barnet, he was a fixture one looked forward to at the end of term. Just now — though Hugh was sure so rational a person had a worthy excuse for this excursion — Mr Collinson supplied no need of his son's.

'But how presentable!' he thought, as the figure of his father appeared among the crowd debouching from the incoming train. 'How decently he's dressed, how workmanlike in shape for a man of forty-two!' And then he thought, 'He's ill or something — there's something wrong.'

'Hullo, Father!'

'Hullo — how nice of you to come and meet me! Sorry I couldn't give you more notice; things wanted a lot of fitting in.'

They went to the station hotel, where a formidable waitress said that lunch was over, really — they didn't expect to do lunches after two; well, yes, there might be some cold — she would try the chef and see what he said.

'That's a pity — I was hoping to give you a decent blowout.' With unwonted nervousness Mr Collinson sat and crumbled his bread. 'Well, how are things? You hadn't anything special on this afternoon, I hope?'

'This afternoon? No, Father. Well, there was a match against Torrington, but they're not a lot of use this year, it wouldn't have been much of a game.'

'Oh . . . Work going all right — as far as you can tell?'

'I think so — fairly. I was sixth in the maths test — I think I told you.'

'The maths test? Oh yes, good! Yes, I used to be not too bad at maths myself.'

The plates of cold beef slammed in front of them, with a dish of mashed potato scraped from the leavings of more punctual diners and a grudging bonus of Worcester sauce — even these were different enough from the cuisine of Saunders's to have counted, on some other occasion, as the symbols of celebration. At least one had a napkin here, and the ginger wine was comforting. But today the faint shyness which had always coloured Hugh's relations with his father seemed to have gripped them both like a Siberian frost; and he answered Mr Collinson's laboured questions almost as shortly as a prisoner under cross-examination.

'. . . Yes, we've had two lectures . . . Well, they were both rather boring . . . One about birds . . . Well, I'm afraid I was asleep.'

Not that his answers appeared to matter: the least perceptive boy could have seen that Mr Collinson, with his mind a hundred miles away, was only trying to break the intolerable silences. Unused as he was to leading an adult in conversation, Hugh made one effort himself.

'How is Mother?'

'Oh, she — she's very fit. And the girls too. I had a letter from Alison yesterday, they both seem to be getting on all right.'

Yes, something was very wrong — it must be to do with business, Hugh imagined. Of his father's working life he knew nothing, except that Collinson & Fairford were an agency for American appliances. He had, however, learnt that a company of any kind can suddenly fail — the father of Tony Salter, in his House, had run a boot-polish factory, it had gone bust overnight and Tony had left at the next half-term. If something like that had happened to Father, why didn't he come across with the news and be done with it? Hugh was ready to face the situation: he would get a job — sell papers if he had to — and keep himself going till he was old enough for the RAF.

'This place gives me the willies!' Mr Collinson said suddenly. The waitress had brought the bill for 11s. 6d. 'Let's go and find some other place for coffee — somewhere we can talk.'

They walked in silence down the High Street and turned into Pansy's Parlour. Coffee was only mid-morning, the spectacled woman who seemed to be Pansy said: well, people didn't ask for tea, not usually, much before four: she would make them, however, a pot of tea.

With his hands folded on the table, Mr Collinson stared at his son's House tie as if the green and magenta bands were a message which had to be deciphered.

'Look, Hugh, I was going to write to you,' he started hesitantly, 'but I thought it might be better if I came and saw you. I've got some news which I'm afraid is going to be a bit of a shock.'

'Yes, Father.'

'There are things you probably haven't had any reason to think about up till now, and really I'd rather you still didn't have to think about them. But — well, it can't be helped. You're — let me see — how old now?'

'Sixteen next month.' ('For Pete's sake,' Hugh thought, 'the Old Man isn't going to tell me the Facts of Life!')

Again, Mr Collinson damped his lips.

'Well, now, look, I think you'd agree that things have always gone pretty well at home. We've been quite a jolly party, I think. I think you and the girls have always had a fairly decent time — I mean, you've been reasonably happy.'

'Yes, Father.'

'Well, that's the way I'd like things to go on. And mind you, I think they will. Only — life doesn't always work out exactly the way one hopes. Look, it's like this. Your mother and I, as you know, we've always got along pretty well. We've had you youngsters to think about, and that has meant working in partnership, and we've managed it — well, I suppose as well as the next couple. I mean, we've been jolly good friends, your mother and I — we still are, for that matter.'

The woman, Pansy, was suddenly beside them.

'I could give you some scones,' she said, '. . . Oh, all right, I see — just the tea! Would you like to pay me now?'

Hugh watched his father fumbling over change and tip in a way that was quite unlike his usual performance. He gazed after the woman as she went off to the back regions, as if, in that homely figure, he might find some safety. She, at least, was real: and the beaded curtain was real, and the menu cards in their stands on the tables. His father's voice, now flowing as steadily as if from a recording, had lost all reality.

'. . . to understand that you haven't got to worry about your own immediate future, I've put aside the money that's wanted to get you through school, and through Cambridge as well. All that side has been properly tied up, so neither you nor your mother will have anything to worry about.'

Upon these words the boy's brain superimposed the ones which had come before. *Jolly good friends . . . still are, for that matter.* But surely, but surely —

'You see, one has to be honest, one has to face facts. Your mother and I are both older than when we married — well, we're practically middle-aged now, I suppose. And at different times of life one needs — well — different sorts of companionship. At least, some of us do. As I say, the home's going to go on, you'll find everything exactly the same as when you get back for the holidays, except that I — I myself — I shan't be there. Of course, Alison and Joan will be there just the same. And then, later on, I hope you'll come and spend at any rate a few days of each holiday with me. With me and Eileen.'

'Eileen?'

'I think, you know, you'll like her. I think you'll get to like her very much. Of course she's — she's a different *kind* of person from your mother. She's — for one thing — she's — well, younger. But — she's a jolly sort of person, and tremendously understanding. Oh, there's another thing I meant to say. There's almost bound to be something or other in the papers about this. It may miss you altogether, but I thought I'd better just warn you. It's one of the most unfortunate features of this sort of business that it has to be so public. But, in fact, it's very likely that that aspect won't concern you at all. I don't suppose the fellows at school read anything but the sports pages, do they, as a rule?'

'No. I suppose they don't.'

Abruptly, as if he had lost the last pages of his brief, Mr Collinson pushed back his chair.

'Well, now, as I am down here, and as we've had a perfectly filthy lunch, I wonder if there's anything you'd like to do. Would there be anything on at the local cinema?'

'Actually, we're not supposed to go in term.'

'We couldn't override that?'

'Well, thank you most awfully, but I ought really to get back to the House, if that's OK with you. There's — there's some work I should have done — I shan't get another chance. It's got to be done before Monday morning school.'

Nothing in Mr Collinson's face showed his relief. He said, 'Well, that's a pity. I'm sorry. But you know the form, of course — I won't try to tempt you . . . Well, in that case I suppose I may as well get the 4.10.'

He was still talking, and Hugh was still trying to listen, while they sat waiting for the train.

'I shall be writing to you — there's a good deal I meant to say, only one can't say it all at once. Of course, naturally, you'll be thinking over this business a good deal. And there are things you won't understand — not at present. Later on — when you're older — you'll get a better sort of general view of things. What you want, for now, is to try and not worry too much about what's happened . . .'

The actual parting was brought into manageable shape by the offer and acceptance of three pound-notes: this was a drill in which they were practised (though the third pound had no precedent) and therefore grateful to them both. Thereafter there was fuss over getting a seat, for the train had come in already crowded, and only a quick handshake through the window was possible.

So that was over, Collinson thought, spreading his *Evening Standard*, wriggling to settle his shoulders between those of two huge north-countrymen; and Hugh would never know what it had cost him to make this journey and break the news in person. The boy had taken it well, he thought — though with an apathy which was rather perplexing. At that age, perhaps, a child accepted the changes of life more equably than adults imagined; the presence at home of a father — one had to face it — was less important to a fifteen-year-old than things like football and getting on with one's friends.

A queer boy; not unlovable but hard to understand; undoubtedly a trifle young — except in physique — for a lad of his years. . . . As the train screamed through Kettering a faint malaise returned like the flavour of an anxious dream, joined with the image of Hugh's curiously empty eyes, the fixity of his cold-looking mouth, against the stripes on the parlour walls; it persisted when the lights of the northern suburbs were crowding past the misted carriage windows. But uppermost in Collinson's mind was a sense of accomplishment; of having performed a formidable task with courage and also with some skill.

By then the boy himself was back at school; where the House Matron, accepting his plea of a headache had given him a glass of

water with an aspirin and told him to go immediately to bed. There
he lay with the light still on, his face composed, rehearsing the
argument which he had drawn like a cloak about his mind on his way
out from the town; that the situation was not abnormal, that at least
two people here in Saunders's had fathers who lived with someone
else instead of those people's mothers. . . . And there Tod Maxwell
found him.

'Hugh, you blister!' It was essential in Tod's love for his closest
friends that he roared at them like a Sandhurst instructor. 'What
d'you think you're doing, sneaking off to bed?'

'Get out!' Hugh got up, still clutching his glass of water.

'Hi, Hugh, what's the matter with you! Haven't you heard?'

'Heard what?'

'The news — they've given you your Colours.'

And then even Tod drew back; for the white passion in Hugh's
face was something he had never seen or dreamed of. He could
scarcely believe it was Hugh Collinson, the shy, the diffident Hugh,
who shouted, almost screamed at him, 'Who wants their bloody
Colours! Get out of here, will you! I said, *get out!*'

How I rose to be an Australian Shoeshine Boy

In my theatre-acting days I used to forget now and then about the matinées. So they said I ought to try another vocation.

'You might get work in Ireland,' they said.

'There's a place called Ballydoggin,' a gentleman in North Ireland said, 'they might have a job for you there.'

At Ballydoggin a gentleman on the railroad station said, 'You might try the constabulary. They're short of cops in this town.'

The police sergeant didn't ask me about my education, or things like that. 'Have you got people depending on you?' — that was what he asked.

'Little wee bairns?' he asked.

'Or a darlin' wee wife?' he asked.

'Or a sweet old widowed mother?'

I told him I was alone in the world, and he said, 'You'll need a uniform.'

'Now this,' he said, trying a tunic on me, 'was Sullivan's. He was down the canal way last week, trying to pacify the boys at The Old Flag.'

It was tight under the arms.

'Try Jimmy Coster's,' he said. 'Jimmy won't be needing it now, poor lad. He was interferin' with a bank hold-up, and there was three of them to one of him.'

It might have been made for me, that tunic. And a pair of blue serge pants that Constable Torrens had been wearing the night he tried to stop an old lady on the council estate from arguing with her husband, they fitted me a treat as well.

'Pluck,' the sergeant said, 'pluck an' anitchitive, that's what makes a Class cop. We're going to be proud of you, my lad,' the sergeant said. 'And by the way,' he said, 'as you go down O'Mailey Street you'd best shoot an eye at Number 48. That's Mr James's house, and he's the Mayor of this town, and he's away with Mrs James in the country. We wouldn't want anything pinched from Mr James's house,' the sergeant said.

I made a note of that. If you want to get on, I always say to young chaps, you need to pay attention to what people say.

In that town they turn off the street lights at midnight to save the rates, O'Mailey Street was like the inside of a railroad tunnel and I couldn't read the numbers. But a pair of gentlemen were sitting in a big car beside the road, and I put the question to them.

'Why, this is Number 48,' they said, 'this one beside you here.'

'You aren't by any chance Mr James,' I asked the biggest of these gentlemen.

'Well, not exactly,' he said. 'I'm Mr Healey, and my friend here is Mr O'Brien.'

'I just wondered,' I said, 'because Mr James is supposed to be away in the country with his old lady. I thought perhaps he'd changed his plans.'

'Well, that's odd,' Mr Healey said, 'because I saw a light flashing in the house not five minutes ago.'

It's little things you overhear like that which act as clues for a keen young cop.

'I'm going to look into this!' I said.

I went and rang at the front door, but no one came, so I went round the back. No answer there either, and the whole place seemed to be bolted up. But I wasn't satisfied. I wanted to have a look around inside, and I tried my pocket-knife to see if maybe the lock of the back door would give — it didn't feel to me like much of a lock.

'You want a better tool than that,' Mr Healey said. He'd come after me to see how I was going on. 'Tim!' he said — because Mr O'Brien had come to see how *he* was going on, 'See if you can find that thing in the car I use for taking off the plugs.'

You couldn't have wanted a better tool than that was. And a neat little flash-lamp Mr Healey had as well, and Mr O'Brien had one too.

'It won't do to put the house lights on,' Mr Healey said, when we were all in the hall.

'Why, surely, that would be like calling *Peekabo* to any chap that's lurking inside,' Mr O'Brien said.

So he went upstairs with nothing but the flash-lamps to show the way.

There was no one around that we could see. But in the main bedroom there was something Mr Healey said I ought to look into, and that was a big tin box standing under the bed.

'Now that's the sort of place people keep their jewels and such,' Mr Healey told me.

'And that's not right!' Mr O'Brien said.

'It looks a safe enough place to me,' I said, meaning to learn from these gentlemen what I could.

'Safe?' Mr Healey said. 'Tim, give me that tool again!' he said.

And then I saw those gentlemen were one hundred per cent right! Why, a child could have opened that box, the way Mr Healey showed me how. And when I saw the diamond rings and the pearl necklaces and all the other gewgaws, why, I could have laughed and cried to think of Mr James's foolishness, trusting all Mrs James's spangles to what was no better than a candy-box.

'We can't leave this stuff the way it is,' Mr Healey said.

'Wouldn't be right,' Mr O'Brien said.

'Better hide it somewhere out of sight,' Mr Healey said.

'Put it in one of the grips we got in the car,' Mr O'Brien said.

'And then put the grip where no house-breakers would see it,' Mr Healey said.

Mr Healey and Mr O'Brien found when they went to look they had three big grips in their car. So besides Mrs James's trinkets we put in some silver sporting cups we found in one of the rooms downstairs, and some silver forks and spoons, and a little old-fashioned clock, and a pile of other things a house-breaker might be apt to lay his hands on. The trouble was to find somewhere safe to put the grips.

'They might go in the closet under the stairs,' I said.

'House-breakers always look in closets,' Mr Healey said.

'Or down in the coal cellar.'

'The coal cellar's where house-breakers begin,' Mr O'Brien said. Not in a superior way. Just putting one wise.

'If they weren't so heavy I'd take them back to the police station,' I said.

'Aye, they're heavy!' Mr Healey said.

'You might borrow Mr Healey's car,' Mr O'Brien said.

'But I've got to finish my beat,' I said.

'Then why don't *I* take them to the station?' Mr Healey said.

'It was a lucky break for me,' I said, as we were putting the grips in the car, 'meeting such gentlemen like you my first time on duty.'

'Why, it was a nice break for us!' Mr Healey said.

'You do get young cops that haven't the sense to cooperate,' Mr O'Brien said.

Nine o'clock in the morning, I was back reporting for duty like the sergeant had told me.

'All correct on beat?' the sergeant asked.

'All OK, sergeant,' I said.

'You took a good look at Mr James's house?'

'Lucky I did!' I said.

And I told him about Mr James's foolishness, and the way I'd used my block to put things right.

'I'll just find out where the Duty Constable's put those grips,' I said.

Then I noticed the sergeant had come over queer. The sergeant's face had changed to the colour of a plum just getting ripe, he was shaking like a road-drill operator, and making little clutching movements with his hands and little noises like a baby with a bone stuck in its throat.

'Hot in here, sergeant!' I said.

He didn't seem to come at me on his feet, it was more as if somebody had turned the force of gravity on its side. And that worked on me as well, for no legs of mine never moved me the rate I found myself outside and half way down the street.

Funny thing, back at the railroad station I came on the same gentleman I saw there the day before.

'What do you want me to tell you now?' he said.

'The place that's farthest off from Ballydoggin,' I said.

'That would be Sydney, New South Wales,' the gentleman said.

Duel at Mont Lipaux

The annual race on the Mont Lipaux circuit was discontinued three or four years ago. As a spokesman of the French police delicately put it: 'The design of the course paid too little regard to the question of competitors' safety.'

For me the motor-car is just a pleasurable means of transport, and I had scarcely heard of the goings-on at Mont Lipaux before the summer of 1952. It was through Trevor St Austell, of all people, that the place became more to me than a name on those pages of a newspaper that I never read. He telephoned from York one evening towards the end of May. 'You may not remember me,' he said. 'We've been out of touch so long. We were together at Catterick in forty-three.'

But of course I remembered him. The hesitant, faintly pedantic voice brought the whole man before me — the heavy spectacles, the prematurely greying hair, the forehead that remained anxious even when the sensitive mouth was smiling.

'You sent me a Christmas card in forty-eight,' he added, as if this would identify and exonerate him. 'It was your own design for a theatre at Shoreditch. I admired it greatly. It was all that a theatre should be.'

When I had convinced him that I knew who he was, and did not consider his trunk call a gross invasion of my privacy, he came by careful stages to his purpose. He was going, a fortnight later, to the South of France, on business of some kind. Would I come with him as his guest?

'I mean,' he said, 'we could stop on the way at Chartres or somewhere. I thought there might be things you wanted to see, professionally or otherwise. It might not be a total loss. I mean, two bachelors together, it makes travelling less of a bore. You still are a bachelor?'

'Yes.'

'Of course I realize that this is a most fearful nerve. You must have hundreds of more interesting things to do.'

I hadn't. My own branch of architecture was suffering a lean period. And I remembered that at Catterick Trevor's conversation had always been stimulating. With the impulsiveness that the telephone promotes in me I gratefully accepted his invitation.

'By the way,' I asked, 'how do we go?'

'Well, I thought we'd use my car, if that's all right with you.'

'Why, that would be perfect,' I said.

But I was puzzled that he should own such a thing. At Catterick we had been caused to handle vehicles of many kinds, and Trevor had loathed them all. He was, by trade, a don at some northern university — a classical historian. In spirit he belonged to the eighteenth century, and I had always imagined that he regarded even the steam engine as a retrograde invention. 'What can you see when you're being whisked past things?' he had often demanded bitterly.

His clumsiness at the wheel had driven instructors almost to insanity. And once he had said to me: 'The thing I must look forward to, at the end of this war, is never even sitting in one of those damned contraptions again.'

And now, it seemed, even he was trundling with the times.

In imagination, I saw the kind of car we should travel in: an elderly tourer, immensely solid and slow, with a complicated hood, a puritanically upright windscreen, the spare wheel strapped to the side. This image was distinct in my mind when — at the very moment he had promised — Trevor rang the bell of my house in Highgate. And he himself, in civilian clothes, conformed exactly with my mental picture. Not so the car which had brought him.

It sat, as it were, low in the water: a two-seater of prodigious length, its shape reminding me a little of a greyhound going over hurdles. The space assigned to driver and mate was small — a narrow trough like that in a dug-out canoe. The rest, in a menacing curve which almost reached the ground, was bonnet; and I trembled to think how many and what size of cylinders that vast prow concealed.

'This?' I asked. 'This is yours? We travel in this?'

'It's not as comfortless as it looks,' he said apologetically. 'One sits on about a foot deep of rubber foam — and the rear pit takes a fair amount of luggage. Of course, if you feel you'd rather not . . .'

'You drive this thing?' I persisted.

'Why, yes.'

'On the road? I thought this sort of missile was only allowed at Goodwood.'

'Oh, it's perfectly legal,' he said. 'They don't race these things on ordinary tracks.'

Yes, he drove it. And as we flicked through the city traffic, as the needle fingered ninety on the Dover road, I began to learn something new to me in the craft of driving. My own car has some pace, which at times, when I am building in several parts of the country, I make use of. But I should never dare to drive as fast as he did. Nor could I do so — as he did — with perfect safety. He was handling this leopard with a superb authority, using with a precise knowledge its brilliant acceleration, calling on its Herculean brakes so shrewdly that when we needed to fall in behind the chain of lorries there was no jerk, only a sense of speed being gently cast away.

I said, as the shyness of reunion thawed: 'You know, I'd never thought of you as a motorist.'

'No?' Most of his mind seemed to be elsewhere. 'I took it up again,' he said vaguely. 'Not long ago — early last year.'

'What made you?'

The question seemed to worry him. But he said at length: 'Well, I don't like being unreasonably bad at things. I was always useless at games — that couldn't be helped, I've got a dicky heart among other things. But I felt it was silly to be defeated by things like pedals and levers, when a perfect fool like Miles Hudson could manage them.'

'Oh, Hudson — yes, I remember him.'

'Do you . . . ? So I got myself retaught, by one of my own history pupils. And then I thought I'd get this thing — I had it made for me by the Watts-Leaver people.'

'And now you enjoy it?'

'No, I can't pretend I do, really.'

'Do you make these business trips often?'

'No.' Again he was remote and hesitant. 'I did this turn last year, I wanted to — look over the ground. Strictly, I shouldn't have called it business when I spoke to you on the phone.'

'It's some sort of research, you mean?'

'No. No, it's just something I thought of doing . . .'

Later, in France, as the road to Amiens tore away beneath us, Trevor said abruptly: 'So you remember Hudson?'

'Yes. I didn't care for him. I ran into him again, just after the war. He'd married then, but it hadn't altered him.'

'No, it wouldn't,' he said, with his teeth together.

'It shocked me, rather,' I said.

'What — that he'd married?'

'That he'd married this particular girl. We'd both known her — she lived near Barnard Castle — Anne Eppingham. Her people were very hospitable, I used to go and play tennis there.'

'Yes,' he said, rather absently. 'I knew her. I used to go there too.'

With that, we banished the subject — or so I thought. For myself, I did not consider Hudson worth our breath: an animal of splendid size and appearance, he had belonged to that small minority who found the army a perfect vehicle for their egotism — one merely thanked heaven, on demobilization, that one need never associate with such people again.

But from Anne, as I had known her, my thoughts would not depart so easily. In the great and hideous house of her father she had always seemed a stranger: a creature so small and framed so perfectly, of such humour and gentleness. There had been, at that time, a score of pretty girls within our tennis-party range — nature furnishes that embroidery to military encampments. I had forgotten all the others; but Anne I had not forgotten.

Talking desultorily about our jobs we had left Amiens and another hundred kilometres behind when Trevor said, as if his thoughts had been linked to mine: 'Yes, I saw Anne again, early last year. She and Hudson gave a party. They were celebrating something or other — some triumph of Hudson's.'

'Was she just the same?' I asked

'More or less, to look at.'

'Happy, did you think?'

He waited to collect his thoughts before he said: 'I asked her that, when I got her alone for about two minutes. All she said was: "When you're married you've just got to be." Of course it was a stupid question — I could see for myself she was almost in tears. Hudson had been treating her like dirt all evening.'

That picture was clear enough to me. And I said with a sudden fury: 'Whatever made her marry him? She had all of us to pick from.'

'It happens that way,' he answered soberly. 'The best fall for the worst, the gentlest women take on the toughest males. Or it may be she thought she could civilize him — some of them marry from a cock-eyed sense of vocation.'

His face remained as calm, as contemplative, as it had been all the way from London. But I saw that his hands had tightened on the wheel, and for the first time the car swerved a little.

I said, lamely: 'There's nothing anybody can do.'

'Perhaps not. But I took the liberty of having a word with Hudson — I told him what I thought of him.'

'Did that make any impression?'

'It made him laugh. You remember how he laughs? I think it's almost the most repellent thing about him. And Anne has to listen to that laugh all day long.'

At my own choice we spent that night at Poitiers. Trevor proved a capable as well as an indulgent host: he was shrewd about food and wine; he taught me, next morning, more about the church of Ste Radegonde that I could teach him. In the afternoon we wandered about the Roman ruins nearby, and Trevor talked of the builders of that place as a humorous squire talks of his neighbours.

Yet I was not totally at ease. There were silences in which his mind left me altogether, and then, from a dozen nervous tricks — a needless cough, the incessant fingering of his tie — I deduced that he had come on this excursion to escape some deep anxiety.

At one point I must have betrayed the fact that his distracted behaviour troubled me. For after one long period of silence he said impulsively: 'You know, I'm most terribly grateful to you. For coming along, I mean. I know I'm a hopeless companion.'

'On the contrary —'

'But I did need somebody. I couldn't have done this trip alone.'

We left it at that. But a little later he said, with increased nervousness: 'Look, I wonder if you'd like to stay at this place and let me go on alone. There's a lot here for you to see. I'd pick you up on the way back — on Friday.'

I told him that by lunch-time next day — when we had arranged to go on — I should have seen all that I specially wanted to see. The rest could wait — I should prefer to stick with him. But this brought a fresh embarrassment.

'I know this sounds idiotic,' he said, 'but I want to push on tonight. It's a sort of engagement. There's plenty of time really, but I keep thinking of things that might go wrong. This place makes me restless, I don't know why.'

A hasty adjustment was needed. I could not say with the smallest appearance of honesty that Poitiers was boring me. Equally, I could not let a man in his state of mind go on alone. By degrees I persuaded him that I had come on this trip first for the enjoyment of his society.

We returned to the hotel to pack our things — he still unselfishly protesting — and shortly after dinner we were on the road again . . .

The Watts-Leaver, as he had said, offered more comfort than one would have supposed: in patches I slept, dreaming that a boat I was sailing in had been caught by a wind which bore it high over trees and hills and cities. That illusion infected the intervals of wakefulness. In the faint light from the dash I could just see Trevor's face as that of a carved figurehead; and it seemed to me that he and the car were a single being, a sweeping force, inanimate.

Once, sleepily, I asked him, 'Trevor, are you all right?'

He did not reply.

Daylight came in a long valley walled by steep escarpments, with a rocky stream threading from side to side of the road. Ahead, from a wilderness of pine, rose formidable hills. We stopped for coffee outside a small *auberge* in a place called Baisereau-la-fontaine, where Trevor appeared to be known and welcome.

At that meal we scarcely spoke: I was still sleepy and he pre-occupied. But when it was finished he said, with the emphasis of one who has come painfully to a firm decision: 'Well, I'm leaving you here — I hope to pick you up again tomorrow night. You don't mind? There's not much to do, but it's good walking country, and these people cook quite well.'

Without waiting for me to answer, he returned to the car, fished out my bag and took it into the inn. I heard him in conversation with the *patronne* and presently he emerged to tell me that he had fixed my room.

At that stage I was shy of asking questions; but I screwed myself to say: 'You're sure you're going to be all right?'

'Why?' he demanded.

'I wondered if you were perfectly fit.'

'For what?'

'Well, I don't know what sort of appointment you're going to. I just thought you might be tired — I thought you might need some sort of support.'

We were standing near the car, and he went on staring at the bonnet as if there were some instruction painted there which he could not quite read.

'Really, I should have told you,' he said at last, 'but I'm ashamed of it, it seems so childish. Mont Lipaux — it's less than twenty kilometres from here — that's where I'm going.'

Mont Lipaux? Vaguely I remembered headlines: *Another fatal crash at Mont Lipaux.*

'Yes,' he continued, as if he had read my thoughts, 'they race motor-cars there. It's an open circuit of thirty kilometres.'

'And you're going to watch?'

'No. I'm entered. I'm going to race.'

'Good God!'

'I know,' he said. 'Yes, I'm thirty-seven years old, and I've only been driving seriously for just over a year, and I'm just as cracked as you're thinking. Well, there it is. I want to prove that a bookworm can do that sort of thing just as well as anybody else.'

'But why? Prove to whom?'

'Oh, myself, I suppose.'

Somehow I knew even then that this was untrue. 'And you'd rather I didn't watch you?' I said.

'Well, yes, I'd rather go alone . . .'

A day or two in such a place as Baisereau-la-fontaine would have been pleasant enough, and I meant to respect Trevor's wishes. But I came under peculiar temptation.

An English party arrived at the *auberge* in a big Humber — two brothers and the son of the elder. They were quiet people whom I should have associated rather with the Chelsea Flower Show than with any more boisterous activities; but I discovered — when they asked me to join them at dinner — that motor-racing was their special weakness.

I also found them most agreeable. They were going on next morning to Mont Lipaux, or, more exactly, to a point on the circuit called *La Tour d'Annibal* which commanded 'one of the most interesting turns'. Wouldn't I come with them? They even had a ticket for the viewpoint (which belonged to the hotel there), since a fourth member of their party had cried off just before they left England.

Fundamentally, I did not want to go: I lack the taste for any sort of dangerous exhibition. But to accept the invitation could do Trevor himself no harm, and I argued that if my company had been of use to him on the journey, it would surely not be valueless at the moment when this foolish business was over — when I should find him tired and defeated, perhaps with his nerves badly shaken.

I asked my new friends to let me think it over, and in the morning I said, in grateful terms, that I would go with them.

The race was timed to start at eleven. We reached *La Tour d'Annibal* just after ten.

The tickets for this point of vantage had cost five thousand francs each. The two or three hundred people who had paid this sum were corralled on a railed terrace about half the size of a tennis-court; but because this terrace sloped steeply — almost dangerously — towards the rails, it afforded everybody a perfect view.

Perfect, that is, for anybody who cared for such views. I myself enjoyed it only so long as it was void of cars.

One saw perhaps as much as ten kilometres of the course. The place where the cars could first appear, on the skyline, was a dip like the rearsight of a rifle on the summit of Mont Lipaux itself. From there, in view nearly all the way, they had to descend 950 metres (so the programme told me), on a road like a crazy ladder with the rungs joined in violent hairpin bends.

The final stage of that descent was a perfectly straight section, known to devotees as *La Plongée*. I quote again from the programme:

> This section is 430 metres in length, and descends through a height of 120 metres. Progress in the same direction would carry competitors into the parapet. They are therefore required at the foot of the slope to make a turn to the right of approximately 110 degrees, and this is followed, at a distance of seventy metres, by a second turn to the right of approximately eighty degrees. Skill and judgment are required of competitors on this part of the course.

With my own uninstructed eyes I could see that this observation was correct. The parapet into which 'progress in the same direction would carry competitors' was only a few yards below me, an affair of wire ropes and sandbags built on the lip of a precipice. Fully two hundred feet below that lip, and invisible from where I stood, the Usère river pursued its broken course between the rocks and boulders which had fallen there through the centuries. It was not impossible to guess what would happen to competitors who, failing to exercise the required skill and judgment, continued their 'progress in the same direction'.

These matters would have been made clear, had I so needed, by the people all round me, who were explaining the hazards to each other in half a dozen languages and with the relish of connoisseurs. The men who had kindly brought me had drifted to another part of the enclosure. Sharing none of my neighbours' fervour, I felt detached and very much alone.

Shortly before the starting-time, I noticed somebody who gave me the impression of being in equal solitude: a woman standing close to the rails. She was fair, very slight in build, and her clothes marked her as English. I could not see her face, but the way she stood — and perhaps the shaping of her neck and shoulders — seemed instantly familiar. I thought, a moment later, that I knew who she was.

I opened my programme again, turning to the list of competitors. Five of the names were British, Trevor's coming last of these. The first — driving a Mansfield Special — was 'Hudson, Miles Q.F. . . .'.

It was, to begin with, less exciting than I had expected and feared. The cars, as they appeared at the summit, were as small as toys, and gave little impression of speed. Even when they came closer they moved with such regularity that it was like watching the marbles falling down a child's helter-skelter — their progress seemed so mechanical that one scarcely realized that each one of them was under individual control.

I did hold my breath when the leader roared down *La Plongée* and took the double turn with a dreadful screech of tyres. But when that was repeated and repeated by the cars which followed, one's sense of wonder and alarm ceased to operate. The thing was done with an apparently automatic precision which made it look almost easy

The circuit had to be covered four times. On the first lap two Italians were leading, the second closely followed by a Frenchman. Hudson, first of the British drivers, was lying seventh. Those first seven were closely grouped; a long gap followed, and then another seven or so came even closer together. Among these I had picked out, as it turned into *La Plongée*, shot down and skidded round the cliff-edge turns, the grey Watts-Leaver in which I had been sitting not many hours before.

By the second round the placings had altered a good deal. Before the cars came into sight I heard from the blower behind me that Hudson, driving with signal daring at the other side of the circuit, had advanced to the fourth place. By the time they reached me, he had overhauled the Frenchman and was closely pressing the second Italian, so that my compatriots in the stand grew suddenly vociferous.

Trevor had improved his position, too: he had drawn away from the rear group, made up the gap between them and the leaders, and was now pressing hard on the German car which was running sixth.

I had achieved by now a certain discernment, and it appeared to me, as I watched his management of the corners, that he had the Watts-Leaver under calm and beautiful control.

It was during the third lap that the French voice on the blower began to pour like a waterfall. First the leading driver went off the road — I gathered that he was unhurt but his machine past using. Then we heard that the second Italian had suffered mechanical trouble and was virtually out of the race. Much that followed came so fast that it was incomprehensible to me; but presently I caught, '*le Watts-Leaver Britannique*', and then a version of Trevor's own name.

Soon Hudson appeared again, now in the lead, with the next car perhaps a hundred yards behind him, and, behind that, another almost on its tail. With only a word of apology I seized the idle field-glasses of a man beside me.

Hitherto there had been no overtaking on the downward serpentine — I had heard a man explaining that it was a technical impossibility. Yet now, through the glasses, I saw it happen. On one rung of the ladder I saw the third car shoot forward as if a rocket had exploded behind it and draw level with the second.

It seemed barely to slacken for the hairpin bend which followed, but seemed to throw itself right up on the sloping wall of rock and travel, twisting, with its flanks almost parallel to the surface of the road. In that moment that car had taken second place. And now, as it came nearer, I saw that it was Trevor's.

That was only a prelude. I had an impression that Hudson, coming once more into *La Plongée*, gave a lightning glance over his shoulder. He came down the slope faster, I judged, than it had been done before, but the Watts-Leaver moved faster still. At the bottom the two cars were side by side. They took the parapet turn together. And it seemed to me a double miracle defeating the laws of motion, that Hudson kept off the parapet by inches and that Trevor kept off him.

The excited movement of the crowd had brought me nearer to the Englishwoman whom I thought I recognized. I pushed in beside her. It was Anne.

I said the first sentence that came into my mind: 'Your husband's a fine driver.'

I thought she had not heard. But presently, without looking at me, she said in a voice as colourless as mine: 'He should be — it's all he cares about.' And then, with only a side-long glance, she asked: 'Who was that cramming my husband's car at the parapet? It looked like a British car.'

I answered: 'It was. It's Trevor St Austell. You remember him?'

'Trevor?' Then she did turn to face me. She whispered: 'Stephen, why? What's he doing here? What made him think of such a thing?'

I said: 'I think he wanted to convince himself that he could do other things besides teaching history.'

'Convince *himself*?'

'And anybody who might be interested.'

With a little nod she said, almost inaudibly, 'I think I understand.' She turned away, and we did not speak again before the cars reappeared.

This time the two of them, having drawn far ahead, were by themselves: in a few seconds I saw that Hudson was leading by what looked like forty feet.

That distance was maintained as they came down the ladder, so precisely that they might have been fixed together: it seemed clear that Trevor, even if he had the power, had no intention of trying to repeat his former *tour de force* by overtaking on one of the hairpins.

Both cars must in fact have been moving at something near the maximum speed which was possible on that section. Yet the descent seemed to take longer than before, and I had the curious impression that what I witnessed was not a duel but a parade of combatants, slow, deliberately prolonged.

At the same distance apart they swung into *La Plongée*. There was a moment when the roar of the two engines faltered. Then Hudson, swinging to the left margin of the road, came down the slope like a falcon swooping.

I cannot have seen his face — it must be a later imagination which makes me think I saw the fear there. But I know — I am certain I know — how his mind was working: he was building speed to the very limit of what he could rein back for the parapet turn — but to him this dreadful risk looked smaller than the one which menaced him from behind.

For, almost incredibly, Trevor was once more coming down *La Plongée* faster than he.

Hudson achieved that turn — a greater feat in driving I suppose nobody will ever see. With twenty yards to go he screwed the car with the wheels locked dead; still on those wheels, the tyres crying hideously, it skidded sideways towards the parapet, touched it, seemed as if it must crash through. Then, answering to a violent burst of engine, the wheels took hold again, the car miraculously leaped forward.

Clear — or it should have been.

Steering on the extreme right of the road, Trevor had waited longer still to put on his turn. Scarcely trying — or so it looked — to check his speed, he could only bend his course to the right through a few degrees. That would have taken him slantwise into the parapet — but the path was not open. At a speed of more than a hundred miles an hour he hurled the Watts-Leaver at the Mansfield's off-front wing.

I saw a cloud of smoke with a flash of flame in it. I caught sight of the underside of a car that burst through the parapet and dropped from our sight. The other car should have followed. But as the first clot of smoke thinned I saw it in the air, turning over in a perfect backward somersault.

Freakishly it landed on its furiously spinning wheels and set off in a crazy zigzag along the road, with the driver — dead or alive — still appearing to cling to the wheel. It had travelled forty yards, giving me just time to see it was the Watts-Leaver, before it crashed to pieces on the wall of rock below me . . .

Anne, when I looked for her, had disappeared. Inquiring at the hotel, I came upon a servant who had seen her setting off by herself on a path which led into the woods nearby.

Following that path I found her, walking slowly, her face pale and quite without expression. I fell in beside her and we went on some way in silence. It seemed to me that she was completely indifferent to my presence.

At last, suddenly, she sat down beside the path, and looking at her knees she said: 'Stephen, tell me — must I pretend to be heartbroken about Miles? I would be if I could — I know one ought to be. But I just can't pretend.'

There was no real answer to that outburst. I said, feebly: 'I can't even tell you my own feelings. I'm too shocked that Trevor killed him — shocked and miserable. There was something better for Trevor to do with his life than that.'

'You mean,' she said, after another silence, 'you think it was deliberate? Why? How could he be as mad as that?'

I answered: 'I suppose because he was in love with you. Ever since Catterick I think he had been.'

At this she nodded. 'I was always afraid so.' And she added in a whisper: 'I wasn't in love with him.'

Something made me risk an audacious question: 'Perhaps, if Miles hadn't turned up, you would have been?'

'No,' she said firmly, 'not Trevor. I was fond of him, but that was all.'

She was standing up again, and we began to walk back towards the hotel.

'And there's been nobody else?' I asked.

'There was one man,' she said reflectively. 'But he got posted to North Africa, and he never wrote to me. So I fell for Miles instead.'

'He didn't write,' I told her, 'because his tank hit a land mine which knocked him out for nine months.'

'I knew that afterwards.'

'And now he'll begin to write again.'

But I saw, later on, that there would be no need for writing.

Anniversary

Yes, I met him — I shook hands with him — shortly before he died, when I was a young graduate doing field research on South American history: the legendary José Alguarte, murderer of General Lugones.

'José Alguarte? Believe it or not, he's still alive,' the Governor said, in the first interview he granted me, 'though he was an oldish man at the time of the outrage.'

He nodded with a certain complacency — the satisfaction of a librarian who instantly produces a rare volume.

'You want to see him? Well, as a rule he doesn't have visitors — the people who look after him feel it might be harmful. But you're in luck, I think. You're here for some time? Well then, Tuesday week is José's birthday party.' He lowered his eyelids, hinting mystery. 'Not his actual birthday, you understand — we don't happen to know exactly when he was born. But every year I invite José to a little luncheon on the anniversary of the assassination. If you, Señor Professor, would care to join us, you shall be my guest this year as well.'

The State Penitentiary was then at Santa Sabeia, some thirty kilometres from the capital. To Santa Sabeia the Governor took me in his vintage Chevrolet, luxuriously upholstered and driven by a coloured chauffeur in resplendent livery.

'In the first two or three years of his imprisonment,' the Governor said, as the car lurched and shuddered on a potholed road through endless banana plantations, 'Alguarte was handled rather roughly. Herrera — the successor to Lugones — was in some respects a simple fellow; he believed that sooner or later any man will tell you what he knows if he's sufficiently hurt and frightened.' He smiled, giving me a generous view of his gold-stopped teeth, expressing with a gesture of his soft white hands a genial contempt for Herrera's simplicity; he himself appeared a man of settled indolence, not subject to emotions of any kind. 'But the next Governor, Colonel Ureña, realized that those tactics might never work with a type who'd clearly been feeble-minded since childhood. Yes, my predecessor Ureña was a man of high intelligence. And in dealing with this problem I have been content to humbly follow him.'

'You mean,' I asked, 'that you're still trying to get information out of Alguarte — more than ten years after the crime?'

'But of course! To you, Señor Professor, history is something to be locked away in school books. With respect, we whose whole business is politics can't afford to look at things like that.'

A new note in his voice made me turn, while he was concentrated on preparing and lighting a cigar, to study his face more keenly. Now I saw that this was not after all an operatic figure, but a man whose outward laziness might clothe an ominous resolution.

'Remember,' he continued softly, 'that José can't possibly have been alone. Imagine the mere physical labour of collecting all the apparatus for wrecking a railroad train, transporting it to a site almost twenty kilometres from the nearest road — do you think that was a chore for one elderly man? And then again, look at the choice of place, the accurate timing. It was no imbecile who made all those calculations. If you care for figures, the experts in the police department have worked out that not fewer than ten conspirators must have been involved — most of them young, tough men, and anything but stupid. What we don't know is their names.'

'And does that still matter, after nearly eleven years?'

'To me, Señor, it matters a great deal. For one thing, I like to feel at ease when I travel on the railroad. You see, I have a wife, and young children. There are always men around who don't care for any sort of government — or governors. I want to keep tabs on those men.'

'And you still hope to get the names from Alguarte, after all this time?'

The Governor slowly nodded; in his somnolent olive eyes I saw (I thought) a fresh gleam of self-satisfaction.

'With a crazy type like José,' he said, holding his cigar to observe the lengthening ash, 'it can take years to make him see his own advantage. And since our last little birthday party my staff have found at least one new argument for me to put to him. I've just a hunch that this time José is going to see things my way — I figure we'll find him playing ball with me today.'

The garden of the Prison Commandant was an irregular oblong of gravel fenced by agaves and tufted with a thin brown grass. There, when we arrived, a table had been set, half in the shade provided by a crescent of raphia palms. It had four places set, faced by four wicker chairs of which one was furnished with a cushion or two to soften its austerity. As soon as the Governor had settled himself on this seat of honour an Indian servant standing in attendance took a hand-bell from the table and rang it loudly.

Almost at once, on the path which came from the Commandant's house through a thicket of bamboo, there appeared a small procession, headed by the grandly-moustachioed Commandant himself in the full-dress uniform of the civil police, while a pair of *mestizo* soldiers, armed with rifles and festooned with bandoliers, brought up the rear.

These figures were, by comparison, commonplace; it was the one walking between them who, as the group drew nearer, fastened my attention. He was tiny, and immensely old, with deeply wrinkled skin and fine white hair which fell luxuriantly about his ears and neck. His salt-and-pepper suit — long in jacket and narrow in trouser-leg — was one that a European landowner might have worn on his country estate in the last decade of the previous century; well-preserved, a trifle foppish to my eye, it was long out of date, and perhaps it was this outmoded dress which gave the old man an appearance of unreality. I felt as if the body of some historic personage, long embalmed in its own clothes, had been taken from the museum, given mechanically a semblance of life and paraded for my inspection.

'Prisoner and escort, halt!'

The little party shuffled to a standstill, then the Commadant took two more paces forward and performed an extravagant salute.

'The prisoner Alguarte, señor.'

The Governor acknowledged the salute with a cursory nod; but as he stood up and turned towards Alguarte he seemed to melt into affability.

'Ah, José,' he said, advancing and extending his hand, 'my congratulations on yet another anniversary — the years pass so quickly! You know, of course, who I am? You remember this is the day you take luncheon with me?'

For some moments it appeared that the old man remembered nothing: he stood blinking against the ferocious sunlight, his lower lip and jaw working as if on a spring. Then the wizened face cracked, a throaty giggle came, and a womanish voice, with what I recognized as an Andean inflexion, said excitedly, 'Yes, yes, the anniversary!'

The Governor beamed. 'But of course — you have an excellent memory, my old friend. Now let me present you to my friend Professor Van Thiel, who has been most anxious to meet you. The Professor wants to put you in the history book he's writing — he's going to make you famous for ever.'

In some embarrassment I held out my hand. With his eyes still on the Governor, Alguarte negligently shook my fingers.

'Famous, yes!' he said, giggling complacently.

Studying his pale and watery eyes, I did not doubt that José Alguarte was far from sane, and the Governor's belief that he had been an imbecile from birth seemed at least plausible. That conclusion relieved my moral discomfort: however distasteful this occasion, there was no need, I thought, to squander pity on a creature so obviously incapable of ordinary human feelings.

To Alguarte was given the place of honour on the Governor's right. I sat facing him, and opposite the Governor sat the Commandant, while the two morose soldiers stood together a yard from Alguarte's back, with their rifles at the port position, their thumbs close to the safety-catches.

Gastronomically, it was an admirable meal, with several courses of diced or shredded vegetables, copiously sauced and artfully spiced, leading to an elaborate dish in the local tradition which somewhat resembled *iscas a Portugueza*. The local port-coloured wine, in generous supply, was excellent of its kind. No fewer than four negro servants were employed in seeing that no one's plate or glass was for a moment empty. And never, as far as I remember, did such luxurious entertainment afford me so little delight.

'Attention, Alguarte!' the Commandant barked at invervals. 'Answer when the Governor speaks to you!'

And on each occasion the Governor rebuked him: 'No, Herculano, leave him alone! José and I, we understand each other.'

He need not have troubled: it was evident that Alguarte was no more sensitive to Herculano's voice than are children in the slums of Salvador to their mothers' incessant scolding.

'Yes, José, the Professor is greatly interested in your historic act,' the Governor said, smiling paternally, as the meal progressed. 'A remarkable act it was indeed. Of course, we must all regret that it meant the loss to the State of General Lugones. But from the point of view of planning — of boldness in execution —'

'Lugones?' Like a dart fired from an air-pistol the name seemed to penetrate the cloak of apathy in which Alguarte had been wrapped. But almost at once his look of alert suspicion gave place to a vapid smile. 'That was the tyrant,' he muttered, and he began repeating in a childish sing-song, 'Tyrant Lugones, Tyrant Lugones . . .'

'Enough of that!' the Commandant interposed.

'Well, for the moment, let's accept your point of view,' the Governor said equably, nodding to Alguarte as if both were entirely reasonable men. 'What seems to me so strange, if Lugones was a hard man, is that no one helped you in getting rid of him. All that planning you had to do, collecting the apparatus, transporting it all the way to the Matzina defile — I'd have thought that among all the men who hated Lugones you could have picked a few to lend a hand.'

Alguarte said nothing. In a spinsterish way he was prodding at the food on his plate, separating morsels of red pepper and finically bearing them to his mouth, one at a time. From his fixed and foolish smile I inferred that his thoughts, if any, no longer had any connection with what the Governor was saying.

Undaunted, the Governor leaned over the table, bringing his eyes and voice to bear with greater intensity on his peculiar guest. 'I've always thought it a pity,' he said softly, 'that those others had to die as well — the Governor's entourage, four of them, the driver of the locomotive, and two or three more. Men with families, most of them. Have you ever thought of them at all?'

No answer.

'I mean, if I myself had been responsible for all those deaths I'd be looking out for someone to share the responsibility. I'd expect my friends — people who thought the same way as me — to come around and give me some support. Not just to leave me in jail, year after year, all alone.'

Still no answer: nothing to show that the Governor's words, slowly and carefully articulated, had any meaning for the man they were addressed to. I had the impression, just then, that I was attending an elaborate ritual which could lead to no conceivable result.

But a little later that view was slightly modified. We had reached dessert, and the Governor's voice had grown lazy, as if, besieged by the dual force of wine and sunlight, he were already half asleep. Quite casually — or so I thought at the time — he remarked, 'Well, José, I've been thinking: you've been in jail for long enough. It seems to me we might just as well send you home now. I mean, after one or two small formalities.'

That brought from Alguarte a movement of the head so small that I may only have imagined it. But the lips did move; and though it was barely audible I distinctly saw them framing a single word: 'Formalities?'

Had the Governor caught that utterance too? He was looking another way, over the Commandant's shoulder, and when he spoke again it appeared that he had forgotten the topic of Alguarte's release.

'I meant to tell you,' he said idly, sipping at a tall glass of coffee, 'I had the privilege of speaking to Señora Alguarte the other day. Your Luisa, I mean. It has taken my staff all this time to find out where she's living — as soon as we knew that, I asked her to come and see me. I must confess, it surprised me to find your wife so young — what, twenty, twenty-five years younger than you are? And once, before her illness, so beautiful — that one can still see.'

It needed no great intelligence to see how the Governor's tactics were developing, and now I was more than ever thankful for Alguarte's insensibility. Once more he seemed impervious to the Governor's observations. As he primly stirred his coffee he turned his eyes to left and right, always slightly avoiding the three faces which were turned towards his; again he was smiling over some private rumination, so that I saw him then as a little old gentleman of the nineties, already for some years senile, surrounded by foreigners who spoke in a language he did not know.

But now there was a further change in his behaviour. His wandering eyes came to rest on the Governor's forehead, with a look of curiosity, as if the Governor had only just arrived there, dropping from the skies. And he said abruptly, 'The driver? You tell me the locomotive driver was killed too?'

It was the Commandant who popped out the answer: 'Well, of course, fool!'

As far as I could see, the Governor accepted the backward turn of the conversation without a tremor of surprise. He said evenly, 'Yes, naturally the loco went off the line, and the driver died from scalding.'

'Not natural at all!' Alguarte retorted. 'A mistake entirely! Second coach — Lugones was in the second coach. That vulture, with all his hangers-on. That was the one we blew.'

' "We?" ' the Governor echoed.

'The timing was absolutely right!' the old man persisted, now sweating with excitement. 'I had the stop-watch, we'd tested all the fuses. It worked perfectly — I challenge you to deny it. Second coach — blown to smithereens.'

'Yes,' the Commandant said drily, 'and it just so happened the loco went off the track at the same time!'

'Who do you say tested the fuses?' the Governor asked.

'I tell you there was nothing wrong with the fuses,' Alguarte rejoined. 'I tell you the timing was perfection — I got the second coach.'

It was an angry little man who said those words, beating the table, glaring alternately at the Governor and the Commandant and then, for good measure, at me. But so frail a creature could not persist in such titanic rage: once more his mood abruptly changed.

'An excellent repast!' he said inconsequently, swallowing the rest of his coffee, energetically wiping his mouth with a big red hand-kerchief. 'The best I've had for a long time. I must thank you, señor — for the moment I've forgotten your name — I must thank you most sincerely. You and I, señor, we have our differences. Lugones — a friend of yours, I think you once told me. In truth a monster, if you want to know — but one can't expect everyone to have a grasp of politics like mine. I thank you, none the less, for your gracious hospitality, which I hope very soon to return.'

'Soon?' the Governor repeated.

'On my little farm,' Alguarte explained, staring with screwed eyes into space as if he could just catch sight of it. 'I have a farm, you know — a modest affair, but quite productive in a good year. Fruit and maize. Hogs, as a rule. Some cotton, a little tobacco.'

'Very nice, José. It sounds a charming property.'

'At any rate you'll get a decent meal. Yes, señor — I'm afraid I forget your name — we'll have a good time, you and I, when I'm back on my farm.' In fresh excitement, he broke into quavering laughter. Still laughing, he darted a contemptuous glance at the Commandant and made the motion of spitting on the ground. 'You and I, señor — not that bastard. He can stay here, he can hang himself any time he likes.'

'And when is it to be,' the Governor asked pleasantly, 'this meal to which you're kindly inviting me?'

'When?' The laughter in Alguarte's face went out like a match-flame, giving place to a pale confusion. 'Soon, I think — quite soon. I was told . . . I understood . . . I think it was you, señor, who said just now I should return quite shortly to my farm.'

The Governor in his turn appeared to be perplexed. 'Indeed — did I say that? Well, I suppose it could be arranged, if that is what you wish. You feel quite capable of managing your farm again?'

A sound from Alguarte's lips may have been meant for 'Yes' — it was scarcely audible. His attention seemed to have slackened once more; his eyes, like the beam of a searching torch, were wandering everywhere except towards the Governor's face.

'I mean,' the Governor said, his tone still rational and friendly, 'it's rather a question whether you could look after your wife as well. She's a sick woman, you know — she's never been well since your son's death. What — didn't you hear? Ah, the letter from my office must have gone astray. Your son died more than a year ago.' He paused to relight his cigar. 'So your wife has to run the farm by herself now. That's hard for her, with her illness. It's a state of affairs that can't last long.'

Once again my own feelings were protected by Alguarte's alienation. His eyes had come to rest on the table; he was dribbling, and though there were tears on his cheeks his mouth was spread in a fresh, exuberant smile, a grin of total vacancy.

'Yes,' the Governor pursued, 'for your Lisa's sake I think you'd best be getting home as soon as possible.' And now he turned to the Commandant. 'I want you, Herculano, to make all the arrangements as quickly as you can. Our friend may need fresh clothes, and any property he has here wants to be carefully packed. Then transport — you'll attend to all that as well. I want Alguarte to be on his way home within one hour of his filling out the necessary form.'

Without moving my head I could read the few words typed on the paper which, as casually as a ticket-clerk, the Governor dropped on the table where Alguarte's plate had been: *The following assisted me in the action against General Lugones* and there were lines of dots numbered 1 to 6, and a further line with the words *Signed* on the left and Alguarte's full name in capitals beneath.

'You see, I've lowered my terms,' the Governor said agreeably, as if this were a game they both played. 'Six names, that's all I want now.'

And he slipped a pencil into Alguarte's hand.

For a few moments Alguarte paid no attention: I should have said he was no longer even aware of his surroundings. Then, watching closely, I saw a movement of his eyes which told me that covertly, suspiciously, he was trying to read the typewritten words. There followed another and longer interval in which I could not even guess whether his chaotic mind was working at all. And it came as a surprise when he spoke.

'Please — you must forgive me, being so slow,' he said indistinctly. 'It's difficult — you understand — it's difficult for me. I've been through a hard time, I'm not clear any more what's happening, my memory's all gone.'

But his fingers, as he said those words, seemed to grow sensitive to the pencil stuck between them. He was still staring at the paper, and now, showing extreme reluctance, he began to write. His left arm, lying across the top of the paper, obstructed my view, but I could see that he wrote uncertainly, like a child or a man with a strained wrist. Once he paused to cross himself, as if that were an integral part of his task. The whole laborious operation must have taken three or four minutes; and then, with a gesture of impatience, he pushed the paper towards the Governor and rose to his feet.

'So — done!' he said.

He made a small, military movement with both his hands, beckoning the two soldiers who, as if this were a daily routine, stepped instantly to his sides. 'Back now!' he ordered; and as the three men wheeled to return the way they had come I had a momentary impression that he and no one else was in command.

Taken, I think, by surprise, the Governor had left the paper on the table. Obliquely, I could now read the large and sprawling sentence: *For murdering innocents with Lugones I look to mercy of Almighty God.* And below, in giant capitals: J. ALGUARTE DOES NOT BETRAY FRIENDS.

I turned to stare again at the retreating trio. Ridiculously small, Alguarte appeared, between the two husky soldiers, and his stiff, bow-legged walk (such as belongs often to the insane) made him look as if he were bestriding a sheep. Yet what remains most vivid in my memory is the curious impression of completeness, of inflexible independence, which came perhaps from the set of his shoulders, the erect and rigid carriage of the small white head.

Afterword
R. C. Hutchinson: a brief biography
Bibliographical notes

Afterword

At the time of his death in 1975 R. C. Hutchinson had published twenty-eight stories, the first having appeared in the *Empire Review* in 1928, the last in *Argosy* in 1965. While his novels are slowly coming back into print, with several now available for the first time in paperback, the short stories remain little known and difficult to locate. (A standard reference book on the modern novel lists only four of the twenty-eight stories.) The present collection assembles all but six of Hutchinson's published stories; of those omitted three were merely 'pot-boilers', designed for newspaper serialization. Four pieces from the early part of his career, previously unpublished and only surviving in typescript, are also included, so that the twenty-six stories that make up this volume represent the bulk of Hutchinson's work in that genre.

Although R. C. Hutchinson was a prolific and generous novelist — seventeen novels in a career interrupted by five years of military service — he wrote little in the way of critical or analytic prose. The few comments he did make, in interviews or the rare essay on fiction, suggest that he thought of the novel and the short story as two very different forms, only united by both being written in prose. Amplitude and leisureliness, in Hutchinson's view, were what distinguished the novel from the short story. Indeed in its brevity the latter was, he suggested, more akin to drama. 'Slowness (the tedium of which ought to be cunningly alleviated),' he wrote in an article on the craft of fiction which appeared in the *Saturday Review of Literature* (New York, 1949) 'is an element essential to the novelistic form — as opposed to the dramatic or short-story form.' Most of Hutchinson's short stories are, as we might expect from this comment, indeed short and conclude with a surprising revelation of character or plot that the writer has withheld from the reader until the end, such a revelation determining the shape of the tale and bringing it to a sharp and abrupt ending.

Several of the other pieces in this collection, however, are not tailored to the need for a concluding surprise or revelation, and these stories possess some of the leisureliness we associate with Hutchinson's novels. 'A Prison in France', 'Excursion to Norway', 'Exhibit

'A', 'Crossroads', and 'Anniversary' belong to this second group and significantly these deal with themes common to the novels as well: the perversion of post-war values; the moral and physical courage of unsung heroes, civilian and military; the intransigence and vengefulness of South American politics; the cruel egotism of the theatrical 'star'. It is also significant that most of these stories are set abroad — in France, South America and the Middle East — for Hutchinson once remarked that he found the English very difficult to write about, 'dealing with foreigners is a kind of challenge and it operates on the imagination'.

And yet, irrespective of their setting and theme, these stories reflect many of the strengths characteristic of Hutchinson's best novels: the compulsive narrative excitement in his account of a commando raid or motor race; the creation of 'atmosphere' — of military tension, moral evil, supernatural haunting; the description of dawn in the Persian mountains; the novelist's admiration of simple courage and his allied skill in creating 'good' characters; and, equally, the skilful, gradual revelation of the evil heart of an admired celebrity. R. C. Hutchinson devoted most of his energy to the novel and regarded the short story as a minor and subsidiary form; nevertheless, the present collection enables us to widen our appreciation of his skills as a writer and in several cases to watch him working up a character, theme or environment that will later be extended and enriched when it appears in a novel.

Robert Green
Professor of English
The University of Swaziland
Kwaluseni, Swaziland

6 October 1983

R. C. Hutchinson: a brief biography

1907	January 23	Ray Coryton Hutchinson born in Finchley, North London.
		Educated at Monkton Combe School, near Bath, where he writes a 20,000-word novel, 'The Hand of the Purple Idol'.
1927		BA, Oriel College, Oxford.
		Joins the advertising department, Colman's, Norwich.
1928	January	His first publication, a short story, 'Every Twenty Years', appears in the *Empire Review*.
	September	Begins writing first novel, *Thou Hast a Devil*.
1929	January	Completes *Thou Hast a Devil*.
	April	Marries Margaret Owen Jones, daughter of Captain Owen Jones, CBE, RNR.
1930		Writes 'The Caravan of Culture', his only unpublished adult novel.
	October	*Thou Hast a Devil* published in London by Ernest Benn.
1931		At work on *The Answering Glory*.
	December	Begins writing *The Unforgotten Prisoner*.
1932	March	*The Answering Glory*, his second novel, published in London by Cassell.
	June	*The Answering Glory* published in New York by Farrar & Rinehart, his first publication in America and a Book of the Month Club recommendation.
1933	March	Completes third novel, *The Unforgotten Prisoner*.
	December	It is published in London by Cassell; 150,000 copies are sold in the first month.
1934	February	*The Unforgotten Prisoner* published in New York by Farrar & Rinehart.
1935	February	*One Light Burning*, the fourth novel, is published in New York by Farrar & Rinehart and in London, where it is a best-seller, by Cassell.
		Leaves Colman's and starts writing full-time.

1936 September   Fifth novel, *Shining Scabbard*, published in
                   London by Cassell.

      December   It is published in New York by Farrar &
                   Rinehart, and is again a Book Club
                   recommendation. 78,000 copies are sold in two
                   weeks.

                   Begins writing his longest novel, *Testament*.

1938 August 11   *Last Train South*, his only play to be produced,
                   opens in London's West End; it closes on 3
                   September after poor notices.

      September   *Testament*, the sixth novel, published in London
                   by Cassell, where it is a Book Society Choice.

      October   It is published in New York by Farrar &
                   Rinehart.

      November   Awarded *Sunday Times* Gold Medal for Fiction.

1939   At work on *The Fire and the Wood*.

1940 February   *The Fire and the Wood* completed.

      March   Commissioned in the Army.

      June   *The Fire and the Wood*, the seventh novel,
                   published in London by Cassell, a Book Society
                   Choice.

                   Signs PEN appeal for support against Nazi
                   Germany.

      July   Posted as Captain, 8th Battalion, The Buffs
                   Regiment.

      August   *The Fire and the Wood* published in New York by
                   Farrar & Rinehart, a Literary Guild Selection.

                   'Designs' *Elephant and Castle*.

1943   Staff College, Camberley.

                   Begins *Interim*.

1944   Serves in the War Office, London, in the Home
                   Guard Directorate.

      December   Writes speech delivered by King George VI at
                   Stand-down Parade of the Home Guard.

1945 March   *Interim*, Hutchinson's eighth novel, published in
                   London by Cassell.

      April   Begins work in Baghdad on the military history,
                   Paiforce, for HMSO.

      May   *Interim* published in New York by Farrar &
                   Rinehart.

	July	Completes *Paiforce*.
	October	Demobilized with the rank of Major.
		Attends some sessions of War Crimes Trial, Nüremberg.
1946	January	Begins writing *Elephant and Castle*.
1948		*Elephant and Castle* completed.
	September	Visits New York to publicize *Elephant and Castle*. Begins writing *Recollection of a Journey*.
1949	January	*Elephant and Castle*, the ninth novel, published in New York by Rinehart & Co. First printing of 25,000 copies, with a further 170,000 for a book club.
		Paiforce published in London by HMSO.
	April	*Elephant and Castle* published in London by Cassell, where it is also a best-seller.
1951		*Recollection of a Journey* completed.
1952	April	*Recollection of a Journey*, Hutchinson's tenth novel, is published in New York as *Journey with Strangers* by Rinehart & Co.
	October	*Recollection of a Journey* published in London by Cassell.
		Begins *The Stepmother*.
1954	September	Completes *The Stepmother*.
1955	April	Begins *March the Ninth*.
	August	*The Stepmother* published in New York by Rinehart & Co. Book Club recommendation.
	September	It is published in London by Cassell.
1957	April	Completes *March the Ninth*.
	October	It is published in New York by Rinehart & Co.
	November	And in London by Geoffrey Bles; a Book Society selection.
1958	January	Begins *Image of My Father*.
	November	Adaptation of *The Stepmother* as a play, by Warren Chetham-Strode, opens in the West End.
1961	January	*Image of My Father* completed.
	September	The thirteenth novel, *Image of My Father*, is published in London by Geoffrey Bles; a Book Society recommendation.
1962	January	It is published in New York by Harper Bros. as

		The Inheritor, a Book Club recommendation.
	June	Elected Fellow of the Royal Society of Literature.
1964	September	*A Child Possessed* published in London by Geoffrey Bles.
		Begins work on *Johanna*.
1965	January	*A Child Possessed* published in New York by Harper Bros.; a Book Club recommendation.
1966	November	Receives W. H. Smith Literary Award for *A Child Possessed*.
1969	April	*Johanna at Daybreak*, the fifteenth novel, published in London by Michael Joseph.
	September	It is published in New York by Harper & Row; a Book Club recommendation.
1971	March	Begins work on *Rising*, his last novel, during a voyage to South America.
	September	*Origins of Cathleen* published in London only, by Michael Joseph; it is rejected by American publishers.
1975	July 3	R. C. Hutchinson dies, leaving the final chapter of *Rising* uncompleted.
	September	*Rising* is published in London only, by Michael Joseph.
	November	It is short-listed for the Booker Prize.

Bibliographical Notes

Every Twenty Years
First published, under the name 'Coryton Hutchinson', in the *Empire Review*, 324 (January 1928), 61–7. Reprinted in E. J. O'Brien, ed., *The Best Short Stories of 1928* (Jonathan Cape, London: 1928). A German translation appeared in *Das Leben* (Leipzig), VII, iii (September 1929), 5–14. Hutchinson received £7 from the *Empire Review* and two guineas from Cape, his total literary earnings in 1928. The story had been written while Hutchinson was an undergraduate at Oriel College, Oxford.

The Wall not made with Hands
After coming down from Oxford, Hutchinson worked for several years in Norwich, where this story, previously unpublished, was written in the late twenties or early thirties.

A Rendezvous for Mr Hopkins
First published in *English Review*, XLVIII, ii (February 1929), 212–16, and later read by the author on the BBC National Programme, 1 August 1937. A German translation appeared in *Neues Wiener Journal* (29 September 1929) and in *Familien-Wochenblatt* (Zurich, 19 April 1930); the story was also translated into Hungarian and published in Budapest in 1929. The version printed here incorporates the many verbal revisions Hutchinson made to the *English Review* text, perhaps when he was preparing the story for radio in 1937.

Mr Harptop rings the Bell
Published in the *Manchester Guardian Weekly* (29 December 1929), 20, as the runner-up in the paper's Ghost-Story competition. A German translation appeared in *Neues Wiener Journal* (6 March 1930).

James returns
Probably written between 1927 and 1931, this story was rejected by *Cornhill*, *London Mercury* and *John O'London's Weekly* and remained

unpublished. Like several other stories of this period and the novel begun in 1931, *The Unforgotten Prisoner*, 'James Returns' indicates Hutchinson's preoccupation with the effects of the First World War.

At Grips with Morpheus
Another unpublished story with a wartime setting and probably written in the early thirties.

The Last Page
Published in *The Bermondsey Book*, VIII, ii (March/May 1930), 65–77.

In the Dark
Published in *English Review*, L, v (May 1930), 635–9. Hutchinson's first novel, *Thou Hast A Devil*, was published in October of that year.

Last Voyage
Published in the *Manchester Guardian* (25 November 1931), 18. In the same year he completed his second novel, *The Answering Glory*.

The Quixotes
Published in *English Review*, LIV, i (January 1932), 51–60, two months before the appearance of Hutchinson's second novel, *The Answering Glory*.

Slaves of Women
Published in *Storyteller* (February 1932), 701–08.

The Tramp with a Visiting-card
Published in *Saturday Review* (5 March 1932), 243–4.

A Prison in France
Published in *English Review*, LV, iii (September 1932), 281–94. Hutchinson was still at work on *The Unforgotten Prisoner*, which he completed in March 1933.

Elosindi's Christmas
Published in *Snapdragon*, Norwich Hospitals Annual (1934), 53–8.
One Light Burning, the fourth novel, was published in February 1935,
its success emboldening the novelist to abandon commerce, leave
Norwich, and write full-time.

A Photograph of Mrs Austin
This story was read by the author on the BBC National Programme,
11 October 1938, the text printed here being the one prepared for
radio. Since leaving Colman's in 1935 Hutchinson had published
two highly successful novels — *Shining Scabbard* (1936) and *Testament*
(1938).

Outsiders: Two sketches
The typescript is undated, but these 'Sketches' were probably
written in the late thirties. Hutchinson was to return to their theme,
the psychological effects of unemployment, in *Elephant and Castle*,
which he designed in 1940 and began writing after the war.
Hutchinson's typescript in fact includes three 'Sketches', one of
which has been omitted from this collection.

Excursion to Norway
Hutchinson's last novel, *The Fire and the Wood*, had been published in
June 1940, three months after the novelist had been commissioned in
the army. 'Excursion' was published in *Atlantic Monthly* (July 1942),
7–13. Hutchinson received $250 for it and his editor, Edward
Weekes, wrote to the Ministry of Information that it was 'the very
narrative I have been hungering for for months. The intricacy of the
raid, the character of the men who undertook it and the authenticity
of what they did, have all been set down without a shadow of doubt.
It is a brilliant piece of writing.' The story was based on a real action
against Vaagsö in December 1940. It was sent to the United States by
wireless and this led to several errors of transcription being
incorporated into the magazine version, but the novelist later
pencilled the corrections into his copy of *Atlantic*, and these have
been incorporated into the version printed here. 'Excursion to
Norway' thus appears here for the first time in the form intended by
its author. Hutchinson's next novel, the short *Interim* (1945), was

written in 1943–4, while he was attached to the War Office in London, and then in 1945 he was sent to the Middle East to write the official history of the 'Paiforce' campaign.

Exhibit 'A'

Hutchinson spent several months in the Middle East, at work on his military history, to be published as *Paiforce* in 1949. 'Exhibit "A" ' was published in Leonard Russell, ed., *The Saturday Book: Seventh Year* (Hutchinson, London: 1947), and is based, as is a part of *Recollection of a Journey* (1952), on the novelist's experiences during that period. Hutchinson was demobilized in October 1945 and three months later started work on the ambitious *Elephant and Castle* (1949), which he had been forced to put aside in 1940.

Crossroads

Published in Leonard Russell, ed., *The Saturday Book: Eighth Year* (Hutchinson, London: 1948). *Elephant and Castle* was published the following year, and was a best-seller in both London and New York.

All in the Day

First published in *Lilliput* (April 1953), 51–5; reprinted in John Pudney, ed., *The Pick of Today's Short Stories*, *IV* (Putnam, London: 1953), and in D. Pepper, ed., *A Time to Fight* (Nelson, London: 1978). Reginald Moore, in *Time and Tide* (2 January 1954), called it a story that 'incises the callous military skin and draws a few drops of warm blood'. Hutchinson's tenth novel, *Recollection of a Journey*, had appeared in 1952.

A Common Tongue

Published in *Evening News* (10 July 1953).

A Question of Value

Published in *Evening News* (8 December 1953).

The End of Innocence

Published in *Housewife* (June 1956), 50–51, 127, 129–30. *The Stepmother*, the eleventh novel, had appeared the previous year.

How I rose to be an Australian Shoeshine Boy
Published in John Pudney, ed., *The Pick of Today's Short Stories*, *VII* (Putnam, London: 1956).

Duel at Mont Lipaux
Published in *John Bull* (8 February 1958), 7–9, 31–2. In both typescript and manuscript the story had been entitled 'A Peculiar Engagement'. *March the Ninth* had been published the previous year.

Anniversary
First published in *Argosy* (December 1965), 91–100, and reprinted in D. Rutherford, ed., *Best Underworld Stories* (Faber, London: 1969). *Image of My Father* had appeared in 1961, and in 1962 Hutchinson had been elected a Fellow of the Royal Society of Literature. His fourteenth novel, *A Child Possessed* (1964), won the W. H. Smith Literary Award in 1966, and *Johanna at Daybreak* was published in 1969. One more novel, *Origins of Cathleen* (1971), appeared before the novelist's death in 1975. 'Anniversary' was the last short story Hutchinson wrote and, with its interest in South American militarism, can be seen as a 'pencil sketch' for *Rising*, the seventeenth novel, published posthumously.